"It would be a
to ask m

Greg spoke quickly, so she wouldn't have a chance to dismiss him. "You know, before the neighbors see a uniformed officer at your door and start to talk."

Beth grinned, looking out at the street in front of her house where he'd left his car. "Oh, yeah, like that thing with that big Sheriff emblazoned on the side isn't going to raise any suspicion?"

"Hell, no." He grinned, too, his hands in his pockets as he stood his ground. "They'll just think the sheriff's sweet on you when they see that."

"Which *won't* cause talk?"

"Well, not the kind I was referring to. You know, the kind where everyone whispers about the secret life you're probably living and they weave fantasies about bank robberies or jewel theft and lock their doors and windows at night."

Beth started to pale at the ridiculous situation he was describing, but then she laughed. "Yeah, that's about as likely as the sheriff being sweet on me."

"I sure hope not," he said almost under his breath. And then wished he hadn't. That was good for a slammed door in his face.

Because he didn't know what else to do, Greg met her eyes. From the first time he'd met her, he'd recognized something in that deep blue gaze. And until he knew what it was, what it meant, he had to keep coming back.

She didn't shut him out or shut the door.

Dear Reader,

Welcome back to Shelter Valley! This visit is going to be a little different, but I promise you'll still find the things that make Shelter Valley so special—the feeling of home, and hope, security and enough love to heal life's deepest wounds.

Beth and Greg haven't been in Shelter Valley during our other visits, though Greg was born and raised here. He attended Montford University. And now he's back, the newly elected sheriff. Beth read an article about Tory Evans (whom you might remember from *My Sister, Myself*—she's the woman who was escaping an abusive spouse and found shelter and solace in Shelter Valley); as a result of that, Beth came here to find safety for herself…and her child.

This story made me take a hard look at reality, at the way each person has his or her own perception of reality—and at the way other people can take control of it. I felt a little tense at times, worrying about Beth and hoping she'd find her solution, but I didn't give up on her, and I hope you don't, either. She won't disappoint you!

I love hearing from readers. Please let me know what you think! Write me at P.O. Box 15065, Scottsdale, AZ 85267 or visit me at www.tarataylorquinn.com.

Tara Taylor Quinn

Books by Tara Taylor Quinn

The Sheriff of Shelter Valley
Tara Taylor Quinn

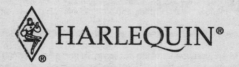

HARLEQUIN®

TORONTO • NEW YORK • LONDON
AMSTERDAM • PARIS • SYDNEY • HAMBURG
STOCKHOLM • ATHENS • TOKYO • MILAN • MADRID
PRAGUE • WARSAW • BUDAPEST • AUCKLAND

ISBN 0-373-71087-9

THE SHERIFF OF SHELTER VALLEY

Copyright © 2002 by Tara Lee Reames.

For me.

CHAPTER ONE

"MAMA! MAAMAA!" Ryan's scream tore through her fog of sleep.

Beth Allen was out of bed and across the room before she'd even fully opened her eyes. Heart pounding, she lifted her two-year-old son out of the secondhand crib, pressing his face into her neck as she held him.

"It's okay, Ry," she said softly, pushing the sweaty auburn curls away from his forehead. Curls she dyed regularly, along with her own. "Shh, Mama's right here. It was just a bad dream."

"Mama," the toddler said again, his little body shuddering. His tiny fists were clamped tightly against her—her nightshirt and strands of her straight auburn hair held securely within them.

"Mama" was about all her son said. All he'd said since she'd woken up alone with him in that motel room in Snowflake, Arizona, with a nasty bruise on her forehead, another one at the base of her skull. And no memory whatsoever.

She didn't even know her own name. She'd apparently checked in under the name Beth Allen and, trusting herself to have done so for a reason, had continued using it. It could be who she really was, but she doubted it. She'd obviously been on the run, and it didn't seem smart to have made herself easy to find.

She didn't know how old she was. How old her son was. She could only guess Ry's age by comparing him to other kids.

Stoically, Beth stood there, rocking him slowly, crooning soothingly, until she felt the added weight that signified his slumber. Looking at the crib—old brown wood whose scars were visible even in the dim August moonlight coming through curtainless windows—Beth knew she should put him back there, should do all she could to maintain normalcy at this stage of their lives.

But she didn't. She carried the baby back to the twin bed she'd picked up at a garage sale, snuggled him against her too-skinny body beneath the single sheet and willed herself back to sleep.

In that motel room in Snowflake, she'd seen a magazine article about a young woman who'd run away from an abusive husband. Like someone drawn in mingled horror and fascination to the sight of a car crash, she'd read the whole thing—and been greatly touched to find that it had a happy ending. The woman had run to someplace called Shelter Valley, Arizona.

Desperate enough to try anything, Beth had done the same.

But after six months of covering her blond hair and hiding her amnesia, she was no closer to her happy ending.

Neither, apparently, was her son. Spooning his small body up against her, she tried to convince herself that he was okay.

Ryan had only had a nightmare. Could have been about monsters in the closet or a ghost in the attic.

Except that the one-bedroom duplex she was renting had neither a closet nor an attic.

No, there was something else haunting her child, giving him these nightmares.

It was the same thing that was haunting her.

Beth just didn't have any idea what it was.

NEARLY BLINDED by the sun-brightened landscape, Sheriff Greg Richards scanned the horizon, missing nothing between him and the mountains in the distance.

A young woman had been rear-ended, forced off the road. And when she'd rolled to a stop, two assailants had pushed her into the rear of her Chevy Impala. She'd never even seen the car that hit her; she had been overtaken too quickly by the men who'd jumped out of its back seat to notice the vehicle driving off.

Stillness. That was all Greg's trained eye saw. Brownish-green desert brush. Dry, thorny plants that were tough enough to survive the scorching August sun. Cacti.

Another desert carjacking. The third in three months. A run of them—just like that summer ten years before. Yet…different. This time, instead of ending up dead or severely injured, the victim, Angela Marquette, had thrown herself out of the car. Made it to an emergency phone on the side of the road.

Greg continued to scan the surrounding area, but there was no sign of the new beige Impala. Not on the highway—patrols had been notified across the state—nor in the form of glinting metal underneath the scarred cacti and other desert landscaping that had witnessed hideous brutalities over the years. In the places it was thickest, a hijacked car or two, even an occasional dead body, could easily slide beneath it undetected.

Patrol cars and an ambulance ahead signaled the location of the victim. Pulling his unmarked car off the road and close to the group of emergency personnel, Greg got out. The immediate parting of the crowd always surprised him; he hadn't been the sheriff of Shelter Valley long enough to get used to it.

As he approached the victim, he noticed that she was shaking and in shock. And sweating, too. The young woman, her brown hair in a ponytail, leaned against one of the standard-issue cars from his division. One of the paramedics shook his head as Greg caught his eye. Apparently she'd refused medical attention.

"Angela, I'm Sheriff Richards," he said gently when her gaze, following those of his deputies, landed on him.

"We've got her full report." Deputy Burt Culver stepped up to Greg. "We just finished." Burt, only a few years older than Greg, had been with the Kachina County Sheriff's Department when Greg had first worked there as a junior deputy. Other than a short stint with Detention Services—at the one and only jail in Kachina County's jurisdiction—Burt had been content to work his way up in Operations, concentrating mostly on criminal investigations. He was one of the best.

Culver had never expressed much interest in administration, had never run for Sheriff, but Greg was hoping to talk him into accepting a promotion to Captain over Operations. No one else would be as good.

Greg glanced down at the report. "This is a number where we can reach you during the day?" he asked.

"Yes, sir," the young woman replied, her voice as shaky as her hands. "And at night, as well. I'm a student at the University of Arizona. I live at home with my parents."

"The car was theirs?" Greg asked her. Chevy Impalas weren't cheap. Certainly not the usual knock-around college vehicle. She would probably have been perfectly safe in one of those. These hijackers didn't go for low-end cars.

"No, sir, it's mine. I also work as a dance instructor in Tucson."

Greg looked over the pages Burt had handed him, confident that everything was complete. That he wasn't needed here, at the scene of the crime. Still, he thumbed through the report.

Two men had done the actual hijacking. Young, in their late teens or early twenties. One Caucasian. A blonde. The other had darker skin, brown eyes and black hair. They'd both been wearing wallet chains, faded jeans—in the one-hundred and ten degree heat—ripped tank T-shirts, medallions. The blonde—the driver—had a tattoo on his left biceps and he'd been wearing dirty white tennis shoes. They'd had her radio blaring.

"Neither of them spoke to you?"

The young woman shook her head, the movement almost spastic. Other than a couple of bruises, she'd escaped physically unharmed. But she'd probably carry mental scars for the rest of her life. Greg stared into the distance for a moment, focusing his concentration. He was the sheriff now. Personal feelings were irrelevant.

The carjackers of ten years ago had been silent, as well. No accents to give any clue that might imply one social group or school over another.

"I just remembered something," the girl said, her brown eyes almost luminescent as she struggled against tears and sunshine to look up at him. "Just after they pushed me...over the seat...one of them said something...about this 'counting double.' They turned the radio on at the same time and I was so scared... I could be wrong...." She shook her head, eyes clouded as she frowned up at him. "Maybe I'm not remembering anything at all."

"Are you sure you wouldn't like the paramedics to take a look at you?" Greg asked.

She shook her head again. "I'm fine...just a little sore..." She attempted a smile. "I called my parents." Her words suddenly came in a rush. "They're on their way to get me."

Nodding, Greg handed the report back to a sweating Culver. "See that I have a copy of this on my desk ASAP," he said, then added, "Wait here until her folks arrive. I want them to be able to get the assurances they'll undoubtedly need from the man in charge, not from a junior officer."

"Got it, Chief."

Unsettled, dissatisfied, glad only that Culver was in charge, Greg gave the young woman his own card with the invitation to call if she needed anything now or in the future, and headed back to his car.

He could keep trying to pretend that this case wasn't personal, but either way, he was going to get these guys. There was simply no other choice. With every carjacking that went unsolved, there was a greater chance that another would follow.

That was the professional reason he wasn't going to rest until the perpetrators were caught.

And the personal one…

His father's death had to be avenged.

He entered Shelter Valley city limits an hour later and drove slowly through town, glancing as he always did, at the statue of the town's founder, Samuel Montford, that had appeared while he'd been away.

There was no reason for Greg to stop by Little Spirits Day Care. Bonnie, founder and owner of the only child-care facility in Shelter Valley—and Greg's only sibling—would be busy with all the "little spirits" in her care, doing the myriad things an administrator at a day care did.

He pulled up at Little Spirits, anyway. It was Friday. After a week of day care, maybe Katie, his three-year-old niece, needed to be sprung.

Even if she didn't, Bonnie would pretend she did. Bonnie understood.

Sometimes Greg just needed a dose of innocence and warmth, sweetness and love, to counteract the rest of his world.

"Dispatch to 11:15…" The words came just as Greg was swinging shut the driver's door. With an inner groan, he caught the door, sank onto the seat again and listened.

Two minutes later, he was back on the road. There was a warrant out for Bob Mather's arrest. As far as Greg knew, the man he'd graduated from high school with hadn't been in Shelter Valley for more than five years, but his parents' place was listed as his last known address.

Which meant Greg had to pay the sweet-natured older couple yet another unpleasant visit, when he should've been watching ice cream drip down Katie's dimpled chin.

This was not a good day.

TOILETS WEREN'T HER SPECIALTY. But Beth made the white porcelain bowl, the fifth she'd faced that day, shine, anyway. A job is only worth doing if it's done right.

Beth squirted a little glass cleaner on the chrome piping and handle to make them glisten, then wiped efficiently, satisfied when she saw an elongated version of what she supposed was her chin in the spotless flush handle. She ignored the pull she felt as the quote ran through her mind again. *A job is only worth doing if it's done right.*

How did she know that? Had someone said it to her? Many times? Her mother or father, perhaps? A boss?

There was no point traveling in that direction. The blankness in her mind was not going to supply the answer. And Beth didn't dare look anywhere else.

But she made a mental note to write the thought down in her notebook when she got home that night. Because these obscure recollections were her only link with a reality she couldn't find, she was cataloguing everything she remembered—any hint that returned to her from a past she couldn't access.

And making up new rules to live by, as well. Creating herself.

Bucket full of cleaning supplies in hand, Beth blew at the strand of hair that had fallen loose from her ponytail. Only one more bathroom to go, and Beth's Basins could chalk up another good day's work. She still had to vacuum the Mathers' carpets and water mop the ceramic tile in the kitchen and baths, but those jobs weren't particularly noteworthy. Beth measured the progress of her day by bathrooms.

The doorbell rang in the front of the house. Stopping only to rinse her hands in the sink she had yet to clean, Beth wiped her palms along the legs of her overall shorts and hurried to the door. The Mathers had told her they were expecting a package, and she didn't want to disappoint them by failing to get to the door in time.

The man waiting outside was uniformed in brown, but he wasn't the UPS deliveryman she'd been expecting.

"Sheriff?" Between the hammering of her heart and the fear in her throat, she barely got the word out. His face was grim.

Ryan! He has to be okay! They can't take him! Have they found me out? What do they know that I don't? The thoughts buzzed loudly, making her dizzy.

"Beth!"

She almost relaxed a notch when Greg Richard's stern expression softened.

"I didn't know the Mathers were one of your clients."

"Just this month," she said. He hadn't known she was working there. So he hadn't come after her.

Thank God.

But then…that meant he was there to see the sweet older couple she'd met in the lobby of the Performing Arts Center at Montford University six weeks before.

"I take it Bob, Sr. and Clara aren't home?" he asked.

He had the most intense dark green eyes.

Still holding the door, Beth told him, "They went

to Phoenix to have lunch and see a movie." She frowned. "Is something wrong?" Bob, Sr. had lost both his parents during the past few months. Surely they'd had their share of bad news for a while.

Greg shook his head, but Beth had a feeling that it was the "I'm not at liberty to say" kind of gesture rather than the "no" she'd been seeking.

"I just need to ask them a couple of questions," he added, "but it sounds like they'll be gone most of the afternoon." His gaze was warm, personal.

"I got that impression."

Hands in his pockets, Greg didn't leave. "I'll catch them later tonight, then. If you don't mind, please don't mention that I've been by."

"Of course not." Beth never—ever—put her nose in other people's business. She didn't know if this was a newly acquired trait or one she'd brought with her into this prison of oblivion. "I won't be seeing or talking to them, anyway. I just leave their key under the mat when I'm through here."

"So what time would that be?"

Beth glanced at her watch—not that it was going to tell her what jobs she had left or how long they would take. "Within the hour." She was due to pick Ryan up from the Willises at five.

Ryan couldn't be enrolled in the day care in town. Not only was Beth living a lie, without even a social security number, but she couldn't take a chance on signing any official papers that might allow someone to trace her.

Especially when she had no idea who that someone might be.

So she left the toddler with two elderly sisters,

Ethel and Myra Willis, who adored him. And she only accepted cash from her clients.

"How does an early dinner sound?"

That inexplicable headiness hadn't left her since she'd answered the door. "With you?" she asked, stalling, putting off the moment when she had to refuse.

He nodded, the movement subtly incorporating his entire body. It was one of the things that kept Greg on her mind long after she'd run into him someplace or other—the way he put all of himself into everything he did. You had to be sincere to be able to do that consistently.

"I have to feed Ryan," she said, only because it was more palatable than an outright no. It still meant no.

Pulling a hand from his pocket, he turned it palm upward. "The diner serves kids."

Beth's eyes were automatically drawn to that hand and beyond, to the pocket it had left. And from there to the heavy-looking gun in a black leather holster at his hip.

"Ry's not good in restaurants." Her mouth dry, Beth knew she had to stop. Too much was at stake.

Yet she liked to think she was starting a new life. And if she was, she wanted this man in it.

If he weren't a cop. And if she weren't afraid she was on the run from something pretty damn horrible. If she were certain she could trust him, no matter who she might turn out to be, no matter what she might have done.

"He's two," Greg said. "He'll learn."

"I have no doubt he will, but I'd rather get him over the food-throwing stage in private."

Greg stared down at his feet, shod, as usual, in freshly shined black wing tips. "In all the months I've known you, I've never done one thing to give you reason to doubt me, but you always brush me off," he said eventually.

"No, I..." Beth stopped. "Okay, yes, I am."

"Is it my breath?"

"No!" She chuckled, relaxing for just a second. With the truth out in the open, the immediate danger was gone.

"My hair? You don't like black hair?" He was grinning at her, and somehow that little bit of humor was more devastating than his earlier intensity.

"I like black just fine. Tom Cruise has black hair."

"Dark brown. Tom Cruise has dark brown hair. And he's the reason you've come up with an excuse every single time I've asked you out?"

"No."

"It's the curls, then? You don't like men with curls?"

"I love your curls." Oh God. She hadn't meant to say that. Her throat started to close up again. She couldn't do this.

And she couldn't *not* do this. Beth's emotional well had been bone-dry for so long she sometimes feared it was beginning to crumble into nothingness. She had no one else sharing her life—her fears and worries and pains; worse, she didn't really even have herself. She was living with a stranger in her own mind.

"Ryan has curls," she finished lamely.

Greg's expression grew serious. "Is it the cop thing? I know a lot of women don't want to be involved with cops. Understandably so."

His guess was dead right, but not in the way he

meant. "I'm not one of them," she said, compelled to be honest with him. About this, at least. "I'd consider myself lucky to be involved with a man who'd dedicated his life to helping others. A man who put the safety of others before his own. One who still had enough faith in society to believe it's worth saving."

"Even though you'd know, every morning when you kissed him goodbye as he left for work, that you might never see him again?"

"Every woman—and man—faces that danger," she said. "I'll bet that far more people die in car accidents than on the job working as a cop."

"Far more," he agreed.

"And, anyway," she said, feeling a sudden urge to close the door, "who said anything about kissing every morning?"

"I was hoping I'd been able to slide that one by you," he said.

"Nope."

"So—" his gaze became challenging "—if it's not the cop thing and it's not my breath, it must be *you* that you're afraid of."

"I am not afraid."

He sobered. "If you need more time, Beth, I certainly understand. We could grab a sandwich as friends, maybe see a movie or something."

More time? She frowned.

"It's been—what?—less than a year since you were widowed?" he asked, his face softening.

Widowed. Oh yeah, that. It was the story she'd invented when she'd come to town. She was a recent widow attempting to start a new life. You'd think she could at least manage to keep track of the life she'd made up to replace the one she couldn't remember.

"Look," she said, really needing to get back to work. Ry was going to be looking for her soon. Routine was of vital importance to her little boy. "If you were serious about the friend thing, I could use some help."

She was testing him. And felt bad about that. But not bad enough to stop herself, apparently.

"Sure."

"I just bought a used apartment-size washer and dryer." Taking a two-year-old's two and three changes a day to the Laundromat had been about to kill her—financially and physically. "I need someone with a truck to go with me to pick it up and then help me get it into the duplex."

He'd know where she lived, then. But who was she kidding? He was the county sheriff—a powerful man. And Shelter Valley was a small town. He'd probably known where she lived for months.

"I have a truck."

"I know."

She'd passed him in town a couple of times, feeling small and insignificant in the old, primer-spattered Ford Granada she'd bought for five-hundred dollars next to his beautiful brand-new blue Ford F-150 Supercab.

"If I offer to help are you going to brush me off again?"

"No."

"You aren't just setting me up here?" He was smiling.

"No!" Beth said indignantly, but she was smiling, too.

"I'm tempted to force you to ask, just to win back a little bit of the pride you've been quietly stripping away for months. But because I'm afraid to chance it, I'll ask you, instead. May I please help you bring your new appliances home?''

Beth laughed out loud…and was shocked by the sound. She couldn't remember having heard it before. Couldn't remember anything before waking up in that motel room in Snowflake, Arizona, with bruises and a child who called her Mama crying on the bed beside her.

"If you're sure you wouldn't mind, I could sure use the help,'' she said, all laughter gone. She had no business even *thinking* about flirting with the county sheriff, but she and Ryan needed those appliances. And she couldn't get them to the duplex alone.

"What time?''

"Tonight? After dinner?''

"Sure we couldn't do it before dinner and just happen to eat while we're at it?''

"I'm sure.''

Beth hated the conflicting emotions she felt when he gave in with no further cajoling and agreed to pick her up at six-thirty that evening for the ten-minute drive out to the Andersons'. They were remodeling the one-room apartment over their garage and no longer needed the appliances, which, while five years old, had hardly been used.

Conflicting emotions—one of the few experiences Beth knew intimately. Intermittent relief. Disappointment. Resignation. Fear.

Peace. That was, and had to be, her only goal. Peace for her. And health, safety and happiness for Ryan.

Nothing else mattered.

CHAPTER TWO

HE'D SEEN HER DOWNTOWN, coming out of Weber's Department Store, at the grocery store, the gas station, and in the park just beyond Samuel Montford's statue. Seen her at Little Spirits once or twice when he'd stopped in to visit Bonnie or spring Katie. According to his sister, Beth Allen never left her son at the day care, but she volunteered once a week so he could have some playtime with the other kids.

He'd seen her at the drugstore once, and at Shelter Valley's annual Fourth of July celebration.

But he'd never seen her at home.

The duplex was not far from Zack and Randi Foster's place. But it didn't resemble that couple's home with its garden and white-picket fence. Her place was very small. One bedroom—the door was shut—a full bath squished into a half-bath space, a living room with a kitchen on the other end. And a closet that would fit either coats or the stackable laundry unit Beth had purchased. But not both.

The closet had washer-dryer hook-ups, and a clothes bar and single door, both of which had to be removed to fit the washer and dryer. The door he could rehang. The clothes bar's removal would be permanent for as long as the closet remained a laundry room.

The entire house was meticulous.

"Where'd you say you lived before coming to Shelter Valley?" Greg asked as, pliers in hand, he attached a dryer vent to the opening on the back of the appliance.

"I didn't say."

"That?" Beth's two-year-old son was standing beside Greg's toolbox.

"It's a hammer," Beth said.

"That?"

"A level."

"That?"

"A screwdriver."

Glancing between the top rack of the toolbox and the little boy, Greg frowned. "How do you know which tool he's referring to?"

Ryan hadn't pointed at anything. His index finger had been in his mouth ever since Greg had collected Beth and her son more than an hour before.

She shrugged, hoisting Ryan onto her hip. "I could see where he was looking," she said.

"You don't have to hold him." Greg returned to the metal ring he was tightening on the outside of the vent. "He's welcome to help."

She held the boy, anyway, as defensive about her son as she was about herself.

Greg still liked her.

"Here, Ryan." he said, standing to give the little boy his wrench "Can you hang on to this and give it to me when I ask for it?"

After a very long, silent stare, the toddler finally nodded and took the tool. He needed both hands to handle the weight of it, meaning that finger finally came out of his mouth—but he didn't seem to mind the sacrifice.

"You changed."

Beth's words threw him. "Changed?" he asked. "How?"

"Out of your uniform."

"I'm off duty."

"I've never seen you out of uniform."

He hadn't thought about that, but supposed she was right. He'd been on duty the Fourth of July. And just coming off duty each time he'd stopped in at Little Spirits. She hadn't been there the afternoon he'd spent building the sandbox on the patio of the day care.

"You look different."

Giving the dryer vent a tug, satisfied that it was securely in place, Greg moved down to the washer. "Good different?" he asked. The jeans were his favorite, washed so many times they were faded and malleable, just the way he liked them.

"Less...official."

He screwed the washer tubing to the cold-water spigot. "So, you going to tell me where you're from?"

"You going to tell me why you're so nosy?"

"I'm a cop. It's my job to be nosy."

"I thought you were off duty."

"Touché." Leaning around the edge of the washer, he grinned at her.

Beth wasn't grinning back. Her expression showed both anger and hurt. And defensiveness—again. She hugged Ryan closer, almost knocking the wrench out of the little guy's hands, but the boy didn't complain. He just held on tighter.

Ryan Allen was one of the quietest toddlers Greg had ever met.

"You think I'm some kind of threat to the people of Shelter Valley?" she asked.

"Of course not!" Greg would've laughed out loud if he wasn't so surprised by the tension that had suddenly entered the room. "I'm interested, okay?" he said, eager to clarify himself before the evening dived into dismal failure. "As a guy, not as a cop."

"Interested." Her hold on the boy loosened, but not much.

"Yeah, you know, interested." He went back to the job at hand, thinking it was probably his safest move. "Men do that," he grunted. He could tell the water spigots hadn't been used in a while. If ever. He was having one helluva time persuading the faucet to turn. "They get interested in women who attract them."

"I attract you?"

An entirely different note had entered her voice. Though the sound of battle hadn't left, he was no longer sure he was the target.

"I haven't made that perfectly obvious by now?"

The room had gone too still. Greg glanced around the washer once more, half thinking he might find he was alone, and his gaze locked with Beth's.

"I need to be more obvious?" he asked. He'd never worked so hard for a woman in his life. Not that he'd had that many. His life had taken unexpected turns, been filled with unexpected responsibilities, but when he'd wanted a woman, he hadn't had to work at it.

"No," she said, looking down. From his silent vantage point, Ryan stared up at her, as though following the conversation with interest. "I, um...guess—" her eyes returned to his "—you have to be *looking* to see the obvious, don't you?"

"You're trying to tell me you aren't looking. Period." He couldn't deny his disappointment.

"No. Yes." She set her son down. "I'm saying maybe I didn't notice your, um, interest because I wasn't looking."

The woman challenged him at every turn—something he particularly liked about her—and yet she'd never, until that moment, been difficult to follow. Just difficult to get any information from.

Of course, she'd been hurt, was wary. Probably loath to risk letting anyone get close again. Greg could understand that. It had taken him a long time to open up after Shelby left.

"And now that I've pointed it out to you?"

"I know."

"And?"

"I don't know." As Ryan toddled toward Greg to see what he was doing, Beth leaned over the washer. "How's it going back there?"

Greg twisted the faucet again and it gave immediately. Probably because exasperation had added strength to his grip. "Good," he told her. "Another five minutes and you can throw in your first load."

"Can I have the wrench, Ryan?" he asked, surprised when he turned his head to see the little guy so close to him, staring him right in the eye. Without blinking, the boy handed over the wrench.

"He's a man of few words," Greg said to Beth.

"We're working on that."

With his only living relative in the day care business, Greg knew a lot about kids. "He'll talk when he's ready."

"I hope so."

Greg made one more adjustment. "Here you go, little bud," he said, handing the wrench back to Beth's son. "You want to drop that in the toolbox for me?"

Ryan put the tool down on top of the hammer.

"I'll bet he has more to say when it's just the two of you," he said as he slid the appliances in place against the wall.

"Not really."

She sounded worried. Greg figured it had to be hard for her, a single mother—all alone in the world, as far as he could tell. She had no one to share the worries and heartaches with, to calm the fears, to share the mammoth responsibility of child-rearing.

More than ever, he wanted to change that.

If she'd let him.

"Did you get to the Mathers'?" she asked as he packed up his toolbox.

Greg nodded. It had been just as difficult as he'd expected.

"Bad news?"

"A sheriff rarely gets to deliver good news."

"Clara told me they lost a daughter."

Resting a foot on his toolbox, Greg leaned his forearm on his leg. "It's been almost twenty years," he told her, nowhere near ready to leave. Ryan was sitting on the floor a few feet away, a toy on his lap, pulled from a neat stack of colorful objects in the bottom drawer of the end table. The boy was obviously occupied, but Greg lowered his voice, anyway. "She and some friends were in a boat on Canyon Lake. They hit a rock. She was thrown and ended up underneath the boat."

Beth's eyes clouded. "They have pictures of a boy in their bedroom. I'm assuming they have a son, too?"

Greg nodded.

"Is he still around?"

"He's still alive." Greg sighed. The Mathers had physically deflated as he'd told them about the latest trouble Bob had gotten into. "After Molly, their daughter, was killed, they focused everything they had on Bob. He became their reason for living. He was a rebellious kid, but they pinned all their hope, love and energy on him."

"You knew Bob?"

"We graduated in the same class."

"Is he good to them?"

Greg wasn't surprised by the compassion he read on Beth's face. He'd been touched by her natural warmth the first time he'd run into her at the day care. He hadn't needed his sister's priming—her point-blank matchmaking attempts—to get his attention. Odd how someone could be so closed off and yet emanate such caring.

"Bob somehow came out of it all believing that the world owes him a living. He's a conniver who works too little and drinks too much."

"He's not good to them."

Most of what Greg knew, he wasn't at liberty to say. "He hasn't been home to see them in over five years." He could tell her that much.

"What a shame. They're such nice people."

"They are."

"It's not right, you know," she said softly, her arms wrapped around her middle as she leaned back against the wall, facing him and the room where her son played.

"What's that?"

"Life, I guess. You have people like the Mathers, filled with unconditional love, great parents in an empty house, and their son, a jerk who's completely wasting one of the greatest gifts he'll ever get in this life. I'd literally give a limb to have what he's just throwing away."

She stopped, stepped away from the wall and busied herself with closing the closet door and picking up the packaging from the dryer vent, the papers she'd been given with the appliances.

She'd said more than she'd meant to. He could tell by the stiffness in her back. The way she wouldn't look at him. Greg knew the signs well. He'd seen them again and again over the years as he'd questioned suspects. Could tell when just another push or two would wring the confession he was seeking.

"How about we take this little guy out for ice cream?" he asked, walking toward Ryan.

"Cweam?" the boy echoed, staring up at his mother.

"He's messy," Beth warned.

It wasn't a no. Greg was elated. Probably far beyond what the situation warranted.

"Messiness is an unwritten rule when you're two," he said lightly.

He could read the uncertainty in her face. Which only made him want her capitulation that much more.

If he was a nice guy, he'd give up. Go away and leave her alone, quit bugging her, as she seemed to want. Except, Greg didn't feel at all sure that *was* what she wanted. From the very beginning, whenever their eyes met, which she didn't allow often, he'd felt the communication between them.

Something about this woman kept bringing him back, in spite of her refusal to have anything to do with him. And he had a pretty strong suspicion that she was drawn to him, too.

Her mouth said no. But he wasn't convinced the rest of her agreed.

"Aren't you worried about what people will think?" she said in a low voice.

As excuses went, it wasn't one of her better ones. "It isn't against the law for sheriffs to eat ice cream with messy kids."

"Cweam?" Ryan asked again. Beth picked him up.

"Greg—" She stopped abruptly.

It was the first time she'd called him by his first name. He liked it. Too much.

"You know what I mean," she said, her shoulders dropping. "I've only been here six months and don't know many people, but I've certainly seen how well-oiled the gossip wheel is in this town. It might make things uncomfortable for you if you're seen with the cleaning lady."

"We aren't snobs in Shelter Valley."

"I know, but I'm a nobody who cleans houses and you're the boss of the entire county."

"I don't think Mayor Smith would be too happy to hear you say that."

"Even I know that Junior Smith is just a figurehead in this town."

"Cweam?"

The boy might not talk a lot, but he was persistent. Greg liked that.

"Why don't you tell me the real reason you're so hesitant to be seen with me," he said.

She didn't. But he had a pretty good idea that she wanted to. Her eyes were telling him so much, frustrating him because, as hard as he tried, he couldn't translate those messages.

She'd mentioned gossip. "You're worried that they're going to see us together once and start planning the wedding."

"I might worry about it if I believed for one second that anyone would think I was good enough for you."

"Bonnie's been trying to hook us up for two months."

"No way!"

"Yes, way. She's invited you to dinner every Sunday for the past five weeks."

"So?"

"I was invited, too."

"Cweam?"

"Just a minute, Ry," Beth said softly, kissing the top of the boy's curly head.

"That's just a coincidence," she told Greg, adjusting her son on her hip. Ryan slid a finger into his mouth.

Katie would've been crying by now, demanding ice cream. Beth's son didn't seem to demand much at all. Something he had in common with his mother.

"Trust me, there are no coincidences with my sister," Greg told her, prepared to stay there arguing the point all night if necessary. "And she wouldn't leave something as important as this to chance, anyway. She's not the least bit subtle or embarrassed about how adamant she is to change my marital status. Nor has she been subtle about telling me what a fool I'd be if I let you get away—I'd be missing my chance of a lifetime." He mimicked the little sister he adored.

"So you're doing this for her."

Greg took more hope from the disappointment he heard in her voice than any other thing she'd said or done since he'd met her.

"No."

He had no idea what had tied Beth Allen up in knots so tight they were choking her, but it bothered the hell out of him. She shouldn't have to fight this hard all the time.

"I noticed you before Bonnie said a word," he said, telling her something he would normally have kept to himself. "In fact, I'd already tried to get you to go out with me before she told me there was someone I 'just had to meet.'"

"Oh."

"Cweam?" Ryan said around the finger in his mouth.

Greg's eyes met Beth's and that strange thing happened between them again. As though something inside her were conversing with something inside him....

"Not tonight, Ry," she finally said, breaking eye contact with Greg.

But she hadn't looked away fast enough. He'd seen the pain in her eyes as she'd turned him down. It was the most encouraging rejection he'd had yet.

"Another time, then," he murmured.

He could've sworn, as he said goodbye and told her he'd be in touch, that she seemed relieved.

Yep, there was no doubt about it.

Beth Allen wanted him.

"BONNIE, CAN WE TALK?" Monday was not her usual day to volunteer at the day care, but Beth had come, anyway. She'd been thinking about this all weekend.

"Sure," the woman said, giving Beth one of her signature cheery smiles. Other than the dark curls that sprang from all angles on her head, thirty-four-year-old Bonnie looked nothing like her older brother. Short where he was tall, plump where he was solidly fit, she could be, nevertheless, as intimidating as he when she got an idea.

Beth knew this about her and she'd only known the woman a few months. Until now, she'd liked that trait, identified with it somehow.

With Ryan in clear view, Beth followed Bonnie into her windowed office and, canvas bag still over her shoulder, sat when Bonnie closed the door.

"What's up?"

"I want you to quit bugging Greg to ask me out."

"Why? Greg's great! You two would have so much fun together."

In another life, Beth was certain she'd agree. It was precisely because she wished so badly that this *was* another life that she had to resist. She'd thought about it all weekend and knew she had no choice.

Yet, how she longed to be able to confide in this woman, to talk through her thoughts and fears, benefit from Bonnie's perspective.

Almost as badly as she longed to go out with Bonnie's brother.

"I just don't want to be a charity case," she said, hating how lame she sounded. "I don't want anyone asking me out because he feels sorry for me or he's forced into it or—"

Bonnie cut her off. "You don't know Greg very

well if you think I could force him to do anything he didn't feel was right. Nor would he ever date a woman simply because I wanted him to. Otherwise, he wouldn't be thirty-six years old and still single.''

''He told me you've been trying to get us together for months.''

''And if he's asked you out, it has absolutely nothing to do with me.''

Bonnie's green eyes were so clear, so sure. She was the closest thing Beth had to a friend in this town. Although she knew it would probably shock the other woman, Beth's relationship with Bonnie meant the world to her.

''Well, just stop, okay?'' she said, standing. Somehow she'd convinced herself that if Bonnie quit pushing, so would Greg.

Or was it because she secretly hoped he wouldn't that she'd been able to take this stand?

''Sure,'' Bonnie said. ''But it's not going to change anything. If Greg asked women out because I pushed them at him, he wouldn't have had eight months—at least—without a real date.''

Beth sat back down. ''He hasn't had a date in eight months?''

''I said *at least* eight months. That's how long I know about. That's how long he's been back in Shelter Valley.''

''Back? I thought he grew up here.'' She didn't care. Wasn't interested. Ryan was playing happily with Bo Roberts, a three-year-old with Down's syndrome. Bo, a moderately affected child, was a favorite at Little Spirits and particularly a favorite of Ryan's.

''He did. We both did. But Greg moved to Phoenix ten years ago.''

"To be a cop?"

Hands clasped together on the desk in front of her, Bonnie shook her head, eyes grim. It wasn't something Beth had seen very often.

"He was already a cop," Greg's sister said. "Our father was severely injured in a carjacking and required more care than he could get in Shelter Valley. Greg moved with him to Phoenix and looked after him until he died."

Beth's heart fell. A dull ache started deep inside her. She didn't want Bonnie—or Greg—to have suffered so.

"What about your mother?"

"She died when I was twelve. From a beesting, of all things. No one knew she was deathly allergic."

"I'm so sorry."

"Me, too."

Beth needed to say more. Much more. And couldn't find anything to say at all.

"So it was just you and Greg and your dad after that?"

Bonnie nodded, and the two women were silent for a moment, each lost in her own thoughts. Bonnie, Beth supposed, was reliving those years. Beth was searching desperately for anything in her life that might help her to help Bonnie. But, as usual, she found nothing there at all.

"Anyway," Bonnie said suddenly, spreading her arms wide, "Greg moved back here to run for Sheriff last January and hasn't had a single date since he was elected. And it hasn't been for lack of trying on my part, either."

"So I'm just one in a long line to you, eh?" Beth asked, trying to lighten the tension a bit, make sure

Bonnie knew there were no hard feelings, and the two women chuckled as they returned to the playroom.

Bonnie went back to supervising and Beth to finding crayons and engaging little minds in age-appropriate activities. On the surface, nothing had changed. But Beth was looking at her friend with new eyes. She'd had no idea Bonnie had led anything other than a blessed life.

There was a lesson in this.

Bonnie had suffered, and still found a way to love life. The other woman's cheerfulness, her happiness, could not be faked. It bubbled from deep inside her, and was too consistent not to be genuine.

Beth had a new personal goal. Peace was still what mattered most—behind Ryan's health and happiness, of course. But she didn't plan to completely scratch happiness off her list. At least, not yet.

The next time Bonnie asked her and Ryan to Sunday dinner, she was going to accept. What was she accomplishing by denying herself friends? She literally didn't know what she had to offer, so there was no way she could embark on an intimate relationship. But where was the harm in taking part in a family dinner? How was she ever going to create a new life for Ryan and herself if she didn't start living?

CHAPTER THREE

LOOKING AT THE PHOTOS WAS GRUELING.

"I think we're wasting our time here, looking in the wrong places." Deputy Burt Culver said. Greg studied the photos, anyway.

It was the third Friday in August, and there'd been a fourth carjacking the night before. This time the victim hadn't been so lucky. A fifty-three-year-old woman on her way home from work in Phoenix had been found dead along the side of the highway. There was still no sign of the new-model Infiniti she'd been driving.

"I understand why it's important to you to tie these incidents together with what happened ten years ago, Greg, but you're letting this get personal."

Anyone but Burt would be receiving his walking papers at that moment. Eyes narrowed, Greg glanced up from the desk strewn with snapshots. "I appreciate your concern," he said, tight-lipped, and turned back to the pictures—both old and new—of mangled cars. Of victims.

"But you're not going to stop," Burt said. In addition to obvious concern, there was a note of something bordering on disapproval in the other man's voice.

Studying a photo of the smashed front end of a ten-year-old Ford Thunderbird, Greg shook his head.

"I'm not going to stop." The front end of a year-old Lexus found abandoned earlier that summer, its driver nearly dead from dehydration, unconscious in the back seat, looked strangely similar to that of the Thunderbird. They hadn't started out looking similar. "Neither am I going to let my personal reasons for wanting this case solved interfere with the job of solving it."

His trained eye skimmed over the image of the nearly nude young woman found in the desert ten summers before. The carjackers had become rapists that time. Her car, a newer-model Buick, had turned up twenty miles farther down the road. Also smashed.

Greg frowned. Another front-end job.

"My instincts—" He paused. "My cop instincts are telling me there's some connection here."

"Why?" Culver asked, barely glancing at the photos. Of course, he'd seen them all before. Many times. As had Greg. "Why these two sets only? Why not look into the rash of heists down south?"

"Those cars were being put to use."

"So?"

"Whoever's doing this is taking brand-new or nearly new cars, expensive ones, and smashing them up."

"Joyriders."

Yeah. It happened. More often than Greg liked to admit.

And yet... "Look at these front ends," Greg said, lining up a few of the photos on another part of the desk.

Burt looked. "They're mangled."

"They're identical," Greg insisted.

"They're smashed, Greg." Burt wasn't impressed.

Hell, maybe he *was* letting it get personal. Maybe he should agree with his deputy and back away. Still...

"They all look like they hit the same thing at the same angle and speed," he said slowly.

Pulling at his ear—something he only did when he was feeling uncomfortable—the deputy leaned his other hand on the desk and gave the photos more than the cursory glance he'd afforded them earlier. "Could be," he said.

It would be pretty difficult, especially after the hard time he'd just given Greg, for the older man to admit he'd missed something that might be important. Greg had no desire to belabor the issue. His eyes moved to the table behind his deputy and the partially constructed jigsaw puzzle there, which gave Burt a moment to himself.

"Let's not write off the past just yet" was all he said.

"I'll order some blowups of these...."

Burt didn't meet Greg's eyes again as he left the room. Standing over the puzzle, pleased to fit in the first piece he chose, Greg sympathized with his friend and co-worker. There was nothing a cop like Burt—or Greg—hated more than to have missed something important.

WHY HAD SHE THOUGHT this was a good idea? With her canvas bag clutched at her side, Beth stood in Bonnie Neilson's sunny kitchen on the third Sunday in August, watching Ryan and Katie ignoring each other as they played quietly in the attached family room. She longed for the dingy but very organized interior of her rented duplex. Better the hardship you knew than one you didn't.

The duplex wasn't much, but for the time being, it was hers. She was in control there. Safe.

"Keith just went to town for more ice," Bonnie was saying as she put the finishing touches on a delicious-looking fresh vegetable salad. Already in a basket on the table was a pile of homemade rolls. Really homemade, not the bread-machine kind she used to make…

Beth froze. She'd had a memory. A real one. She had no idea where that bread machine was, no picture of a kitchen, a home, a neighborhood, a town or state—but she knew she'd had a bread machine. And she'd used it.

And been chastised for it?

"Can I do something?" Beth asked, probably too suddenly, reacting to a familiar surge of panic. She needed something to occupy herself, calm herself.

Staying busy had worked for months. As far as she knew, it was the only thing that worked.

"You can—"

"Unca!" Katie's squeal interrupted her mother.

The ensuing commotion as Katie tossed aside the magnetic writing board she'd had on her lap and jumped up to throw herself at her newly arrived uncle—and Ryan dropped the circular plastic shape he'd been attempting to shove into a square opening on the shape-sorter to make his way over to his mother's leg—served to distract Beth. She was so relieved, she didn't have nearly the problem she had anticipated with the arrival of Greg Richards.

Instead, she was almost thankful he'd come.

LATER THAT AFTERNOON, Beth had very mixed emotions about Greg's presence at his sister's house. Bonnie and Keith, her husband, had left to drive over to his grandmother's. Katie was asleep in the new trundle bed in her room. Ryan was also asleep, his little body reassuring and warm against her. He'd climbed in her lap after lunch, when they'd all migrated to the sitting room before trying the new chocolate cream cheese dessert Bonnie had made that morning.

That was when Keith's grandmother had called and Beth had suddenly found herself alone with a man who launched her right out of her element.

Not that she had any idea what her real element was. These days, all she had to go by was the Beth Allen Rules of Survival. A notebook with frighteningly few memories. Plus the perceptions she'd had, decisions she'd made, since waking up in that motel room.

He lounged on the leather couch, dressed in jeans and a cotton-knit pullover that emphasized the breadth of his chest. He was surveying her lazily, and appeared content to do so for some time to come. Beth didn't think she could tolerate that.

"Bonnie said you'd explain about Grandma Neilson," she reminded him. His younger sister had begged that Beth stay, insisting they'd only be gone a few minutes and she'd hate it if their day was ruined.

"She refuses Bonnie's invitation to join us for dinner on a fairly regular basis, insisting she doesn't want to impose, and then, inevitably, has some kind of mock crisis that's far more of an imposition than her acceptance of the dinner invitation would've been."

"Mock crisis?" Soothed into an unusual sense of security, Beth leaned back against the oversize leather chair she'd fallen into after lunch.

"Something that seems to need immediate attention, but that she could handle perfectly well by herself—or that turns out to be nothing at all. A toilet that *might* be clogged, for example. Or a strange noise in the attic, due to a loose shingle." Greg was smiling.

"But today's call—a seventy-five-year-old woman who's lost electricity in half her house, including her refrigerator—sounds pretty legit to me."

"Most likely a blown fuse."

"Still, for a woman her age..."

"Baloney," Greg exclaimed.

Ryan stirred, but settled back against her, his auburn curls growing sweaty where his head lay against her.

"She might be seventy-five years old, but she's as feisty and as manipulative as they come—and I've loved her as long as I can remember."

"You knew her before Bonnie and Keith got married?"

"She used to be the librarian at the elementary school. Every kid in town knew Mrs. Neilson. And loved her, too, I suppose. She's been a widow since Keith's dad was little. She's also the strongest person I've ever met. She'd go to the wall for any one of us if she believed in our cause. Nothing as trivial as a blown fuse is going to get in her way. Lonna Neilson could rewire that whole house if she put her mind to it."

"Then, why do Bonnie and Keith keep running over there?"

Greg's shrug drew her attention to the width of his shoulders. Shoulders a woman could lay her head against...

If that woman wasn't Beth Allen. Or Beth Who-ever-she-was.

"In the first place," he said, "because they never know whether she's crying wolf or whether it might be the real thing."

She liked that. A lot. That they didn't give up on the old woman.

"And more importantly, because what's really driving her to call is the need to know she's loved. That's why Bonnie always goes, as well. It takes both of them to either make her feel good enough to be happy at home, or to convince her to join them here."

Beth smiled, praying he couldn't see the trembling of her lips. "So you're used to being left here with Katie every Sunday?" she asked. *Keep talking, don't think. Don't envision a vacant future, or, maybe worse, one that isn't vacant, only intolerable.*

"Nah, Grandma Neilson comes over about half the time she's asked, and then there's the occasional Sunday when no crisis arises."

His words were something to focus on. Something to take her thoughts away from the fact that her past held a threat so great she'd taken her baby and run.

"But I'm used to time alone with Katie," Greg continued lazily. "She's a big part of my life."

"Have you ever thought about having kids of your own?"

Beth's gaze shot down to Ryan as soon as she heard her own words. She'd broken a major Beth Allen rule. *Never ask personal questions.* Doing so was often taken as an invitation by the recipient to ask questions, too.

Damn. Give her a good meal, a comfortable chair and she lost all sense of herself. Which was scary when one didn't have much of that to begin with. When one was making things up as one went along...

Lifting an ankle to his knee, Greg slouched down farther. He looked more like a college kid than the head of an entire law enforcement organization. "I used to think I'd have a whole houseful of kids by now," he said. "You've probably noticed that Shelter Valley families tend to be rather large. You don't have to live here long to figure that out."

His grin was sardonic, half deprecating, half affectionate, as he spoke about the people he protected day in and day out.

"Especially if you spend any time at Little Spirits," Beth said, his easy tone allowing her to continue a conversation she'd meant to shut down. "It seems like everyone in Shelter Valley is related."

"Either by blood or by a closeness of the heart," Greg agreed. He sounded proud of the fact. "Everyone in Shelter Valley has family of one sort or another."

It was the perfect opportunity to ask why he didn't have that houseful of kids he'd envisioned. She badly wanted to know.

Only the very real threats she lived with every second of her life kept her silent. The threat of being found out. And of never finding out. Never learning who she was. What she was hiding from.

And why she hadn't been strong enough to solve her problems rather than run from them.

The threat that he might ask questions she couldn't answer. Or find answers she didn't want him to have.

"Did you and your husband plan to have more children?"

Blank. That was the only way to describe the mental picture his question elicited. But there was nothing blank about the instant panic that accompanied the emptiness. As the dull red haze blotted out her peripheral vision—a reaction she'd long since recognized as her body's danger signal—Beth again looked down at her son.

She could do this, get through whatever life required, for Ryan. Without a single memory, she knew he was the reason she'd run. And she'd keep running forever, from her memory, her needs, her heart, if that was what it took to keep him safe.

"I'm perfectly happy with Ryan," she said.

"So you'd planned for him to be an only child?"

"Not necessarily."

"Did your husband spend a lot of time with the boy?"

I don't know! "What's with the inquisition, Sheriff?" Guided by survival instincts, she stared at him, chin raised, as she offered the challenge.

And then turned quickly away. Those dark green eyes scared her with their intensity. When he looked at her, Greg Richards saw more than she could allow. She didn't know how or why; she only knew it had to stop.

"I'm just trying to get you know you, Beth, but for some reason you make that very difficult. I can't help wondering why."

Because if she told him the smallest thing—truth or lie—he'd be able to find out more. Because she couldn't afford to trust. Not even him. No matter what her heart said.

The red haze was back. "I notice you didn't answer my earlier question about your own empty house," she said, making a quick amendment to Beth Allen's Rules of Survival. Avoiding personal questions was no longer the issue. Sidetracking him was.

"A couple of things happened to change my plans."

"What things?" The fact that she really wanted to know made the query a dangerous one. But she had to keep him talking—about him. And not her. It wouldn't be much longer before Bonnie and Keith returned. "You haven't met the right woman?"

It was a common enough excuse.

"I met her."

Oh. Beth frowned. "Was she from Shelter Valley?" Had the woman died? Why hadn't Bonnie told her?

"Born and raised," Greg said, his thumb tapping a rhythm on the couch beside him. "Shelby and I met in grade school. Dated all through high school. I think I always knew I'd marry her someday."

"What happened?" And why was she taking this so personally?

"I asked her to marry me, but I wanted to wait until after I graduated from A.S.U. and the police academy."

Beth didn't think she'd have agreed to wait—and was bothered by that thought. Did it mean she was impatient by nature? She certainly hadn't had any indication of that up to this point. But she'd been so busy surviving, self-discovery hadn't been much of an option.

As life in Shelter Valley grew more routine, things were starting to slip out from her hidden past, her hidden mind. She wanted that so badly.

And yet...she didn't want it at all.

Ignorance allowed her to stay safe in Shelter Valley and raise her son.

Of course, maybe the reason she wouldn't have agreed to wait had nothing to do with her; maybe it was just because of Greg. She couldn't imagine having him in love with her and agreeing to wait a week, let alone years.

"During my last year of college, Shelby went to Los Angeles to visit a girl who'd lived with her grandparents in Shelter Valley during our senior year in high school. Shelby met some guy in California and was married within a month."

"What?" Beth sat forward, completely forgetting that Ryan was sound asleep. Disturbed, the child lifted his head, eyes unfocused as he opened them. He fussed for a second and then settled against her and went back to sleep.

"She wanted out of Shelter Valley. Didn't want to be trapped in this small town, raising a bunch of kids. She just hadn't bothered to tell me that."

"She was an idiot." The words weren't conciliatory or polite. Beth honestly couldn't think of any dream better than a real home in this town, shared with a loving man. One who'd love Ryan, teach him the things a son should know. One who'd give her another baby or two...

But was it the *real* Beth thinking these thoughts? Or were they simply the desperate longings of a lost woman on the run?

"I like to think so," Greg said, grinning at her.

"Anyway," he added, growing more serious, "that kind of put a kink in my plans for home and family."

The softly spoken words lured her further into the dangerous conversation.

"That must've been at least ten years ago," she said. "I can't believe there haven't been opportunities since then."

"I spent the past ten years taking care of my father."

"Bonnie told me," Beth said, compassion welling up so strongly she wasn't sure what to do with it. "I'm so sorry."

Tight-lipped, Greg didn't say anything. Beth could almost feel his frustration...and pain.

Which was ridiculous. She barely knew this man.

She adjusted Ryan, moving him to her other shoulder. His sweaty hair had left a damp spot where his head had lain.

"So you didn't date for ten years?" The superfluous words were probably all wrong, but what else could she ask?

"I dated," Greg answered with a dim version of the grin he'd given her earlier. But he looked relieved, too, to have been rescued from whatever thoughts had been hounding him. "I just couldn't find a woman willing to take on a paraplegic senior citizen."

And Greg was not a man who would put his father in a full-time care facility unless there was no other choice.

Beth had never wished more than she did in that moment that she was free to like this man—and maybe let something develop between them. Something more than liking...

DR. PETER STERLING and Houston prosecuting attorney James Silverman faced each other in the elegantly furnished waiting room of Sterling Silver Spa, in the newly incorporated town of Sterling Silver, Texas. The spa's last client had just left for the evening.

"Damn, it's hot." Dr. Sterling pulled at the collar of his pristine white shirt. He'd just walked over from visiting a new resident in the apartment complex a couple of blocks away. "August has got to be the worst month of the year."

Silverman didn't agree. He thought January's cold was pretty miserable. But it wasn't worth an argument to say so. Loosening his tie, he unfastened the top button of his dress shirt. How did Sterling do it? Just keep going every day, always looking perfect?

Didn't the man ever get tired?

And what did it say about Silverman that he was damn exhausted?

"It's time to hire someone new," Sterling said, his eyes black points of steel as they pinned Silverman. "Winters isn't working out. We should've heard something by now."

"I know." James undid a second button. He'd been unhappy with the private investigator for weeks. But he didn't know whom he could trust. There was too much at stake.

"Every day that goes by puts us all in more jeopardy."

"I know."

"We can't think only of ourselves," Sterling reminded him, as he did in just about every conversation the two men had these days. "We have many, many good people relying on us."

"I know." No one knew that better than James

Silverman. He didn't need Sterling reminding him, pressuring him. He carried the burden of his mistake every waking—and sleeping—moment of his life.

He wasn't going to fail his new family, his friends. If nothing else, he believed in the cause. In them. He might have lost his faith in most things, but he still believed in a better tomorrow, a world free of negative energy and aggression.

They'd worked too hard, for too long, and come too far to let a traitor ruin everything for them now.

"Beth's dangerous."

"Yes." James felt sick.

"There's no telling what she's capable of."

Silverman nodded.

"She has to be stopped," Sterling said, his voice colder than any of his patients had ever heard. "At all costs."

"I know."

Satisfied, Sterling got to his feet. The meeting was over.

"We'll get through this together," he said, his tone softer. "Together we always find the cure, don't we?"

James nodded, more because it was expected of him than because he was in a trusting mood that night. As he locked up, he wondered if the doctor's cures were losing their effectiveness. For him, anyway... And that made Beth's defection more dangerous than ever.

CHAPTER FOUR

AS HE LOCKED THE DOOR of his office, Greg thought about how he couldn't lock away the impressions that continued to bombard him. There were puzzle pieces that definitely fit together—as clearly as the myriad jigsaws he'd worked on over the years. If only he could figure out how... Culver was right, there'd been many carjackings in the past ten years. No reason to believe that this year's series had anything to do with the ones that had happened ten years ago. Except that in both cases, there had been a series.

Of course, Burt was also right in his claim that the occurrences near the border had been a series, too.

But...

The pieces floated in and out, settling, moving around, changing location without offering him a single answer.

He was outside Beth's nondescript apartment on one of the older streets in Shelter Valley. Greg chuckled to himself. Considering where he was, his thoughts seemed fitting. Because, judging by past experience, he wasn't going to find out any of the hundred things he wanted to know here, either.

And just as he did with any other puzzle, he kept looking at all the pieces. Turning them this way and that, trying to fit them here or there to create the whole picture. When something mattered enough, when the feeling was strong enough, there wasn't any other choice.

"Greg. Hi." It wasn't the most welcoming tone as Beth opened her door to him that Wednesday night. He hadn't seen or spoken to her since she'd left his sister's right after dessert, late Sunday afternoon.

She'd blamed her early departure on Ryan's grumpiness on waking, but Greg wasn't convinced that was the only reason.

Maybe he should've taken time this afternoon to stop at home and change out of his uniform.

"I knew that if I asked you to dinner or a movie— or anything else, for that matter—you'd say no, so I decided to just come by."

Face softening, though not quite into a smile, Beth leaned against the door. She was wearing a black tank top and black sweats cut off just below the knee. One of the sexiest outfits he'd ever seen.

"If you know I don't want to go out with you, why bother?" she asked.

She hadn't shut the door. Nor did her question seem nearly as off-putting as it could've been. As a matter of fact, she sounded curious.

Good.

"I don't think we've established that you don't *want* to go out with me. Only that you'd say no if I asked."

"Isn't that the same thing?"

Glad he'd come, Greg shook his head. "I don't think so." He paused, pretending to consider. "Nope, not at all."

She straightened. "Well, it seems like the same thing to me," she said.

She'd tensed again.

"It would be a good idea to ask me in," Greg said quickly, before she had a chance to dismiss him. "You know, before the neighbors see a uniformed officer at your door and start to talk."

Beth grinned, looking out at the street in front of her house where he'd left his car. "Oh yeah, like that thing with the big 'Sheriff' emblazoned on the side isn't going to raise any suspicion?"

"Hell, no." He grinned, too, hands in his pockets as he stood his ground. "They'll just think the sheriff's sweet on you."

"And that won't cause talk?"

"Well, not the kind I was referring to. You know, the kind where everyone whispers about the possible secret life you're living and they start to weave fantasies about bank robberies or jewel thefts and lock their windows and doors at night and give you a wide berth anytime they run into you at the grocery store."

"Oh, that." Beth started to pale at the ridiculous situation he was describing, but then she laughed. "Yeah, that's about as likely as the sheriff being sweet on me."

"I sure hope not," he said, almost under his breath. And then wished he hadn't. That was good for a slammed door in his face.

Because he didn't know what else to do, Greg met her eyes. And that was when *it* always happened with them. From the first time he'd met her, he'd recognized something in that deep blue gaze. And until he knew what *it* was, what *it* meant, he had to keep coming back.

She didn't shut him out or close the door.

"May I come in?"

Beth just stared. Her eyes were trying to tell him something…if only he could decipher what it was.

"I won't stay long."

Still without a word, she stood back, holding the door wide. Greg quickly stepped inside and followed her into the small living room. It was as neat as it had been the last time he was there. Neat and bare.

"Where's Ryan?" he asked. He'd expected the boy to be playing quietly on the floor, had expected to see some toys out, stacked along the wall, something.

As far as he could tell, Ryan Allen hadn't discovered the terrible twos yet.

"He's asleep already. Normally bedtime isn't until seven-thirty, but I had a cancellation today and we spent the afternoon at the day care. He was beat."

"Did he and Katie acknowledge each other?" Greg asked, taking a seat on the edge of an old but relatively clean tweed couch, elbows on his knees.

"Nope."

"Your son doesn't like my niece?"

"More likely, your niece isn't interested in giving my son the time of day." She had a challenging glint in her eyes.

God, he loved it when she was feisty. And wondered why he saw that side of her so infrequently.

"No way," he said, shaking his head as he grinned up at her. "Katie'll make friends with anyone."

"You make it sound like she shows no discrimination at all."

He shrugged. "She's a day care kid," he said. "She really will play with anyone. So the problem has to be Ryan. The boy's stuck on himself." He was being outrageous and didn't care. He'd made her smile.

"Or maybe Katie thinks since she's *so much older,* it would be beneath her to play with a two-year-old."

"Were you that way in high school? Too good to go out with the younger guys?"

"Probably not."

"Why just probably?"

She looked away, her shoulders hunched as she rested her arms along the sides of her chair, an old but sturdy rocker. "Oh, you know," she said, "you never see yourself in quite the same way other people do."

True enough. "Tell me what you think you were like in high school."

It took her a long time to answer. "Not one of the stupidest kids in class, but not one of the smartest, either."

"I'll bet you never failed a single test."

"Not that I can remember."

"And you had dates every weekend."

"Well, I don't recall a single weekend without one." She grinned, but was still evading his eyes.

"Did you have a steady boyfriend?"

"Nobody who stayed with me."

She was finally talking to him. Sort of. He wondered what she'd been like before the loss of her husband, before his death had locked her so deeply inside herself.

But Greg wasn't going to let her reticence deter him. He understood the grieving process—from personal experience—but he also knew you didn't stop living.

"What do you enjoy doing?" For someone who interviewed people regularly, he was doing a pretty lame job of gaining his subject's trust.

But then, Beth wasn't a subject. She was a woman who had insinuated herself into his thoughts so thoroughly that she was interfering with his calm, predictable life.

"I'm good at business. Numbers. That kind of thing."

Not quite what he was looking for. And yet, perhaps the first piece of personal information she'd given him.

"So did you go to college?"

He'd just assumed she had no higher education—based solely on the fact that she was cleaning houses for a living. Yet Greg knew better than most how often things turned out to be exactly the opposite of the way they appeared. He knew what a mistake it was to assume anything. To judge anything by appearances.

"I sure didn't learn about business law in high school."

"You majored in business?"

"As long as I can remember, I've wanted to own my own business." She was so passionate in what she was saying that Greg almost missed how adeptly she'd sidestepped his question.

"I don't know how we got that far off topic," she added, before he could attempt to wade any further through the vagueness surrounding her, "but maybe Katie just doesn't like kids who are a little more serious in their endeavors and that's why she won't play with my son."

No matter how beautiful the teasing grin she shot him, it didn't cover the fact that she had, once again, completely turned the conversation away from herself.

From his probing.

"I still think Ryan's the problem," he said, quite purposefully egging her on.

"My son is *not* a problem." The teasing glint remained in her eyes, but she'd crossed her arms over her chest. Usually a defensive gesture.

At least, when you were a suspect being questioned.

"Okay, *problem* is the wrong choice of word. But if the kid's anything like his mom..."

"Ryan plays with other kids," she said. She'd lost the glint.

Sobering, Greg said, "Bonnie told me the reason you volunteer at the day care in exchange for playtime is that you're trying to draw the little guy out more."

"I want him to have a homelike environment during the day when I work, but I did think being around other kids his age might encourage him to talk."

Greg nodded. He knew how much Bonnie and Keith—and he, too, for that matter—ached over every little glitch in Katie's life. A measurement that wasn't right in the middle of the chart. Teeth coming too soon, steps taken too late. Fevers, ear infections, runny noses. An aversion to vegetables. Shouldering all those worries alone had to be hard.

And that on top of losing the man you'd meant to spend the rest of your life with...

"If there's ever anything I can do—teach him to play catch, empathize with you when he's sick—you know I'm here, right?" he asked, certain that he was crossing a line he shouldn't cross.

"Thanks." Beth smiled again. A sad, very real

smile, instead of the quick assurance he'd been expecting.

It wasn't agreeing to a date. But in Greg's book, it was far better than that.

And even though she'd given him more information about herself than he'd ever had before, he still didn't have a clear picture of who Beth Allen really was.

"SO WHAT DID YOU DO TODAY?" Beth asked Greg when silence fell between them and she was afraid he might take that as a sign to leave.

She felt buoyed up and wasn't ready to be alone.

He sat back, his uniform creased from a day in the August heat. That uniform made her uncomfortable. It reminded her of everything she couldn't have. Freedom from fear. Freedom to speak openly. Sex.

"I can't be sure, but I might have wasted the majority of it." The words, accompanied by a tired sigh, completely surprised her.

Greg always seemed so on top of things. In control. Able to handle anything.

She couldn't believe how quickly she wanted to help when she found out that wasn't the case.

"Anything you can talk about?"

"I'm attempting to find a connection between some recent carjackings and the one involving my father ten years ago."

Knowing how close Greg and Bonnie were, how much family meant to them, that couldn't be an easy job. "You think there is one?"

He clasped and unclasped his hands. "I'm sure of it. Problem is, the deputy in charge—the best man in the whole damn department, as far as I'm concerned—doesn't agree with me.''

"What does he say?"

"That I'm making it personal."

"Are you?"

"I don't think so."

Beth didn't know much about herself, but thought she had a pretty good sense of this man. The type of person he was. "You're a smart man, Greg. And an honest one. I don't think you'd kid yourself about something as serious as this."

His eyes were grateful when he looked over at her, making Beth feel elated for no reason at all.

"I don't think so, either," he murmured.

"So what are the similarities you're finding? Anything you're free to discuss?"

"In the first place, we're dealing with a *series* of carjackings in both cases. There are other random occurrences, but these fit an identical pattern—several assaults with the same MO over a relatively short period of time. Two guys, late teens–early twenties, just after rush hour—either morning or evening."

"It's the same two guys every time?"

"No." Greg looked more than frustrated when he shook his head. "In fact, they aren't always even from the same ethnic background."

"So what else?" There had to be more. Greg wasn't the type to be this concerned over flimsy evidence.

"They only take place in the summer, for one thing. I have no idea what that means, but it has to mean something. They start midsummer, there's a rash of them, and then, inexplicably, they stop. No arrests. Not even any real suspects. They just stop."

"What about the drivers?" Beth asked. "Could they be the tie-in somehow?"

With another shake of his head and a raised brow, Greg said, "I don't find a single thing to connect them. Not age. Not where they work or live. Not their religion, where they bought their cars or even their injuries." A shadow of pain crossed his face.

She winced inside, thankful suddenly for the blessing of amnesia. "They weren't all hurt?"

His brows drawn together, Greg gave her an apologetic glance. "You don't have to do this."

"What?" she asked, a bit afraid of how important it had suddenly become to talk this through with him. To do something to help him. "Talk to a friend?"

"Is that what we are? Friends?" His expression lost none of its seriousness.

"I don't know." Beth had to be honest. After a pause, she returned to her earlier question "So, they weren't all hurt?"

"Of this current group, all but one," Greg said. His voice was tightly controlled but she could hear the anger.

"Most were killed," he went on. "But not in the same way. One was shot. Another raped and strangled. One was left unconscious in the desert to either succumb to the heat or die of dehydration, whichever came first."

Beth swallowed.

"I can stop now."

"No, go on," she said. "It's okay, really. I'm not squeamish. I'm just sorry for these people and their families."

She wasn't squeamish. Another characteristic to add to the list she was keeping in her memory notebook. This was a good one. The kind she liked to add. Rated right up there with orderly.

"This summer, a college girl chose to throw herself out of the back seat of her moving car rather than submit to whatever else her abductors had in mind. She was a dancer and knew how to land and roll. She was miraculously unhurt."

Beth frowned, struck by an uncomfortable thought. Could something like this have happened to her? Had she merely been the victim of a random crime and not the runaway she supposed herself to be?

Of course, that didn't explain the canvas gym bag, obviously grabbed in a hurry with a couple of diapers and a change of clothes for Ryan stuffed in with various sweats, T-shirts and socks that fit her, or the two-thousand dollars. Not many people traveled with that much cash. And no identification.

Not smart people, anyway.

Beth didn't know what that bag signified. But she always kept it close. As though it somehow connected her to the self she'd lost.

As for the two-thousand dollars—part of it she'd invested in equipment and supplies to set herself up in business.

"There's something else," Greg said slowly. "The front ends of all the stolen cars—ten years ago and now—were smashed in such a way that no matter what make or model, they look remarkably the same."

"Like they all hit the same thing? Or something similar?"

Greg's brow cleared as he nodded. "Yeah. Odd, huh?"

"Very. Your deputy didn't think so?"

"Didn't seem to. Nor did he seem impressed by the fact that they were all new-model cars. Most car-jackers are looking for quick transportation. They aren't usually so picky."

"You're sure this guy knows what he's doing?" Beth asked, somehow not surprised at the thought that this deputy might not be all that he seemed.

What she found startling was that she was so cynical. She'd just naturally assumed the man was up to no good. People didn't think that badly of the human race without reason, did they?

Oh God. She was cynical. Two things for the list in one night. This second one was not a characteristic she was particularly eager to have.

These past months of almost no self-revelation at all weren't looking as bad as they once had...

"I know he does," Greg said somberly, his words rescuing her from the familiar dark hole she'd been sinking into.

"WERE YOU IN THE MIDDLE OF WORK OR SOME-THING?" Greg asked, pointing to the piles of papers, receipts and ledgers on the scarred desk at one end of the room. Beth had grown silent, and he was kick-ing himself for bringing up such a personal subject. But then, it was difficult to tell *what* she considered personal. He'd worked so hard for so long to get in the door, and he hated the idea of losing the little trust she'd given him.

"Just doing my books," she said, sounding com-pletely relaxed. Maybe for the first time in their ac-quaintanceship.

He smiled. "Looks like you've got enough stuff

going on to be running a business the size of the Cactus Jelly plant.''

"I told you I liked numbers. I'm actually keeping a tally of month-to-month percentages on the variance in cleaning supply costs. I check at the local Wal-Mart and at several places in Phoenix. I then keep track of how much cleaning I can do per ounce of solution. I'll bet you didn't know, for instance, that Alex Window Cleaner does linoleum more cost effectively than any of the ammonia-based floor cleaners.''

"No, I didn't know that.'' There was apparently much more to cleaning than he'd ever realized.

But what was of far greater interest to him was the woman who was rattling off dollars and ounces as easily as he did police radio codes.

"I take it your business is doing well,'' he said, when she'd given him a rundown on the benefits of bulk purchasing versus storage costs. Not just for cleaning supplies, but for business in general. Beth hadn't been kidding. She knew her stuff. More than any business student he'd ever known.

"As a matter of fact, this is the first month that Beth's Basins—and the Allens—are completely in the black! The bills are paid, money's put aside for emergencies and Ryan's education, and I even have some to spare. Ry's been wanting this balsa wood airplane he saw downtown, and even though it's really for older boys, I'm going to get it for him.''

"He told you he wants an airplane?'' Greg couldn't believe the change in her. She could have been any normal woman.

Certainly she was a beautiful one. Beth's loose auburn hair falling over shoulders left bare by the tank top she wore was driving him just a little crazy.

"Ryan hasn't said so, of course," she was telling him, her bare feet pushing off the floor as she rocked gently. "But his eyes light up every time we pass it. Hopefully I'll have time to take him tomorrow."

"You really love that little guy, don't you," Greg said. About that, at least, she was completely open.

"More than life itself."

Somehow one hour became two and Greg was still there, sitting on Beth's couch while she rocked in her chair. She'd gotten up once to get them both cans of soda and to check on Ryan, but that was all. Greg, who usually had a hard time staying in one place, was surprised by how much he enjoyed just sitting there looking at her.

Maybe that was why he didn't push his luck with any more personal questions. He didn't want her to show him the door.

Even now that she was more relaxed, Beth's eyes were still inexplicably expressive. Was it just her intelligence he saw there? He didn't think so.

The woman was a contradiction. Vulnerable one moment, and completely in control the next. Able to accomplish anything. Needing no one.

Teasing—and instantly defensive.

Insecure. And then confident.

And those breasts. He was ashamed of how much he was noticing them, how many times he thought about touching them.

Greg stayed long into that night, talking, mostly about growing up in Shelter Valley—including his college years at Montford University, the Harvard of the West, Shelter Valley's pride and joy. Beth had a million questions, making him wonder if she'd been storing them up for the entire six months she'd lived in town.

A million questions, but very few answers.

He got to know nothing at all about the circumstances and facts, the history, that made up Beth Allen's life.

CHAPTER FIVE

SHE WAS GOING TO HAVE TO LIE. Driving her old Granada to Bonnie's for her second Sunday dinner in three weeks, trying to distract her thoughts with the grand beauty of the mountains surrounding them, Beth finally accepted that she'd have to make up a past—not just the couple of lines she'd recited anytime anyone asked about her. Up until now, the fact that she was a grieving widow had sufficed. Recognizing that her recent past was painful, people were sensitive enough not to ask further questions.

But that was when those people were only acquaintances.

Bonnie Neilson and her family—her brother—wanted to know Beth Allen. Where she came from. Where she went to school. Her most embarrassing moment. Happiest moment. The men she'd dated.

The man she'd married.

They wanted to know it all.

They had no idea how badly she wanted to know all those things herself.

What she didn't want was the rest of the memories that would come as part of the package. She was scared to death to find out she might have stolen her son.

If that was the truth, and if she remembered it, she'd be forced to give him back.

Still, before she'd left home today, she'd read over the few entries in her memory notebook, trying to piece together a picture she could give people.

"We're going to Katie's house, Ry," she told her son, sending him a big smile. His feet, hanging over the edge of the sturdy beige car seat, were still. But his eyes were alert, intent, as he looked back at her, straight-faced.

"You remember Katie from Little Spirits," she continued, knowing that Ryan understood everything she was saying, even if he wouldn't respond. "We went to her house for dinner a few weeks ago and you fell asleep on Mommy's shoulder. You played with Katie's blocks. And she has a Magna-Doodle, too."

Ry's little voice filled the car, but Beth couldn't make out the words. From his intonation it sounded like a question.

So Beth replied to what she could only assume he'd asked. "Yes, I think she'll let you play with the Magna-Doodle, but I want you to promise something, okay?"

Ryan nodded.

"I want you to promise that you'll play with Katie today. Okay? Just like you play with Bo and Jay and Bethany Parsons."

Ryan watched her lips and then her eyes.

"Okay?" she repeated.

He nodded again. Slowly, deliberately, his little chin moved up and down. The chin that had the same cleft in the middle as hers.

Ryan might not say much, but when he agreed to something, she could count on it. Soon after they'd arrived at the Neilsons he picked up one of Katie's puzzles and took it over to sit by the little girl. He dumped the wooden pieces and, with the hand-eye coordination of a two-year-old, he started putting them awkwardly back on the board. Within seconds Katie turned around and placed another piece. Not a word was spoken between them.

Beth wished her own interactions could be so clean and simple. She spent the first five minutes staying out of the way, clutching her canvas bag.

Dinner was excellent—another cold main-course salad in deference to the weather. It was the first Sunday in September, and still too hot to even think about turning on the oven. Or eating anything warm, for that matter.

She was saved from having to sit next to Greg by Katie's last-minute insistence that she get to sit by "Unca" which resulted in Grandma Neilson and Greg switching chairs to accommodate Katie's booster seat.

"Lou can lose my high chair, Wyan," the little girl said importantly as she climbed up and set her little bottom down in her new blue plastic booster.

Well before the end of dinner, Beth had fallen in love with Grandma Neilson. The white-haired, barely five-foot-tall woman didn't let anything—not age, infirmity nor death—get in her way. She'd reduced life to its simplest terms. Being loved and loving others were what mattered. Anything else was simply an inconvenience to be dealt with as quickly as possible.

"So, Bonnie says you've got a cleaning business here in town," Grandma said to Beth as she chomped on her Chinese chicken salad.

Dressed in a long-sleeved button-up blouse and

pair of navy slacks in spite of the heat, Keith's grandmother looked like she was ready to go to the office.

"I do," Beth said, on edge that afternoon as she waited for a question she couldn't answer.

Maybe this was too much of a life for her—having friends, trying to have family experiences. And yet, seeing Ryan sitting there in his high chair, pulled up to the table as though he belonged, watching him grin at Keith and babble a sentence to Bonnie, she wasn't sure she had any choice.

She had no idea what she'd taken Ryan away from. Aunts, uncles? Maybe a grandmother or two like Grandma Neilson?

A father?

How could she not do everything possible to provide him with some of the same now?

"Good for you," Grandma was muttering. "Get on with it, that's what I say."

Head bent over her plate, Beth nodded.

"Use your spoon, Katie, not your fingers," Keith said. Greg leaned over to help his niece do as her father directed.

"Losing a husband is hard," Grandma said. "I'll grant you that, but you still have to get on with it, or the Good Lord would've taken you, too."

"Sorry about that," Keith said. " Grandma just tells it like she sees it."

"I don't mind," Beth said. She had a feeling that if there was ever a time she needed someone to confide in, Keith's grandmother would probably be her most sympathetic audience.

The least judgmental, anyway.

She'd understand how a woman could love her baby so much she'd do anything for him.

"Do you have room for another customer?" Grandma asked. "I've gotten myself on so many committees, I sure could use some help keeping up the house."

Beth didn't miss the way Bonnie, Keith and Greg shared surprised looks. But she didn't really care.

"What committees?" she asked.

She gave up even trying to keep them straight after Grandma described the fifth one. The woman seemed to run the entire town single-handedly.

With a little help from Becca Parsons, apparently. Little Bethany's mother had been mentioned several times during Grandma's dissertation. Beth had yet to meet the woman who was not only a prominent member of Shelter Valley's city council, but wife to the president of Montford University, as well.

"So, you got the time?" Grandma asked.

"I do," Beth said. She didn't really, but she'd make time. She really needed to be putting away more for Ryan's education than she was currently able to allot each month.

If she were anyone else, she could just hire an employee or two. But she wasn't. She was Beth Allen, nonexistent person. While she was diligently figuring out her taxes and setting aside the money to pay them if she was ever free to do so, she couldn't actually file. She didn't even know her social security number.

"I don't accept checks or credit cards," she said.

"Smart woman." Grandma nodded approvingly. "Cuts down on bank fees."

"You want to do my house, too?" Greg asked. "I could—"

"Forget it, buddy," Beth interrupted before she was somehow trapped, in front of the sheriff's family, into doing something she knew would be far too dangerous.

Greg Richards was in her thoughts too much already. She didn't need to see where or how he lived. Didn't need to know where his bedroom was, what his sheets looked like.

Didn't need to know if he kept his refrigerator clean. If it was empty. If he picked up his clothes and left open *TV Guides* lying around.

But Grandma Neilson's house was a different matter. Beth had a feeling there was a lot she could learn from Keith's resilient grandmother.

THERE WASN'T SEATING for everyone in the family room, with Grandma Neilson added to the Sunday party. Conscious of the fact that she was the one who didn't belong in that house Beth quickly pulled out the piano bench and sat down after dinner when they all trooped in to watch a movie on Bonnie's large-screen TV.

"Afraid you might have to sit by me?" Greg whispered on his way to the couch.

It was only because he was carrying Katie, who would have overheard, that she refrained from calling him a name she wouldn't have meant, anyway. But it sure would've been good to say it. To at least pretend she wasn't aware of every move the man made.

If she didn't get control of her reactions to Greg, she'd have to stop coming to Sunday dinner. She could not be influenced by the woman inside her who wanted to love and be loved. Too much was at stake.

"You know how to play that thing?" Grandma asked, settling herself in the armchair next to the piano. Her wrinkled face was alight with interest as her watery blue eyes rested on Beth.

"Maybe."

A rush of tears caught Beth by surprise, she blinked them away and turned to face the keyboard. Lifting and pushing back the wooden cover with practiced ease, she wished so badly that she had a mother or grandmother of her own. Someone to love and comfort her, someone who'd counsel and watch over her... She wondered if she'd left either—or both—back home. Wherever home might be.

No, she decided. Surely if she'd had someone like Grandma Neilson to run to, she'd have done so. She certainly wouldn't have awakened, badly bruised and alone, in that nondescript motel room. Registered under the name of Beth Allen but with nothing to prove who she really was.

Unless she *did* have a Grandma Neilson someplace, and she'd had to run to protect her, too?

The ivory and black keys did not look strange. Or feel strange, either, as she rested her fingers lightly upon them.

"You know how to play?" Bonnie asked, stopping beside the piano bench. "Keith's parents bought that for us when Katie was born, but none of us plays."

"A little, I guess," Beth said, confused. She caressed the smooth white keys with the pads of her fingers, comforted by their coolness.

And their familiarity?

Did she know how to play? Have lessons as a child?

"All I can play is chopsticks," Keith said, standing beside his wife.

"Mama. Uh. Mama. Uh." Ryan toddled over to the bench, both hands grabbing hold of it.

"You want to watch Mama play?" Greg asked. Handing Katie to Keith, he picked the boy up.

"Pway," Katie said.

"You heard her." Grandma's voice brooked no argument.

Beth looked down at the keys—and panicked. She had no idea what to do. The people around her faded as the red haze filled her peripheral vision. She recognized the feel of those keys. Didn't think she could take her hands off them, her need for them was so intense.

And yet…what was she supposed to do now? No picture came to mind of ever having done this before, of what keys to press to make anything close to a song.

Did she use two fingers? Or all ten?

"Mama," Ryan said, not quite whining. But he sounded close.

Heart pounding, Beth knew she had to do something. Some force in her, deep and elemental, wouldn't let her get up without doing *something*. And Ryan wasn't going to give her much time.

Closing her eyes, Beth took a deep breath and stopped thinking. Focusing on that inexplicable drive buried deep inside her, she poised her hands and pushed down. The first sound that came crashing from the instrument was harsh. And yet—right. Completely right. The sounds that followed were perfection, flowing together in a rush of turbulent and compelling music. Beth's hands moved over the keys—flew over them—of their own accord. She hadn't listened to music in months. Never turned on the radio in the car. Had that been on purpose?

Someone gasped just behind her right shoulder, but she was only vaguely aware of it. Only vaguely aware of herself. Again, without her prompting, or even her understanding, tumultuous chords gave way to poignant ones, filling the room with sweet longing. And filling Beth with a longing she barely understood.

She couldn't stop. Music flowed out of her, gushing, it seemed, from every pore, the notes chasing each other almost faster than she could release them. She didn't know what was happening. Didn't know how.

She only knew she'd just discovered something very vital. For the first time in six months, Beth Allen was alive. Living.

The person she was meant to be.

She had no idea how much time had passed before her fingers, sore and almost raw, dropped to her lap. She was afraid to turn, to break the spell.

"My God." The whisper was Keith's.

Embarrassed, Beth glanced halfway around. Ryan was asleep on Greg's shoulder. Another pang of familiarity shot through her. Her son had done that before. He'd fallen asleep while she played to him.

She'd soothed him with her music when he was sick.

The knowledge came and went so quickly—just a brief impression, really—that she wasn't sure, in her oversensitized state, whether she'd imagined it.

Wishful thinking?

It was hard to know what was real when you didn't know your own mind.

"Thank you." Grandma Neilson's voice, soft and uncharacteristically reverent, broke the long silence.

Somehow, Beth wasn't surprised to see tears in the stalwart old woman's eyes.

"You're a concert pianist." Greg, standing just off to her left, was staring at her, his expression a mixture of awe and scrutiny. He was going to want answers.

And that was something she couldn't give.

Beth turned, and started to play again.

GREG WAITED ONLY LONG ENOUGH to be sure Ryan was in bed that night before parking his truck outside Beth's duplex. He leapt over the couple of steps leading to her front porch before delivering a purposeful knock.

"I had a feeling you'd come," she said, holding the door open for him, resignation in the droop of her shoulders, her bent head. Sinking down into her rocking chair, she grabbed a pillow, angled perfectly in the corner of the couch, and hugged it.

She glanced over at him as he slumped on the couch, looking as dazed as he felt.

"Why?" He didn't bother with preliminaries.

"Why am I not surprised you came? Is that what you mean?"

Greg bit back a curse. Even now she was delaying, avoiding a response. What was it with this woman? And why in the hell did he care?

"Why didn't you tell me you're a pianist?"

"I play the piano," she said, although there was an odd note in her voice.

He didn't understand it. Doubt? Where there should've been confidence?

"That doesn't mean I'm anything more than a lady who cleans houses and once took piano lessons."

"That was more than piano lessons. It was an entire repertoire. A concert. Pieces very carefully chosen and arranged to express every nuance of emotion. The peaks and valleys, the passion—it was the most incredible musical experience I've ever had."

Beth met his gaze for a moment. He thought she might cry. And then she looked down, saying nothing. Her foot pushed gently against the floor, slowly rocking the chair.

"Why, Beth? Why hide such a remarkable talent?"

"I don't know."

Her eyes, when she looked up at him, were tortured. Tearing at him.

Greg sat forward, needing to touch her, yet knowing he couldn't—although he wasn't sure why. "Help me understand," he said gently.

She wanted to. Greg could see that in the way she held his gaze, honestly, hiding none of the pain or compassion she was feeling.

"I...can't. I just have to keep me to myself."

What the hell was driving her? What had happened to trap her so deeply inside herself? Was it the shock of losing her husband? Or something more?

"Can't or won't?" He deserved that much, at least.

"I don't know, Greg," she said. "I..." She swallowed, closing her eyes. "I hurt..."

Every word was difficult. Greg wanted to tell her it was okay. That she didn't have to do this.

But he couldn't.

It was too important.

"So badly," she continued. "But I'm still here, you know?"

Tears glistened in her eyes. And suddenly Greg did know. He'd had that feeling, too. Of having something essential taken away from him, and yet enduring because there was no other choice. First with Shelby. And then for the ten years he'd looked after his father or, more accurately, the shadow his father had become.

"I have Ry to think about," she said. "I have to go on. And somehow, in the process of making that happen, I just froze inside.

"It wasn't anything I consciously chose. Or even recognized at the time." Her voice was a whisper, each word an obvious effort.

He nodded. "Self-preservation," he said. He'd seen it dozens of times on different levels. Had experienced it himself.

Beth's arms rested on the sides of the chair as she rocked. The pillow was in her lap. Greg had a sudden and very unusual urge to lay his head there, too. Just for a moment.

To know that she was there, watching over him. To take comfort, for once, instead of offering it.

Unusual reaction. Odd. Embarrassing. *She* was clearly the one in need of comfort. Not he.

"I don't know how to get out," she said. The duplex was quiet. The street outside empty.

"Isn't that what you did today? Playing like that?"

"Maybe." Drawing up her legs, she pulled the pillow to her chest.

"Can you tell me a little about yourself?" he asked, hoping with a hope he thought he'd lost. "About the things that made Beth Allen the person she is now?"

His heart plummeted when she shook her head.

"I'm not ready for emotional risk, Greg. If I don't open up to people, I can stay safe."

"Just tell me where you're from."

She peered at him above the pillow, her eyes moist. "I came here from Snowflake."

Instantly at attention, Greg forced himself not to budge from his relaxed position. "You lived there with your husband?"

She shook her head again.

"Is that where you grew up?"

"No."

"So where *did* you grow up?"

"In the south."

"Alabama? Louisiana? Georgia?"

She nodded.

He could sense how hard she was trying. And he didn't want to push her. "Did you have brothers and sisters?" he asked mildly.

Beth shook her head for the third time. Greg wondered if it was merely reaction to being questioned or an actual answer.

"Are your parents still alive?"

Another brief shake of the head.

God, it was worse than he'd realized. He couldn't imagine how horrendous it would be to face life knowing you were so totally alone. Even in the worst of times, he'd always had Bonnie. And Shelter Valley.

"You can trust me," he said.

"I know."

"I want to help."

"Then, please be my friend, Greg. Be my friend until I can work through this."

Her words brought him a surge of joy. Yet he

couldn't take a chance on being mistaken. "You're sure that's what you want?" he asked, his gaze direct, probing.

"Yes."

"You wouldn't rather I just disappeared and let you get back to the business of surviving?"

"No."

"Why?"

Beth grinned, her eyes filled with tears that pooled but didn't fall. "I'm afraid I'm going to freeze to death and not even know it."

He had no sense of what he should say. What he should do.

"You make me *feel,* Greg. For the first time in six months, I'm feeling."

He needed her to continue. To explain herself. He waited.

"And the feelings are…good."

"I'm attracted to you." He wasn't going to pretend.

"I know."

"And I think you're attracted to me, too."

"I know."

She knew she was? Or that he thought she was? Somehow it didn't matter. Either way, they'd just established something important.

"I'll be your friend for as long as it takes." The words were a promise. One he was determined to keep.

"Thank you."

Her tremulous smile was beautiful. And young. Almost innocent. It planted itself in Greg's heart.

"I'd like one thing, though," he said.

She frowned. "What?"

"I'd like you to be my friend, too."

"Oh." Her brow clearing instantly, Beth met his gaze with clear eyes. "I can do that."

He felt hopeful. Capable. Strong. "Does a friend get to do any touching?"

The frown was back. "What kind of touching?"

"Any kind," he said. He was willing to take anything. "A hug. Maybe—" he paused, reached over and took her hand "—just this." Her hands were slim, feminine. And had elicited such intense and powerful music from Bonnie's piano that it still reverberated in his head.

Looking down at their joined hands, Beth smiled. There was hesitation in the tentative way she turned her hand, taking hold of his. "This is okay," she said.

Then, he'd leave it at that. For now.

CHAPTER SIX

DEPUTY BURT CULVER SHUT HIS OFFICE DOOR when the number popped up on his caller ID. It was Wednesday. He'd been waiting since Monday morning.

Picking up the receiver, he leaned against the edge of his desk, staring out at the Native Reservation that stretched for miles on the other side of the road. "It's not good," he said in lieu of hello to the retired sheriff on the other end of the line.

"Tell me."

"Richards is looking at those photos from ten years ago."

"There's nothing for him to find."

Culver relaxed slightly at the lack of hesitation in the older man's reply. Everything he cared about—his job—was at stake. And for once, he wasn't in complete control. He was being driven to do things, make choices, he wouldn't ever have thought he'd make.

But he couldn't lose his job. Being a cop was his only reason for living.

"We're talking about the magic man here," he reminded his ex-superior, tugging on his ear. "Richards is always pulling stuff out of thin air."

"Only if it exists. Richards is a great cop. He won't

waste taxpayers' money looking for something that's not there.''

''He's studying the front ends.''

''Don't wimp out on me now, Culver. I'm telling you there's nothing for him to find.''

''You'd better be damn sure about that.'' Culver didn't usually talk to his mentor like that. Remorse silenced the rest of what he'd been about to say. ''I'm a good cop,'' he said instead, by way of apology.

''You'd give your life to see justice upheld. Same as me. And Richards, too. Relax, Deputy. You've done nothing wrong. You have nothing to fear.''

Culver nodded, gritting his teeth. All he'd ever wanted was to be a cop. If he loved anything at all, it was his work. With a dissatisfied grunt, he dropped the phone back in its cradle.

Reaching behind him, he yanked out his top drawer, grabbed the bottle of antacids and gulped down a couple.

All he'd really done was plead the Fifth. He wasn't going down for that.

BETH WOKE UP SWEATING. Her eyes immediately went to the night-light by Ryan's crib, then to the mattress where her son lay sleeping. His breathing was even.

Thank God.

Heart pounding, shivering, Beth stumbled from the bed. Scrambled for the notebook in her underwear drawer, but couldn't make herself do more than hold on to it.

A glass of water might help. Might bring reality into focus, chase away the demons of a darkness she didn't understand.

She'd had the dream again. Not that she remembered it. Ever. But it always left her with this debilitating sense of impending death. She carried around a fear she couldn't conquer. Couldn't even identify.

The dime-store plastic tumblers were neatly arranged in two colorful rows on the bottom shelf of one of the three kitchen cabinets. She would've preferred glass, but wasn't going to waste money on purchasing two sets. And Ry needed plastic. She supposed this told her something about herself—that she didn't like mixing and matching, craved complete sets. Something to write in her notebook.

A half bag of ice remained on the shelf she'd designated for ice in the freezer. She'd have to buy more in the morning. It seemed odd to her, this practice of buying ice. She was pretty sure that where she came from, they just used the ice most freezers produced automatically. And those who were in less financially advantaged situations, like hers and didn't have a newer refrigerator, made ice by filling trays with water from the kitchen faucet and freezing it.

In Shelter Valley the water didn't taste right for drinking directly from the tap.

Ice in the glass, water from the gallon jug she'd purchased at the grocery, a sip. Then two.

And still, book in hand, Beth found her limbs were shaky, her skin tingling with unease. She could only take one sip at a time, needing to stop between swallows for air.

"Nights are the worst," she said aloud. Sometimes hearing a voice helped bring her back. Even if it was her voice. "In the morning, when the sun's shining and the sky is blue, you'll be okay."

She wanted to believe herself.

Except…did the light really make a difference to anything other than her sense of total isolation? It didn't change the loneliness, the fear and the uncertainty. Daytime only made it easier to be distracted from them.

Rubbing her arms, Beth stood barefoot and nearly naked in her kitchen. She couldn't afford to turn the air-conditioning up very high and although it was the second week in September, the heat was still unbearable. So were the shivers.

She'd watched an action-adventure movie once where the hero was thrown into a dungeon crawling with bugs. She had no idea when, where or with whom she'd seen that movie, but she remembered the scene, the character's horrific panic. His inability to cope.

That was how she felt. Surrounded by stone walls crawling with black things. And the walls were moving in on her, getting steadily closer.

No one could help. She'd done a lot of reading on memory loss and she knew there was nothing anyone could do. Her assumption was that she was suffering from some kind of retrograde psychogenic amnesia. There was a combination of factors; the damage was organic in nature due to the blows to her head and psychosomatic in reaction to acute conflict or stress. Retrograde in that "events preceding the causative event" were forgotten.

Slowly sipping water she didn't want, Beth silently recited the words she'd read in the *Encyclopedia Britannica* many times over the past months. *Causative event*. Scary words.

The imaginary bugs started to fade as she concentrated on the things she'd read. Her type of amnesia was reversible. But it had to happen in its own time. Amnesia was a coping mechanism, the mind's way of giving her time to heal or grow strong enough. When her mind was ready to cope with whatever it was hiding from, she would remember.

In the meantime, she was supposed to keep her life as stress-free as possible. To fill herself up with as many positive feelings and ''events'' as she could.

A tall order for someone living all alone, in fear, not knowing if she was in trouble with the law, if she belonged in prison. Or if there was a maniac out there looking for her. Wanting to hurt her or Ryan.

Not knowing who she was or where she came from.

And not sure she wanted to know. As much as she hated the darkness, she wasn't sure it was any worse than what she'd left behind. It must've been something pretty terrible for her mind to have resorted to such drastic measures. She couldn't escape the instinctive thought that she should just trust her own mind and leave things alone.

But could she?

After washing the cup, Beth dried it and put it back in the cupboard. How much longer was she going to be able to cope if she couldn't sleep a full night? If the nightmares continued? Every morning now, she got up exhausted—in mind *and* body.

It had been just over a week since she'd played that piano at Bonnie's house, and Beth still hadn't recovered from the traumatic emotions the incident had stirred inside her.

She didn't understand the emotions. Didn't know why they were so disturbing. But they were eating away at her insidiously, mostly at night when she was trying to sleep. Driving her slowly insane…

What if she lost her mind completely? What was going to happen to Ryan then?

Sitting on the floor of the bedroom by her son's crib, her knees pulled up to her chest, Beth opened the notebook and read by the dim glow of the night-light.

And forced herself to think.

SHE KNEW NOTHING about finding missing persons. There was the Internet. And in Phoenix, birth records. But the first thing asked at either of those places was *Name, Last.* It was a piece of information she didn't have.

Still, Beth was desperate enough to try. There had to be a reason she'd used the name Allen; maybe it would lead her to her past.

Leaving Ryan at the Willises' on Thursday afternoon, the second week in September, she finished her last cleaning job and drove over to the university. The place had become like a favorite vacation spot during the past few months. A second home of sorts, as she searched for answers to unending questions. The shelves of books seemed like a lifeline, offering information her mind withheld from her.

It was in that library, browsing the business shelves, that she'd discovered she had more than a passing knowledge on the subject. She'd recognized titles and authors. She'd found, upon pulling out some books and reading a bit, that she was familiar with many of the facts and theories.

She'd done most of her amnesia research at the famous Montford University Library, too.

Today, canvas bag tucked securely on her lap, she was there to use the computer. To log on to her free

Internet account, set up with bogus personal information, trying to find out if there was a Beth Allen living in Snowflake, Arizona.

She got 144 hits when she typed in the name. But when she perused all of them, none of the corresponding addresses meant anything to her.

She wasn't really disappointed because she hadn't expected much.

She just knew that, safe as anonymity was to her, she was no longer sure it was completely safe for Ryan. As long as she was here to protect him, he'd be fine. But what if she wasn't?

There were ways of providing a guardian for him in case something happened to compromise her life or stability, but to be legally effective they had to be filed.

And without a name or a background—without a legal identity—she couldn't file.

The red haze had been with her almost constantly since that afternoon at Bonnie's house, more than a week before.

Beth locked up from the computer screen, needing to connect with the life around her for a moment—remind herself that life was going on. She experienced a moment's respite from her panic when she saw the couple who'd just come into the library. Ben and Tory Sanders. She'd never actually met them, but she knew who they were. She had, in fact, made it a point to find out who Tory Evans was when she'd first come to town. It was the article about Tory that had brought her to Shelter Valley, Tory's happy ending she had held on to all this time.

She watched as the couple chose a table and sat down together, and took comfort from the intimate smile they shared before opening the books they had with them. And then Beth returned her attention to the computer screen in front of her. The news hadn't gotten any better.

Frustrated, she closed the people-finder screen. She knew someone who could help her. Who'd know just where to turn next.

She'd seen him a couple of times since that Sunday night after her impromptu piano concert. Once they'd run into each other at the day care. And he'd stopped by for an hour this past weekend.

Both times she'd felt a confusing onslaught of comfort and unease. She needed his unconditional friendship more than he'd ever know. And yet she feared everything about having him in her life. Feared his job. His intelligence. His desire to know about her. His affection.

His sexuality.

Snowflake. She should look up newspaper articles on Snowflake, Arizona. Maybe her advent, while apparently unnoticed, hadn't occurred without incident. Quickly typing, clicking and searching through files, Beth read carefully, diligently, looking for any mention of a car accident, an attempted rape or murder, a robbery, a domestic disturbance. Anything that might have occurred about the time she'd found herself alone in that motel room.

Searched, too, for any mention of a woman named Beth. And ran a search on the names Allen and Ryan.

All turned up nothing relevant.

So, how about a missing person report? Either an article or a mention in a police log. On a woman. A child. A kidnapping.

Hits flashed up with links. Glancing at her watch,

Beth grimaced, her sweaty palm tightening on the mouse as she clicked on the first one. She was running far later than she'd meant to, but she couldn't stop now.

"What's a woman like you doing in a place like this?"

The mouse flew from her fingers and landed on the carpeted library floor.

"Greg!" Beth said, seeing red everywhere as she pushed keys, removing words from the computer screen before the Kachina County sheriff had a chance to read them and start asking questions.

Greg was a smart man. Who was already suspicious.

Picking up the mouse, he set it on the pad and sat down at the computer beside her. He was in uniform. Which always made her just a little more uncomfortable around him.

"I didn't realize you'd discovered our hidden treasure here at Mortford," he said, surveying the library.

The entire facility incorporated many floors and separate areas, which included meeting rooms small and large, conference rooms, a couple of different computer labs such as the one she was sitting in, group study areas, no-conversation areas, and rows and rows of books on every subject imaginable.

She nodded. Had he seen the child custody article she'd been perusing? "I've been coming here for months."

It was because of far too many sleepless nights that she couldn't come up with a plausible reason for her library visits. "To find myself" didn't work.

But it was the truth.

While most people were there to learn new things,

Beth had been visiting to find out what she already knew.

"We've got a state-of-the-art computer lab at the SO," he said.

He couldn't have seen what she'd had up on the screen. He wouldn't be making small talk otherwise.

"SO?" she asked.

"Sheriff's Office." He grinned at her, a devilish light glinting in his eyes. "I have a system in my shop, too."

"Your shop."

"My place of business," he said, nodding at an older woman dressed in a skirt and blouse, who walked by with her hands full of folders. "In other words, my car."

"So what are you doing in here?" she asked him. There were no reference books in the computer lab.

"I was returning a book and I saw you."

His eyes were warm. Familiar.

"Oh."

She loved that look. As though he had a right to know her, to ask questions, to be with her. As though they belonged together. And she was deathly afraid of it, as well. The tightrope she was inching her way along was getting more and more frayed, and she was afraid the person who'd really be hurt when it broke was a little boy who had no ability to help himself.

"Why are you looking up custody cases?" Greg asked, casually leaning his forearms on the computer table beside him.

Shit.

She'd closed the screen she'd been on. But behind it had been the original search request.

"I wasn't...originally," she said, focusing her energy. Focusing on what mattered most: being calm, keeping Ryan safe.

"I'm here looking for options for Ryan," she told him, deciding that honesty was the best way out of this one.

"Custody options? With his father dead, isn't that a given?"

"Unless something happens to me."

They were speaking quietly, in deference to their surroundings, and Greg stood suddenly. "Let's go for a walk," he said, taking her hand.

Beth shut down the computer and picked up her bag—the canvas gym bag she'd found with her in Snowflake—allowing herself to be led out into the Arizona sunshine.

Montford's campus was beautiful. The cultivated grass was as green and manicured as any golf course. The big old trees, pretty uncommon in this part of the country, threw shade on benches placed all over the university grounds.

Greg led them to one such bench, not releasing her hand as they sat. Beth was more than a little embarrassed by the cut-off sweats and T-shirt she was wearing.

"I love a woman who polishes her toes to clean house," Greg said, grinning as he stared down at her flip-flops.

"I polish them for me," she murmured. "They just come along when I clean house."

Polishing her toenails was almost a ritual for Beth. She'd had red-polished toes when she'd awakened in Snowflake. Keeping them that way seemed like a way to keep herself—the old self she didn't know—alive.

It seemed disloyal, unfaithful to that woman, not to do so.

He rested his arm along the back of the bench. "So, why the sudden worry about Ryan?"

And that was one of the reasons she was uncomfortable around Greg. He had a way of jumping from topic to topic with absolutely no warning. From serious to comic. And back again.

It was a trait she had a feeling she'd have liked if she'd met him in another lifetime.

Greg waved at a distinguished-looking man striding purposefully on a sidewalk across from them.

"Who's that?" she asked.

"Will Parsons. He grew up in this town, went to school here, and is now the president of Montford."

"His daughter is at Little Spirits with Ryan...." Which brought her right back to the question he'd asked her. Why was she worried about her son?

Flicking her hair over her shoulder, Beth resisted the urge to lean into the crook of his arm. She straightened, looking directly ahead of her.

"I've been worrying about what would happen to him if anything happened to me. I don't know what took me so long to think of it, but now that I have, I'm not going to rest until I've made some kind of arrangements."

And that meant she might not be resting for a good long time.

"Your husband's been gone, what—eight, nine months? A year?"

"Yeah."

"Not such a surprise that you're just thinking about this now. Starting over is tough. It can only happen a little at a time."

He was speaking as someone who knew. Who'd been there. "Was it hard for you, coming back here after so much time away?" she asked. "Or did growing up in Shelter Valley make the transition easier?"

Greg shrugged, gazing out over the expanse of lawn. He seemed to be watching a couple as they made their way hand in hand down a walkway that cut through the middle of campus.

"Change is always hard," he said eventually. "And Shelter Valley was a double-edged sword. It's my home, and it welcomed me."

"But?" Beth loved the curls at his forehead. She'd always longed to run her hands through his hair. Sensuously, seductively...

Right now, though, she had the urge to run her fingers through those curls as she would Ryan's, to offer comfort. Solace. A promise of peace...

"My life here was with Shelby," he told her. "We'd been friends since kindergarten."

"You must have known her very well."

She couldn't imagine the luxury of having someone know her that well. But she imagined she'd love it.

"I thought I did. Almost as well as I knew myself."

Hurting for him, wishing she were stronger, more in control of life, Beth met his eyes. "I remember you said she didn't want to wait to get married. That she met someone else in L.A."

He shrugged. "I guess what I saw in Shelby and what was really there were two different things. I trusted her to be honest with me. She wasn't."

"So you...created an image you fell in love with?"

"Worse than that," he said, looking over at her, his eyes lacking their usual spark. "The things I loved about her were real enough to keep that love alive and burning. And to work against me, blinding me to the ways she was changing. What I didn't want to see.''

''Maybe she helped that along by hiding them from you.''

''I don't think so,'' Greg said. ''I almost wish she had, because then I could just chalk the whole thing up to the fact that she was a jerk. But it wasn't like that. Shelby's a good woman who tried her best to do what was right. And what turned out to be right for her—leaving Shelter Valley—wasn't right for me.'' He shook his head. ''When I left, it wasn't by choice. But Shelby decided she wanted a different kind of life.''

''So the moral of the story is that you can't trust anyone?''

''I don't want to believe that.''

''What, then?''

''Maybe what you can trust is that people will change. No one's going to stay the same forever.''

She could attest to that. ''Just living changes people,'' she said slowly, watching a girl who was reading a book under a tree. She'd been highlighting so much, Beth had to wonder if she should even have bothered. From a distance, it appeared that she was including everything on the page, so none of it was going to stand out from the rest, anyway. ''Each decision, no matter how small, each interaction, can have repercussions that affect your whole life.''

''Living in a town like Shelter Valley,'' he said, ''sometimes you forget that.''

''Maybe it's different in a town like Shelter Valley. There are an awful lot of people here who've known each other all their lives and are still happy living side by side, supporting and loving each other. I don't think I've ever seen so many happily married couples.''

"In a perfect world, people grow together, flowing along with each other's changes, rather than letting those changes tear them apart."

"Could you and Shelby have done that?"

"Maybe," he said. "I know I sure would've tried if she'd given me the chance."

For a split second, Beth was sick with jealousy. Who was this woman that had evoked Greg Richards's eternal love?

And was there any hope that she, Beth Allen, would ever be able to grasp even a crumb of it for herself?

She couldn't even be honest with him about the most basic realities of her life. If she told him the truth, he'd have to start looking for her identity. And if he found something bad, she'd be forced to run before he could turn her in.

But in that moment she wanted him to know her.

Better than she knew herself.

CHAPTER SEVEN

GREG WALKED BETH TO HER CAR in the visitors' parking lot. She was late picking up Ryan or he'd have tried to get her to stay longer.

"This is your alma mater, isn't it?"

"Yeah," he said, his hands in his pockets as he walked beside her. "Got a degree in criminal justice."

"I try to imagine sometimes what it would've been like going to school here. It makes me yearn to be twenty again."

"They were good times." Greg thought back to some of the parties. The friendships. The feeling that the world was waiting at his feet.

Beth nodded, a yearning look on her face. It puzzled him.

"Probably not much different from wherever you went," he said. "Unless you studied business at New York University and did Juilliard at the same time."

He was baiting her.

She didn't bite.

He pretended that her reticence didn't bother him. He couldn't figure out how telling him where she'd gone to school, grown up, been born, involved any kind of risk.

But then, he'd never been so completely alone in the world. And he'd given her his word....

"Ryan doesn't have any other family, besides you?" he asked as they left the classroom buildings behind and walked across the gravel that led to the free parking lot.

"Not that I know of."

An odd answer.

"Wouldn't you know if he did?"

"I don't know much about my husband's family."

"He wasn't close to them?"

"I guess not."

Greg frowned. Beth was too warm, too intelligent, not to have probed more deeply than that.

"Is there anyone who could serve as his guardian? A close friend from home, maybe?"

"No." She stopped at her car, looking up at him, eyes filled with concern. "There's no one, Greg, and it's scaring the hell out of me. If something happens to me, he'll become a ward of the state, won't he?"

He wished he could tell her differently, but he couldn't. "Yes."

"And because he's not an infant, that probably means he'd be in and out of foster homes."

She was scaring herself. And yet, there was some truth to what she was saying.

"Maybe."

"The thought of that's been making me sick for two days."

"Foster homes aren't all evil," he said. "Don't borrow trouble, Beth. You're young, healthy, and you live in a town where law enforcement has substantial success in keeping down crime and keeping citizens safe."

She grinned, as he'd meant her to. But sobered quickly.

"Promise me something?"

"Of course."

"Promise me you'll take him if anything happens to me."

She wasn't kidding. Nor did she appear to be reacting to runaway emotions.

"You really think there's a possibility something might happen." It wasn't a question.

Beth looked away—her evasion a sickening confirmation of what he thought he'd just read in her eyes.

"It's always a possibility, isn't it?" she whispered.

He grabbed her arm as she climbed into the driver's seat of the old Ford Granada. "Beth, look at me."

"What?" Her demeanor was suddenly that of a defensive child. She couldn't get away from him fast enough.

And he hadn't yet granted her request. Hadn't made the promise she'd asked.

"Are you in some kind of trouble?"

"No! Of course not."

The denial came too fast. Was too effusive.

"I'm not, Greg," she said, meeting his eyes. "Or put it this way—if I am, I certainly don't know about it."

He believed her—which made the entire conversation, the woman, that much more confusing.

"You'd tell me if you were, wouldn't you?"

"Of course."

"Come to me for help?"

Her expression completely serious, she stared up at him. "I think that's what I've just done, isn't it?" she said softly. "Please promise me you'll take Ryan if anything happens to me."

"Of course, but..."

"Thank you." She interrupted him before he could tell her there was little he'd be able to do, that he'd have no power whatsoever to keep the boy unless she put something in writing.

But almost as though she knew it was coming, she forestalled even that. Standing on tiptoe, she pressed her lips to his in a kiss so tentative it was almost virginal.

And before he could do more than soak up the flood of intense desire her touch had evoked, she'd climbed in her car and was gone.

"WHAT DO YOU MEAN the photos are ruined?" Greg yelled into the phone. It had been two days since he'd seen Beth. Which only added to his frustration.

"I'm sorry, sir, the developer overheated and when I jumped up to tend to it, I knocked the envelopes into the sink...."

"But you've got the originals," Greg said. He was at home, hadn't yet left for work when the lab technician called.

"Well, that's just it, Sheriff. We used the pictures you asked for, but the images weren't clear enough to get the exact marks you highlighted. The only way to—"

"Tell me it wasn't the originals that were just demolished."

"Yes, sir, they..."

The expletives that flew from his mouth didn't make Greg proud. Didn't help his temper much, either. He pounded his fist against the wall, restraining himself enough to prevent punching a hole in the plaster—but not to save his hand from a well-deserved bruise.

"What about negatives? Previous prints? Even if you can't produce the exact image I want, we can take them somewhere else. Get them digitally restored."

"They were all in that pile, Sheriff."

Jaw clamped against scathing words he'd regret, Greg stared out the huge window over his kitchen sink to the landscaped pool and barbecue in his backyard.

"You're telling me we don't have one single image left of any of those cars? Not from ten years ago?"

"Or this summer."

Greg frowned, every nerve on alert. "What were you doing with the ones from this summer? I marked only the four from ten years ago."

"Deputy Culver brought the rest, sir. Said something about comparing measurements of the horseshoe-shaped dents in the lower right front ends."

So Culver was suspicious, too.

"What you're telling me is that we've somehow managed to lose all visual record of those cars."

"The victims, too."

Greg hung up before he fired the bastard on the spot. He'd have to deal with this incompetence—if incompetence was all it was. But not before he'd had a chance to powwow with Culver. They might want to have the technician remain on staff just to keep track of him.

One thing was for sure.

Something was very wrong.

GREG ASKED BETH OUT TWICE that month. Both times she refused. He'd wanted to take her to Phoenix, to the theater. And to a campfire steak dinner in Tucson.

Beth didn't dare leave Shelter Valley. Not until she had some idea of who might be looking for her.

And what *she* should be looking for. Prepared for.

Not while she was still so obsessed with the feeling that she didn't want to be found. Until she'd regained her memory, she had to trust that her mind, even while it withheld information, was telling her something.

She just couldn't take any chance on anything happening to her. Or leading anyone to Ryan.

Of course, there was no guarantee that she was safe in Shelter Valley. But after more than seven months in town, she felt an aura of security here.

It was the only home she knew.

And then Greg asked her to a concert at a casino on the Indian Reservation that bordered Shelter Valley. She was familiar with the band, knew the lyrics to their songs, but didn't have a single memory attached to them.

She wanted to go. She was afraid that if she kept turning Greg down, he'd give up on her. It shouldn't matter. But it did.

There were days when thinking about him, about the hopeful anticipation he sometimes instilled in her, about the warmth she felt when he was around, were the only things that kept her sane.

The casino was set in the middle of nowhere, and while it was bound to be crowded, it wasn't a crowd she'd need to fear.

She was still planning to refuse. Until Bonnie offered to keep Ryan for the night and Ryan, having heard that he might get to play at Katie's house again, looked at her and said "pwease?" Just like Katie did when she wanted something.

Beth was too busy blinking back tears to say no.

And that was why, on the fourth Friday in September, she was sitting beside Greg in the lounge of the Kachina Grounds Casino. She was dressed in her only pair of nice slacks—black stretch denim she'd bought at Weber's Department Store, just for the occasion— and a new gauzy red-and-black top. She had no idea if the outfit was anything she'd have worn in her previous life, but she felt good in it.

The cigarette smoke, on the other hand, felt like death to her.

"Will it bother you if I tell you how beautiful you look?" Greg asked, his arm around the back of the booth. The lonely woman inside Beth wished he'd touch her.

She was relieved he didn't.

"No," she answered honestly. "I'm the only other one who'd tell me something like that and it sounds much better coming from you."

"You tell yourself you're beautiful?"

"Only when I'm feeling desperate."

She was only half joking. "Times like those, I'll believe just about anything." She grinned at him. She'd had a glass of wine, the first she could ever remember. Maybe it had gone to her head more than she'd realized.

"Let me know next time it happens. I've got a few other things to tell you," he said. He looked so good sitting there in jeans and a navy-and-white plaid button-down shirt. The top button was undone and the shirt kept drawing her eye to what it covered.

She wondered if the hair on his chest was as thick and black and tightly curled as that on his head.

"Like what?"

"Uh-uh." He shook his head, taking a sip from the beer he'd ordered.

His grin made her warm in places that had no business feeling warmth.

"I'm not giving them up until you're in a believing mood," he said.

Thankfully she was saved from any further flirtation when the lights went down and then, on the stage, a single white spot appeared. In the shadows there were instruments set up. Really expensive-looking drums. Some guitars and amplifiers. An alto sax.

But on center stage, beneath the white spotlight, was a beautiful black baby grand.

Beth's heart started to beat so hard she could feel its rhythm. In the semidarkness, Greg's shadow took on a reddish hue. She could hardly breathe. Felt surreal, disconnected. Weak.

And very, very frightened.

She had to get out of there. Find a safe place.

She had to breathe.

"What is it?" Greg's whisper in her ear startled her so much she jumped.

"N-n-nothing," she said, her voice loud, competing with the sudden thunder of applause as the band took the stage. "I need some cool air."

Without another thought, Beth slid from the booth and hurried out. She had no idea where she was going or what she'd do when she got there. She didn't know how she'd explain herself. Or how she'd even get back inside the lounge.

She didn't care.

She had to get out.

Just outside the lounge wasn't far enough. Beth barely heard the cacophony of slot machines, coins dropping, people cheering, bells ringing as she searched, frantic yet completely focused, for a way out.

Fresh air. That was all she needed. She'd be fine as soon as she had air.

It might've made more sense to stop long enough to seek a door, to read a sign, to remember the way she'd come in. Beth didn't have time to stop. She charged in one direction and then the next, cutting through rows of slot machines, behind a tuxedoed woman dealing blackjack, through a series of roulette tables, back to what might have been the same slots. The room was filled with smoke and noise. She bumped into people and hardly noticed.

Finally, she found a revolving door. She shoved through in her haste to get out.

And then she was free. Outside. Sucking in balmy desert air. And choking back a deluge of tears she neither recognized nor understood. Beth didn't ever sob. As far as she knew...

Gasping, she ran down the sidewalk, not sure if she was heading toward the desert or the parking lot. Not caring. She didn't have a destination in mind. She'd arrived. Nothing else mattered.

"Beth!"

Greg came running up behind her, and she realized then that it wasn't the first time he'd called out to her.

"What?" She turned.

"What happened? What's wrong?"

"Nothing's wrong. I'm fine."

"I see more than my share of adrenaline rushes," he said, keeping pace beside her. "I know it when I see it."

She should slow down. Act normal. And she would. Just as soon as she got some air.

"I'm seeing it now," he went on.

"You're imagining things." Her voice was too high. Too fake. She'd work on that next.

"Should we check your pulse and see just how much I'm imagining? My guess is it's running at about 220."

"I'm fine." She was hyperventilating.

Grabbing her arm, Greg pulled her to a stop, cupped his hand over her nose and mouth and commanded, "Breathe."

She had no choice.

After a few seconds, she was no longer seeing stars. Red, maybe, but no stars.

"Where'd you learn to do that?" she asked, not pretending quite as hard that she was in complete control.

"I'm a sheriff, Beth. I know CPR."

"Oh." Yeah. She started to walk again, but more slowly now.

Maybe, if she was really lucky, she could wipe away the impression of a raving lunatic she'd obviously given him.

"It's a nice night, isn't it." Her voice was sounding more normal.

"Yes."

"I've grown to love the nights these past few weeks. The days are still hot, but the nights are more temperate than they were during the summer. Reminds you of summer days as a kid, doesn't it? Carefree. Playing hide-and-seek until ten o'clock."

"Is that what you did?"

She didn't know. "Yeah." She hoped so. Had no

idea why she'd said such a thing or where the thought had come from. It didn't feel personal.

But then, at the moment, her own feet and hands felt like they belonged to someone else.

They walked for a while, neither of them speaking. Eventually Beth calmed down. She no longer felt as though she was going to be sick any second.

"So what happened?"

"Sometimes I have…memories." She chose her words carefully.

A double-wide sidewalk ran a large circle around the grounds of the casino. They strolled slowly through the darkness, not touching, but close enough to give her strength.

"Memories of your life before you came here?"

"Yes."

"And they're painful?"

"Very."

"So that's what happened back there? A painful memory?"

Beth couldn't think about what had happened back there. Not until she was safe at home, in her duplex, where she could fall apart in private.

She'd remembered something important. Or at least she'd started to. Until panic had taken over and shut her down again.

She'd been on a stage before. Much larger than the one in there. There'd been a piano similar to that baby grand. No other instruments, though. Only a piano.

And then the spotlight had come on….

Beth stumbled. She couldn't go any further than that. It wasn't there. Maybe she'd already lost the rest of what had come storming back.

"I'm really sorry," she said now, proud of how

normal her voice sounded. "I told you I wasn't ready—"

"You miss him that much?"

She shook her head. "I think I just hurt that much. It's not all about him. At least, I don't think it is. It's just about the uncertainty, you know?"

"The 'no guarantee' clause that comes with life?"

"Yeah, only they don't put it on your birth certificate. They wait until you're in all the way before they let you know about the risks...."

"But if we knew up front, we'd never take risks."

"Sounds good to me."

"If life involves change, it involves risk, too. Doesn't it?"

Beth didn't, couldn't, respond. Brushing against him as they turned a corner, she took his hand. "Thank you."

"For what?"

"Not hauling me away in a straitjacket."

"There was no reason to. You were upset, not insane."

It sure *felt* insane.

"It's just that I go through so much of my life these days not feeling anything at all, and then suddenly I feel something so intensely, it hurts so intensely, and I don't think I can stand it."

She couldn't believe she was telling him these things. And yet, she felt completely safe doing so.

"I think I get that. Only, instead of feeling hurt, I'm overwhelmed with anger."

"About Shelby?"

"No, that mostly just hurt." He sent her a wry grin. "I was talking about my father."

"Bonnie told me he'd been injured in a carjacking."

Greg nodded. "He was on his way home from Phoenix one evening after a round of golf with some of the guys he served with."

"He was a cop, too?"

"Volunteer fire department. My father was an economics professor at the U."

"Wow." She'd had no idea.

"As far as we've been able to piece together, he was rear-ended about twenty miles outside Phoenix. When he pulled over, he was jumped. He remembered nothing else until he woke up in the desert, unable to move. The bastards had broken his neck and left him there to die. By some miracle, a couple of teenagers had gone out to the desert and stumbled upon him." He stopped, and Beth, walking close beside him, squeezed his hand.

"They were afraid to move him, but even more afraid to leave him there. Between the two of them, they got him to their car and drove him into Phoenix. He didn't have any ID on him, but one of the guys I'd gone through the academy with answered the call."

"Were you close by?"

"I was at his house, waiting to drive him to Tucson to see a choral performance Bonnie was in."

They rounded another corner and reached the back of the casino. Just the two of them among Dumpsters, empty boxes thrown out the door, the rancid smell of trash that should have been emptied.

Beth figured that was a true metaphor for life.

"I'm so sorry," she said. It was weak. Useless. But there wasn't anything else.

"They never caught the bastards."

"Did they find the car?"

"Oh yeah. So far, we've always found the car. But the interior had been burned out leaving no clues. Dad couldn't remember anything. And eventually the case, considered a random carjacking, was closed."

"But it's not anymore."

"It's not anymore," he said, conviction in every line of his taut body. "I'm going to get those guys, Beth."

"I believe you."

She tripped, a smaller surge of fear darting through her. She was pretty certain Greg Richards always got his man—even if it took him years.

If the need ever arose, she hoped that would work in her favor. Not against her.

CHAPTER EIGHT

GREG WAS WALKING beside Beth, talking to her about his job again. And then he wasn't.

A movement between two of the Dumpsters caught his attention. He'd just barely glimpsed a shadow in the dark, out of the corner of his eye, but whatever was there was too big to be a rat. With an arm in front of Beth to prevent her from walking into the path of whatever was just ahead, Greg slowed and put his finger to his lips. It could be a javelina down from the nearby mountains, and he didn't want either of them to startle it. The four-hundred-pound wild pigs were not known for their placid nature.

Motioning for her to back up, he slid his hand in hers and took a couple of steps with her.

"Hold it." A gravelly voice came from behind them.

Greg froze, his only thought of the woman beside him.

Beth stopped, her hand squeezing all the circulation out of his. He could feel her trembling and willed her his strength.

He didn't have to see the blade to know that he had a knife at his back.

"What're you doin' back here, man?"

"Trying to have a private conversation," Greg said, shifting just a fraction of an inch, concentrating on his peripheral vision as he tried to determine whether there was only one knife.

There was.

Greg moved without further deliberation. Giving Beth a shove to get her safely out of the way, he spun around, his hand locking immediately and with force around the arm that was stretched toward his back.

His assailant was young. Strong. Fast. Greg wasn't intimidated. Martial arts, street-fighting, hand-to-hand combat, shooting—he could do them all. His body seemed to move instinctively, twisting, blocking, maintaining his iron hold on the hand wielding the knife.

The man grunted, used the force of an attempted spin to knock the two of them to the ground. Hitting the hard earth with his shoulder, Greg rolled with the fall, knowing that if he was going to keep Beth safe, he had to make sure this man did not get loose.

He couldn't think about her beyond that.

On the ground, he kept his eye on the potentially lethal six-inch blade gleaming in the darkness. The knife came close to his chest, and Greg rolled again, pinning the man beneath him. Then, with a swift lunge, he knocked his attacker's hand against the dirt. The knife flew. Greg twisted, rolled one more time, and the man was facedown in the dust, his arm twisted behind him.

Greg had his belt off and around the man's wrists in one swift action.

"Move and you die."

Heart pounding from exertion, Greg turned at the sound of the strange female voice.

Beth was standing there, discarded knife in hand,

pointing it at a second figure crouched and trembling beside the Dumpster.

A teenager. Obviously strung out. A quick search of his prisoner revealed a vial of amphetamines that told Greg he'd just interrupted a drug deal. It was a classic. Some poor frightened kid, in too deep, and the intimidating dealer who owned him. There were few questions left to ask.

Except where Beth had learned to be so tough.

And how a woman who'd barely been able to stand half an hour before was suddenly single-handedly holding a drug addict at bay.

Emotional battles knocked her off her feet, but apparently physical ones did not. He couldn't help wondering what that said about the past Beth was so adamantly hiding.

"YOU SURE YOU'RE OKAY, MA'AM?"

Standing on the outskirts of the small crowd that had formed around the blinking police lights, her arms crossed, Beth nodded. Greg was there in the middle of the fray, giving his report.

"If there's anything we can get for you—a drink, an extra sweater..."

"Really, I'm fine." Beth smiled at the casino manager, hoping to convince him she wasn't going to fall apart. Or worse, sue him.

Frowning, he maintained his protective position next to her.

The truth was, at that moment, Beth felt better than fine. She'd been in danger and come up fighting. A huge entry for her notebook. But more, an enormous reassurance. She could count on herself; she could safeguard her child. She wasn't some weakling who collapsed at any sign of trouble.

She'd actually, without conscious thought and without hesitation, held someone at knife point.

The impact of that realization was huge. Suddenly, the unknown dangers lurking in the darkness of her mind weren't so threatening. There was a chance she was equipped to handle them.

"What's going to happen to that kid?" she asked the manager, as the Indian police led away the kid she'd found huddled by that Dumpster. He was just a fourteen-year-old boy.

"If it's his first offense, he'll probably just be handed over to his parents." The man shook his head. "You see this so much. These jerks hit up kids in schools with the promise of a cheap and completely harmless good time. Before they know it, the kids are addicted and doing anything for their next fix."

The harsh-looking man Greg had apprehended elbowed an officer as they led him to a patrol car. In one swift movement the officer had his hand on the back of the drug dealer's neck and had shoved his head against the car.

"He'll be back on the streets before school starts on Monday," the casino manager said, shaking his head again.

Beth hoped he was wrong—and feared he was right. She had a feeling that was the way the world worked. So often, evil prevailed.

"You, Sheriff Richards, are one hell of a fun date," Beth teased later that night. He'd talked her into coming back to his house where he could take a shower and continue their evening. Maybe with dinner or a movie in Phoenix.

Somehow they'd ended up staying at his place instead, grilling steaks in the backyard.

"Yeah," Greg said sarcastically, still kicking himself for how close she'd come to being hurt. He flipped the steaks, needing them to cook quickly. The potatoes he'd put on the top rack of the grill were almost done.

Sitting on a lounge beside the pool, Beth sipped from a glass of wine. Her slim body was beautiful, and the landscape lighting spread a silvery glow over her, giving her a mysterious, almost fairy tale aura.

"Next time I'll just take you down to the prison and let you have your pick of criminal action."

"With you there to protect me, I wouldn't worry a bit."

The night air was soft, cool against his skin. He was too agitated to enjoy it.

"I'm flattered you think that, Beth, but what I did tonight was so dumb I can't even come up with an excuse." He rubbed his shoulder. "Never, never, never is it wise to walk into a dark alley at night. And especially not on a mostly deserted reservation."

"It was hardly deserted with three hundred cars in the parking lot out front."

"Which was why we had no business not staying out front."

He absolutely did not understand what had gotten into him. Being aware of his surroundings was second nature—or should have been. He'd allowed them to stray into danger.

"Let up on yourself, Richards." Beth's soft voice held no humor, just a hint of affection. "You risked your life to save mine. Enough said."

Taking a sip of beer, Greg checked a steak; the middle was still too red. He'd let the night's fiasco go, but not before he made a silent vow never to lose perspective like that again. And to make sure that if Beth's life were ever in danger, he would not be the cause.

He vowed to protect her always—even if that meant protecting her from himself.

He'd let it go, but he wasn't going to forget.

"I HAD NO IDEA that Indians have their own law enforcement and legal system," she said later, as they sat at the white patio table eating steak and baked potatoes.

He'd turned on the waterfall on the far side of the pool, and the gentle lapping of the water added a romantic ambience to the classical music playing softly from the outdoor speakers.

"In some ways, the reservations are like countries unto themselves," Greg said. "Thanks for waiting while I handed the guy over to them."

"No problem." Her voice was light. Almost cheerful. Amazing considering the evening they'd had.

He topped off her glass of wine. She was no heavier a drinker than he was; he was still nursing his first beer.

"You've got this place looking great, especially since you've been here less than a year," she said, looking at the desert landscaping surrounding them.

Greg cut a big bite of filet mignon, ignoring the twinge in his shoulder. "Thanks."

All she'd seen of the house was the front hallway and kitchen, which they'd walked through on their way to the patio. She'd opted to wait outside while he showered.

Greg rubbed at his shoulder. "It was like this when I bought the place," he admitted.

"You could have some great parties out here."

"That's one of the reasons I bought it. With three bedrooms, it's a little bigger than I needed, but I liked the idea of being able to have my deputies and their families here to kick back now and then."

"How many times have you done that in the nine months or so you've been sheriff?"

"Three."

"I'm impressed."

"Cops are a close-knit group. We have to be. Our lives rest in each other's hands."

Beth sighed, the dim lighting giving her a wistful look. "A family."

He supposed that was what they were. "In terms of unconditional trust, I guess you're right. Though—" he grinned "—I certainly don't love those jokers like I love my sister."

Gazing pensively at him, Beth said, "But then, if you had a brother you probably wouldn't love him in the same way you love Bonnie, either."

She had him there. "So what about you?" He didn't expect an answer.

"I don't have a lot of memories of my family."

Well, it was an answer but not much of one. "You're adopted?"

"Just not very close." She put down her fork. Took a sip of wine. "I'm sorry you didn't get to hear the band tonight."

As upsetting as the incident at the casino must have been to her, speaking of it was preferable to speaking about her life before Shelter Valley. Greg couldn't help but file that information away.

"I've got a couple of their CDs and they probably sound better on those, anyway." The band had met with substantial success a decade or two ago, but their music was soft rock. As far as Greg was concerned, they were music's version of a chick flick. He'd chosen the date for her, not himself. "I'll bet you've got more than just two of their CDs," he said, smiling at her. Last he knew, Bonnie and every one of her friends had the entire collection.

"Nope."

"You didn't spend your high school years crooning with them?"

Beth's look was blank. "I don't think so. I don't croon." And then, "You've been rubbing your shoulder a lot. Is it bothering you?"

He hadn't realized he'd reached for it again. "Not really."

"You hurt it in that fall tonight, didn't you."

Greg shrugged, determined not to wince as the movement pulled on the muscles just above his shoulder blade. "Bruised it a little, maybe." It wasn't a big deal.

Beth's expression was just short of a glare. "It's your trapezius," she said. "From watching that fall you took, I'll bet it's got one hell of a knot."

"I don't feel anything," he said. Her fussing made him uncomfortable; getting bruised was just something that happened—if not at work, then when he went to the gym or had a good sparring with a fellow black belt. A guy straining a muscle was as much a part of life as eating, sleeping and going to the john.

"It's gotta be spasming, too."

That sounded painful. "No. It's fine."

"Whatever you say, macho man."

Greg wasn't sure he liked the way she'd said that. But he was willing to let it lie.

Pachelbel's "Canon" came on. One of the few pieces of classical music Greg recognized by name.

The music was haunting. Evocative. Sensual. Mixed with the cool night air, the semidarkness and Beth, it bordered on dangerous.

And then, suddenly, he was reminded of that Sunday at Bonnie's. Beth could probably play this song.

He wanted her to play it for him. That piano tonight...

"Tell me what happened at the casino. When you ran out."

"Nothing, I—"

"Don't, Beth," he interrupted. "Tell me it's none of my business, but don't insult me with a lie."

Beth looked out over the pool toward the waterfall. "I don't lie."

"Never?"

"Not if I can help it."

"So what happened?"

Her gaze, filled with so much he couldn't decipher, locked with his. For a moment neither of them spoke. Greg braced himself not to say a word when she told him it was none of his business.

So why did he feel it was?

"I can't tell you exactly what happened," she said, her eyes steady on his. "I'm not sure I even know."

When he looked into those beautiful blue eyes, there was no doubting the truth of what she said. "What can you tell me?"

"When I saw the piano... I don't know..."

Wanting to reach for her hand, he reached for his beer instead. "What?"

"I used to play the piano professionally."

Her performance at Bonnie's had made that rather obvious. He wanted to ask why she'd denied being a concert pianist that night at her house.

"Seeing that piano there tonight, in the spotlight, brought it all back to me so forcefully..."

"It's okay," Greg said, although he didn't know if that was true. He didn't know what "it" even was. What kept her so locked inside herself? Her hand lay on the table next to her wineglass, and he covered those talented fingers with his own. "After dinner at Bonnie's you said you were starting to come out of a deep freeze. I imagine this was just more of the same. Starting to feel again. Reacting to all the particulars in your life."

"I guess."

Her brows lowered, not quite into a frown, just into a lost look that made Greg feel powerless. He was afraid of no one. But how could he fight what he didn't know?

"It's just so overwhelming...." Her voice trailed off.

There was so much more Greg needed to ask. And, just as badly, he needed her to tell him without his having to ask. He needed her to trust him.

SHE WASN'T GOING TO SUFFOCATE. Not out here in the cool evening air. Not twice in one night. Blocking her mind to the memories that had overwhelmed her earlier, Beth wondered if she should leave.

"You're doing that thing with your shoulder again," she said instead, watching as Greg rubbed ineptly at the knot that had to be tightening his trapezius.

Just how she knew that, she had no idea. And didn't dare investigate, either. Not at the moment.

She'd write everything down later. All the glimmers of memory. And all the internal enemies that had attacked her that evening, rendering her virtually helpless for perhaps the most frightening half hour of her life, would get their time.

When she was home alone, in the safety of her bedroom, she'd write everything down in her journal.

And then would come the responsibility of trying to make sense of it. To search further and see what she knew, what she remembered.

Until then...

"Let me do that," she said. Jumping up, she stood behind Greg's chair. A couple of minutes and she could ease his suffering.

"Right here?" she said, her hands instantly finding the knot in his upper back. Measuring its size, the exact point in the muscle where it lodged, Beth began to massage. Her fingers worked automatically, moving over Greg's body as mindlessly as they'd moved over the piano keys a couple of weeks ago.

"Oh yeah," he said, "that's the spot." His head dropped.

Beth grinned, surmising that he must be too macho to grimace. Or say *ouch*. What she was doing had to hurt like hell.

But it wouldn't for long.

"Deep muscle spasms, just like I thought," she said, rubbing from the outside in.

"Mmm." Eventually Greg started to move with her. "That feels good."

"It would feel a whole lot better if you'd take off your shirt," she said. She was used to doing this on bare skin. With the proper oils within reach.

Beth's fingers faltered. Where? *Where* was she used to doing this? On whose bare skin? And what oils were the proper ones?

Apparently taking her limp fingers as a command, Greg slid out of his shirt. And because she didn't know what else to do with that bare expanse of smooth back, she began to administer a deep-tissue massage.

When she was done, she kept right on massaging. The waterfall, the music, the soft lighting were all part of a distant scene, a vague background, as Beth continued to use skills that belonged to a person she didn't know.

"You can stop now." Greg's voice came from far off.

Beth kept working the musculature of his back. Sometime during the past few minutes she'd moved from his right shoulder to his left, and was now down to his latissimus dorsi.

"I guess it probably wouldn't do any good for me to ask where you learned to do that?" His voice sounded strained.

Nope. No good at all. She'd already tried and there'd been no answer forthcoming.

"Piano players have strong fingers." Beth found herself saying the words. Thought they were words she'd heard before. Some kind of explanation for the skill she was now displaying?

Or a defense of it?

A concert pianist. Masseuse. Other than the obvious requirement of strong fingers, the two professions had absolutely nothing in common, as far as she could tell.

Knotted bruise aside, Greg's back was beautiful. The muscles textbook perfect. In placement. In size.

And his skin...

As her thoughts took her in unprecedented directions, Beth's fingers worked harder. She knew one thing: she couldn't have done *this* as a profession. She was far too aware of the skin beneath her fingers, far too lacking in emotional detachment, not enough professionally removed to have done this very many times.

But then, how had she become so adept?

WHETHER IT WAS THE BEER that made him take the chance or the adrenaline still pumping from the evening's events, whether it was the night and water and soft music or the sheer torture of her fingers against his body, Greg didn't know. He just quit thinking.

Reaching back, he grabbed Beth's burning hand, placing his palm over hers as he guided her fingers through the hair on his chest and held them against the taut pectoral muscles straining for her touch.

Gently pulling, he brought her around until she was standing between his spread thighs.

"I..." Her eyes were wide, filled with uncertainty.

And with something else.

The something else was all he saw. "Shh," he said softly. And before she could say anything, he tugged once more, bringing her down to his lap, and covered her mouth with his.

If she'd resisted, even for a second, he would have stopped. Could have stopped. But when Beth's mouth opened over his, his reactions no longer seemed to be under his control. He took his time with slow, soft kisses, exploring her. Her taste. Her softness. The shape of her lips.

Her kisses started out hesitant, though by no means resistant. But as he continued to move his mouth against hers, her response grew tantalizingly ardent. There was no doubt that Beth was a hungry woman. Hungry to be touched. To be loved.

He forgot where they were, pretty much forgot *who* they were. He was thinking with his senses. Feeling her. Driven by a desire more intense than any he'd experienced before. Lost in a sensual fog.

"Hold me." Beth's words pierced the fog. And then became the fog. Greg held her as close as he could. And when the chair hindered his attempts to deepen their closeness, he picked her up and carried her to the padded chaise longue she'd been lying on earlier.

It might have been made for one person, but it accommodated two quite nicely. Greg laid Beth down and then lay down between her legs, bolstering his weight on his forearms on either side of her. Cradling her.

"You are so beautiful," he whispered.

Her tremulous smile scared him a little, and Greg bent to her lips. Doing what he knew he could do well. What he already knew she wanted.

He kissed her.

And kissed her again. His lips trailed to the corner of her mouth. To her chin. Onto her eyelids. Down to her neck. He had to know every part of her, had to have some kind of claim on this woman who held everything back from him.

His groin ached with a tension far worse than he'd

felt in his shoulder. Knotted and spasming and crying for attention.

Moving his hips against hers, Greg let her know what he wanted.

"Greg?"

"Yeah?" His voice sounded dry, parched.

"I want you so badly I'm aching."

He groaned. Ready to throw away everything he had for one night in this woman's arms.

With all his weight on one elbow, he caressed her side. Her neck. Burning hotter as she moved her head, eyes closed, making herself more accessible. Her gauzy top made it easy to slide his hand beneath the neckline and down, until he had one perfectly rounded breast in his palm—

"But I can't."

Greg shook his head, wondering what he'd missed. Somehow Beth's eyes had opened, were staring straight at him.

His hand still on her breast, he ran a mental slow-down over his body.

"Can't what?"

"Can't do this." She shuddered. "I want to so badly, but I can't. Not yet. Not while I'm still trying to figure things out. It's not fair to either of us...." Only the fact that she sounded as devastated as he felt allowed Greg to handle the situation like the man he purported to be.

"Okay."

"I'm sorry."

"It's okay."

"Greg?"

"Yeah?"

"You're...um...still holding my breast."

Damn. She was right.

Using far more physical strength than he'd needed when capturing the drug dealer, Greg dragged himself off Beth. And then, because he didn't trust himself not to fall down on top of her again and because he was in almost unbearable pain, he turned and dived, headfirst and fully clothed, into the swimming pool.

Even the brutal plunge into sixty-degree water didn't cool his ardor.

Of one thing he was certain. Beth Allen was more than just a woman.

She was a need.

CHAPTER NINE

THE SUBJECT GRADY MULLINS, was ready. He sat straight and tall on the leather sofa in a private back wing of the spa, a big, athletically fit man in his late twenties. He'd shaved off his beard and cut his hair.

Tired as he was, Dr. Peter Sterling still felt the surge of renewed energy as he took in their newest recruit. This was what people on the outside wouldn't understand. It wasn't that they did anything evil—or even secret—at Sterling Silver. It wasn't that they wanted to be exclusive. Exactly the opposite, in fact. Their goal was to have everyone in the world live as they lived at Sterling Silver. Positively. Happily. Productively.

People in the outside world just didn't understand. But they were beginning to. Slowly. One soul at a time.

They had another worthy soldier for the cause in Grady Mullins. All the hard work, the fatigue and the frequent loneliness were worth moments like these.

Peter might not be able to save the world, but in his protected little corner of it, life was damn near perfect. Clean and free from hostility and negativism.

After weeks of relaxation training, Grady had fallen into an altered state of consciousness, almost without Peter's help.

"Grady, you believe in Sterling Silver, don't

you?'' Peter asked, his voice low as he sat facing the man who'd declared his readiness for cleansing.

"I do. I know that the work here is right and good.''

Peter smiled. *Right and Good.* That was one of several sets of key words used at Sterling Silver. Continually repeated trigger phrases that helped them all stay focused, lest they be wooed by the ways of the world.

"Why is it right and good?''

Grady's eyes met his. "Today's world is full of evil,'' he said, his voice ringing with the intensity of sure knowledge. "It's everywhere. In white-collar lives and blue, corporate structures and the ghetto. Gangs. Road rage. Terrorism. In politics. The Bible promises us that if we let evil forces—which we know to be manifested in negative energy—rule our lives, they will overtake us. The only way for any of us to overcome it is to rid ourselves of the negative energy. The hostility.''

Yes. Heart thumping, Peter nodded. He'd sensed from the very beginning that this young man would be a powerful convert. Grady's fervor was validation for Peter's own faith in the rightness of his work.

Outsiders wouldn't understand what was going to take place there that day; they would probably be horrified by the things Grady was subjecting himself to. But that was because outsiders saw only the surface. They didn't understand the meaning, the purpose, the benefit, the motivation.

"The Bible also promises that good will win out over evil if we make right choices. The best choice is to rid ourselves of the negative energies we were born with.''

Grady understood. And after him, there would be more. Slowly they were reaching the world.

"You're sure you believe that?" Peter had to ask. Beth's lack of faith had been disastrous. He couldn't take a chance on having that happen again.

"With all my heart," Grady said, looking him straight in the eye. "I want cleansing more than anything, Dr. Sterling."

Peter believed him.

"You have faith that it will work?"

"I know that it will."

"My son, we've talked a little about the process, but there is much that you cannot know until you actually experience it. The mind is a curious thing and—given the chance—while still filled with negativity, it can take a right and good concept and turn it into something evil. We can't risk this or we've lost all power to do our work. We become devoid of influence and the rituals become meaningless."

"I understand."

"Then, we shall begin." Peter stood, anticipation filling his lower belly. "You must permit no doubt to enter your mind from this point forward. You do not question. You have to trust me completely. Negative energy does not give up easily. We have to render it powerless." The words lost none of their ardor even as Peter repeated them for the three-hundred and forty-ninth time.

Grady didn't even hesitate. "I'm all yours, sir."

That was just what Peter had been hoping to hear since first meeting the young man several weeks before.

"And you've made arrangements for afterward?"

"Yes, sir." Grady nodded. "I'll be working twelve-hour days just as prescribed so that my endorphins flow and fill my body with positive energy. I have always understood that hard work produces positive results.''

"Prosecutor Silverman tells me you've moved out here to our little community."

"Yes, sir," Grady said. He smiled as he described his new apartment—in the complex Peter and James Silverman had contracted to have built just eight months before. It was already at capacity.

"I've given up my old job, as well."

This was something Peter already knew. He and James discussed each applicant in depth before ever letting things progress this far.

"I was a high school teacher and football coach. Pay wasn't much and the levels of testosterone-induced aggression couldn't have been higher. Instead, I'm going to be working in the cannery here. And doing some things with Prosecutor Silverman, as well."

While James put in many hours at Sterling Silver, he still worked for the D.A.'s office. His contacts there were too important to give up.

Moving closer to the door he'd indicated as the beginning point of the ritual, Peter paused. "And your outside activities?"

There was much to sacrifice in order to be part of the Sterling Silver community.

"I'm fully content to find my recreation right here," Grady said. "I know the more I move among nonmembers, the faster I regain negative energy, which would require more work from you. I intend to do all I can to protect your time, sir. You need to be helping outsiders enter our community, not wasting time on those of us who've already been cleansed.''

Hand on the door, Peter stopped. ''You'll still need cleansing, son. It's part of life. Evil forces are constantly trying to win us back.''

''I know, Dr. Sterling. But I'm going to strive every day of my life to someday be like you.''

''Like me?''

''You don't need cleansing.''

''I don't get the benefits of cleansing, Grady,'' Peter said, injecting every bit of pain he'd ever felt into that statement. ''There's no one else to perform the procedures. And even if there were, it takes two full days. Think of the number of people I'd miss helping every time I participated.''

''I know, sir.'' Grady bowed his head. ''I have to tell you how thankful I am for your willingness to do this. We all owe our lives to you.''

Peter hoped so. He needed to make that much of a difference. He resisted the urge to hug Grady. Not everyone appreciated the power of touch.

''You have no illnesses?''

''None.''

''Remember, after today you will never seek conventional medicine.'' Peter had to control the natural antagonism he felt at that moment. ''Physicians take ownership of patients' bodies and interfere with energy forces. They prescribe medicines and treatments that pollute the body with negative influences, which makes my work here that much more difficult as I must then rid you of those influences.''

''I understand.''

''Okay, son.'' Peter finally opened the door, allowing Grady a brief glimpse of the darkened room.

"Wait," he said, just as Grady was about to step through the doorway. "You haven't eaten today, have you?"

"No, sir."

"There will be no food for the next forty-eight hours."

"Fasting is good for the soul, sir."

With a nod, Peter moved aside, inviting Grady to enter the room. There was nothing but dark walls, a medical examining table and a dialysis machine. On the far side was a blackened door, through which Peter would come and go.

For the next two days, Grady was going to get the benefit not only of physical cleansing, but of thought reformation, making it easier for him to follow the mandates. He'd be reminded of the loyalty he'd promised, the contract he'd signed, stating that he had not been forced into anything against his will, that he was of sound mind and body and certain that he wanted the benefits of membership in Sterling Silver. During the two-day session it would be repeatedly stressed that he'd agreed to pay Sterling Silver two hundred thousand dollars, collectible throughout his lifetime, if he were to break any of the rules either then stated or in the future agreed upon.

Those rules would be repeated to him over the next hours until they became virtually hypnotic suggestions, orders that he simply followed while living life with the appearance of complete normalcy. He would never eat excessively—a benefit that the majority of the worldly population spent billions of dollars a year trying to obtain. There would be no consumption of alcohol or tobacco—both negative substances that weakened the body.

And henceforth, Grady—like all men at Sterling Silver—must engage in sexual activity twice a week—no more, no less—as scientific studies had proven that biweekly orgasm would build disease-fighting energies, but that any more activity would begin to diminish them. Grady had agreed that, if at any time he was not in a relationship, he would take care of that last requirement himself.

There was a lot to do during the next two days. Among other things, Peter was going to remove and replace Grady's energy, something that could only be done in this sterile atmosphere, devoid of outside influence.

"I'm going to leave you now to disrobe. Put all your clothes, including underthings, in the drawer by the door."

"I'll be back in ten minutes," Dr. Sterling said. "And remember, what you're about to do is right and good. Those who belong to Sterling Silver are above the rest of the world. Due to our diminished negative energies, our superiority is a given. We are 'as angels.'"

James Silverman was waiting for Peter out in the corridor. He didn't speak. After all their time together, he didn't need to. His raised brow was enough.

Peter didn't speak, either. He merely nodded.

And both men smiled.

BETH MIGHT NOT KNOW where she'd come from, but she didn't have to be out in the world to know that Shelter Valley was exactly the type of place she wanted to be. Which was why, twice a week when she'd finished cleaning houses, she spent a couple of hours in the library at Montford University, while the Willis sisters looked after Ryan.

Until she knew what she was running from, she wouldn't know if she could stop running.

And until she knew what she was running from, she couldn't tell anyone she wasn't free. She couldn't take the chance that someone—especially the sheriff, who was starting to play a rather prominent part in her make-believe life—might put out feelers. Not until she had an idea where they might lead.

She had no idea if Greg's finding out who she was, where she came from, would put her and Ryan, or even him, in danger. No idea what kind of pain and hardship were waiting for her back where she'd come from. Indications were pretty clear that she'd been on the run from something serious—filling her with the vital need to hide. From everyone.

And yet she wanted so badly to tell him the truth. To tell him she wasn't *choosing* not to share information about herself, but that she simply didn't know the answers to his questions. Or her own...

But if she told him she had amnesia, he'd need to find out who she was. It would be his duty as a lawman to determine whether or not she was wanted somewhere, by someone. It was his nature as Greg Richards, fix-it man, to take matters into his own hands.

Unless she asked him not to. Could she trust him that much? Could she expect him to take a chance on her, harboring her, when she might, indeed, be a criminal? Could she be certain he'd even do it if she asked?

Could she stay in this town, putting them all in

danger, if it turned out she was on the run from a maniac?

Beth didn't know. And she hated that.

Whether it was right or wrong, she was on her own and she had no idea where else to look for information. With days' and days' worth of research, she'd exhausted every Internet source she could think of.

The hours spent searching had netted her one thing. The knowledge that on or about the day she and Ryan had awakened in that motel room, there had not been one single article in the United States about a missing child fitting Ryan's description, a missing woman fitting hers, or an accident involving victims of either description.

She'd also discovered she needed glasses. After all the reading, her eyes were killing her.

SHE'D DONE NOTHING to warrant a background check.

Watching Beth's cute butt in the saddle in front of him, Greg gave himself a firm talking to. It was a continuation of the conversation he'd had while shaving that morning. Okay, so the woman he was falling in love with refused to give him any personal information. That was not a good reason to invade her privacy.

So what if she was the first woman he'd felt instinctively able to trust since Shelby? A fact made more incredible by the secrets she kept...

No matter that she was everything he'd always dreamed of in a mate. She loved Shelter Valley as much as he did. Clung to the little town in a way he'd need his woman to cling after Shelby's defection. She had an adorable little boy who needed a father almost as badly as he needed a son.

He knew it hadn't been long enough, but he wanted to marry her. He'd always been a man who knew what he wanted.

Other than Shelby, he'd always been a man who got it, as well.

"Hey!" he called out to her, as her horse cantered away in front of him. If he couldn't get her to talk about her past, maybe he could interest her in the future. "I thought we were going for a relaxing ride," he said, catching up.

"She wanted to run," Beth said, nodding at her mare. "I didn't have the heart to tell her no."

"You have a thwarted compulsion to run now and then?" he asked, finding her comment far too ironic, considering the thoughts he'd just been having.

"None whatsoever. I honestly think I'd be happy never to leave Shelter Valley."

"That's because you've never tried to get all your Christmas shopping done here," he said. "I'm a firm believer in malls for that."

"Okay," she amended with a sideways grin. "I'll amend my remark. I'd be happy never to leave Shelter Valley except to go to a mall in Phoenix once a year."

"Ryan was okay when you left him at Little Spirits?" he asked, enjoying the quiet of the desert trail they were riding. Beth had had a cancellation that morning and she'd found herself with a free day.

Beth nodded, her bobbing ponytail making her look like a teenager. "It's Wednesday, which means Bethany Parsons was there playing with Katie."

"Ryan's two favorite women in the world."

"Next to his mother, you mean." She stuck out her tongue at him.

He'd seen cowboys grab women off horses in movies. He'd never had the desire to do it himself.

Until now.

"So, you'd be happy to stay in Shelter Valley. What do you see yourself doing here? Expanding the cleaning business?"

"That, and maybe other things," she said slowly, as though she might actually be thinking about confiding in him. "It's as though, for the first time in my life, I'm exploring my options. Finding out what I want to do when I grow up."

"You were pressured as a kid?" The question simply emerged. Followed by a silent expletive. He'd promised himself he wasn't going to push her.

In case he pushed her right out his door.

"Yes," she said, staring out at the desert in front of them. "It feels like I've been pressured my whole life to *reach my potential*." She said the words in an ironic tone. "Funny thing is, I'm not sure I ever knew what I was reaching for. What *is* potential, anyway?"

Those blue eyes turned on him and Greg wondered if this was how a prisoner felt when he was being cuffed. Like his fate was sealed, somehow. Or his life had been irrevocably changed.

"I guess I've never really thought about it," he said. The October sun was warm without being too hot, shining down from a typically blue Arizona sky that was a daily gift, no matter how commonplace. "Maybe it's a combination of making the most of your physical and mental talents and yet doing what *you* want to do."

"If that's it, I don't think I've reached it." Her mare—or more accurately Burt's mare—broke into a trot, and Beth rode the saddle expertly, her jeans-clad lower body lithe and sexy.

"Take this, for instance," she said, grinning back at him. "I love to ride, but I know I haven't done it as much as I'd like."

"You've done it enough to get damn good at it."

"I guess." Beth's gaze grew distant.

"You think you'll ever get married again?" He couldn't think of a quicker way to get her back from whatever past she was hiding from him.

Or maybe he just had marriage on the brain.

"I hope so," she said. And then wouldn't look at him.

Greg hoped so, too.

"I sure don't want to live the rest of my life alone."

She had no idea how damn glad he was to hear that.

"How about you?" Her body was tall and straight—a good rider's posture—but stiffer than it had been. She was no longer sending him sidelong glances.

"I don't want to live the rest of my life alone, either."

The response garnered him a nod.

"You think you'll ever want more children?" he asked.

"If everything else was in place, I know I would."

So how could he help her get things in place?

Of course, what was to say that even if he *did* help her, he was the one she'd want to be with? He knew so little about her. Had so little to go on, so little basis upon which to judge.

The thought did nothing to make his day.

"CAN I TALK TO YOU?" Beth asked as they left Burt's small ranch and rode farther afield.

"Always."

Greg turned off onto a dirt path leading back to an old abandoned cabin. "Used to be an illegal distillery back here," he said by way of explanation. "Caught on fire when I was kid. My dad was in on the call."

"You don't talk about him much." Beth's voice softened.

Greg wondered if her eyes had done the same. Wished for a brief second that he could just drown in them and get it all over with.

"I guess it's still hard to think about it without the rage."

"Because he was paralyzed?"

"It wasn't just that," he said. Even Bonnie didn't talk about their dad much. Those years had been so heartbreaking. "He lost his short-term memory, as well," he told Beth, the words sticking in his throat. He gave her a quick glance. Her eyes had softened just like he'd imagined they would. And they were encouraging him to tell her this. Promising in some unspoken way to share his pain.

It was an unfamiliar concept. Greg wasn't usually the recipient of anyone else's help. He didn't usually need—or want—help. "All that intelligence," he murmured. He pulled the horse to a stop in a clearing in front of the old wooden structure, or what was left of it. "He could give you dissertations on profit and loss, on market shares and the benefits of going public as opposed to staying privately owned. The information was all there. He just couldn't put it together. The man was a genius and spent the last ten years of his life sounding like a blithering idiot."

"Did he know?"

"What?" He looked back at her.

"Did he know he wasn't making sense?"

Greg shook his head, wishing he'd never brought this up. "It wasn't that he didn't make sense in a single moment. It was when you pieced the moments together that clarity disappeared. He'd say the same thing over and over and over again. Or string two completely unrelated thoughts together. And no, he didn't know."

"Then, you should be very, very thankful."

Beth's words shocked him. "How do you figure?"

"If he didn't know, Greg, he didn't suffer. He died feeling just as intelligent as he'd always been. And what are we, after all, except products of our own reality?"

For the first time in ten years, Greg felt a ray of real peace. He still hurt for himself and Bonnie—and the hundreds of other people who'd lost a great man too soon. But Beth was right. He was incredibly thankful that his father hadn't suffered his own loss. He'd just never thought of that before.

The woman was definitely a miracle.

"What was it you wanted to tell me?"

Her face twisted with what looked almost like a grimace of pain. "Speaking of our own realities…"

She didn't go on. As though she couldn't rather than that she didn't want to. Greg had a bad premonition.

"Yeah?" he said softly, bracing himself.

"I can't let you form a picture of me that isn't real."

"You're going to tell me what kind of picture we're talking about?"

"One in which a man and a woman live outside the present."

"As in planning a future?"

"Maybe."

"Any guesses as to who this man and woman might be?" he asked. But of course he already knew.

"You and me."

CHAPTER TEN

THE REINS WERE STICKY between her fingers. Old leather and sweat. Beth loosened up on them.

Why was it so hard to do what was right? To *know* what was right?

"I like you." The words came out too loud, seeming to echo over all the shades of brown and green that were the desert, to the huge mountain in the distance and back again.

Greg didn't say anything. Just rode slowly and silently beside her.

"A lot," she added.

The trail narrowed, curved through a thicket of sagebrush. Greg let Beth go first. Pulling to the left on the reins, she nudged her horse—and then had to forcibly lighten up on the leather straps again.

She was losing the battle for words. Beth concentrated on the sound of the leather saddle and stirrups creaking, the smell of horse and old leather. They were comforting to her.

Was there a reason for that? Some memory attached to those smells?

Or was she just particularly drawn to the scent of old leather?

"I can't lead you on." She'd meant to deliver her message with a little more finesse.

"Meaning?"

She glanced over at him. The bright sun shining down gave his hair a blue metallic sheen. His face, eyes focused straight ahead, was stern.

"That night at your house…" Beth looked straight ahead, too. She felt uncomfortable. Wary. And turned on just by the thought of what they'd almost done out by his pool.

She'd been thinking about it ever since. Wanting him.

And wanting to run again, as fast and far away as she could get. Except that no matter where she went, she'd never be able to escape herself. Or the past that imprisoned her.

More and more she wanted to know about her past. Because she was finding it impossible to live with the constant fear, because she couldn't stand the dishonesty, because she wanted to be armed in every possible way to keep her son safe. And without knowing the enemy, she couldn't be sure of the risks.

She hated not being completely honest with Greg. Hated that she *couldn't* be. There was so little definition in her life that she held tightly to those things she knew to be important to her. Honesty was one of them. And Greg, she was afraid, was another.

So maybe the months in Shelter Valley had helped her heal enough to handle whatever she'd been hiding from.

Yet, if she *was* ready to handle it, wouldn't she just remember? From everything she'd read about psychosomatic amnesia, even when brought on by a blow to the head, regaining memory would be the natural course of events once the mind was ready to remember whatever it had blocked.

Should she trust her mind and just wait? Or…

"You've admitted you're attracted to me," she blurted out into the stillness. She felt as though she were riding next to a cardboard likeness of the man whose presence she'd started to crave.

"I am."

"And you keep asking me out."

"Can't argue with you there."

"I'm not saying no as much."

"I've noticed."

This wasn't going at all the way she'd scripted it in her mind. She was not supposed to be warring with herself at this point. The decision had been made. Beth's horse snorted, pulling on the reins. She'd been holding them so tightly she almost flew over the mare's head.

"Under the circumstances, a relationship could develop," she went on when she'd settled back in her saddle.

"Yeah."

"Though at the moment, I'm not so sure," Beth said, grinning at him in spite of the tension stiffening every muscle in her body. "You aren't being very kind here."

"I have a feeling I'm not going to like what's ahead," he said quietly, seriously. "I'm just waiting to find out."

His words spurred her on. "I don't want to presume anything," she said, "but because I know that, at least on my part, there's a real danger of wanting more from our relationship than friendship, I have to be honest with you and let you know that it isn't an option for me. No matter how much I want it."

She wasn't going to say any more. She wasn't. "Which I do," she said. And then, "But I can't,

Greg.'' She drew her horse to a stop and sat there facing him when he did the same. ''I mean it.''

His gaze locked with hers for several excruciating seconds. Then he nodded. ''I believe you.''

She was relieved and desperately disappointed all at once. The wasted possibilities seemed criminal. Especially in a life that offered no possibility, no love, at all.

''I need to know why.''

The statement was soft, and so honest.

She didn't look away. He deserved much more than a partial answer to a statement that she should never have had to make. Sitting there, looking at him, she needed so badly to tell him. But there was too much at risk; she couldn't take a chance on making a mistake. More than anything, she was confused.

His horse lifted his head, then danced around for a couple of seconds before settling back. Beth's mare, standing placidly in the October sun, ignored him.

''I'm not free,'' she finally said.

''Not free how? You aren't married. You're a widow.''

Beth shook her head. ''Inside me, Greg, I'm not free. I'm trapped and afraid. I can't trust or find faith. There are so many things I don't know, so many things, I can't feel. I'm not whole.''

When those intense green eyes darkened with compassion, Beth was afraid she'd be lost. Addicted to that look, she couldn't shift her eyes away from him.

''Sometimes, most times, it's relationships that are the cure for those kinds of wounds.''

Beth shook her head. ''Not when I feel like this, like I'm all chained up inside,'' she said, wishing he wasn't a cop. Wishing she knew what had made up her life before Shelter Valley, knew what she was going to be accountable for if they ever found her— or she found herself. "I can't stand the guilt, Greg. I can't stand not being fair to you. I can't let you think we're building something together when it's taking everything I've got just to hang on to me."

"Why don't you let me decide what's fair?"

"Because you're too nice for your own good. Someone has to watch out for you."

"I watch out for an entire county," he said sardonically. "I think I can manage to take care of myself."

"I don't. Not about this." She took a deep breath before plunging into the most dangerous territory of all. "I care about you. And with that caring, however tenuous it might be, comes responsibility. I can't let you walk blindly into something that's bound to hurt you."

"I'm walking in with my eyes wide open."

"No, you aren't. There's so much you don't know. So much I don't know."

"Why don't you know?" he asked with a puzzled frown. "It's your life."

Beth froze. She tried to find a quick reply that wasn't false without telling him a truth that was too precarious to divulge.

"I don't know why I'm handling the…tragedy— my husband's death—like I am. I understand grief, but this is more than that. I don't really understand why I'm so afraid. It's like I don't even know myself, anymore."

"So we'll discover it together."

Beth shook her head, bending over to pat her mare's neck. "This is something I have to do alone."

"I'll be here to cheer you on."

God, please don't be so cruel, Beth pleaded. The things life required of her were already too hard. She turned her mare, intending to go back.

Reaching out, Greg grabbed her mare's bridle, preventing her from leaving. Pulling her closer.

"There's risk in every single thing we do, Beth. Pain is inevitable now and then. But if, in the between times, we find love and goodness, they'll sustain us through the hard times. It's worth the pain to have you in my life.

"Granted, Shelter Valley has a comparatively low crime rate, but what there is, I deal with. My job doesn't give me the opportunity to see much of the good stuff, and Lord knows, the last ten years with my father weren't chock-full of fun...."

"And before that was Shelby's defection."

His gaze was compelling. So earnest it would have broken her heart—if she'd still had a heart that was intact and whole and capable of love.

"Katie's been my only salvation in the past few years," he said. "When life gets too overwhelming, I go pick her up, spend a couple of hours with her, just soaking up that innocence—and then I return to work."

Tears filled her eyes. Beth wouldn't blink, wouldn't let the tears fall. How she wished she had the capacity to give this man the love he deserved. She might not remember much, but her heart was telling her there weren't too many men like Greg Richards.

"And then I met you," he said, leaning forward, putting his hand gently behind her neck. Caressing her for a tender moment before he straightened.

Her neck, her entire body, tingled from the too-brief contact.

"When I'm with you the world makes sense," he told her.

Beth chuckled. But inside she wept. "How can that be, when I don't even make sense to myself?" she asked.

"Because you make everything fit," Greg said, resolute. "You bring an inexplicable happiness to my life."

Her chest was so tight, Beth couldn't breathe. The desert brown was lost in a red haze.

"But I might not always," she finally managed to say.

"I'm sure you won't. That's human nature. There's balance in all things—and you know something? We value the good that much more when we've experienced its opposite."

He was right about that

Could he possibly be right about some of the other things he'd said? Was it okay for her to let this relationship take its natural course?

"You've been honest with me," Greg said. He grabbed her hand, held it beneath his own against his thigh. "You're struggling. There are no guarantees for the future. You might be gone tomorrow…"

That was true enough.

"But you might not be."

It was her greatest dream. One she didn't dare dwell on.

"Chances are just as good that you'll wake up one day and find yourself healed and ready to marry me."

The jolt his words caused shot itself all the way from her stomach out to her fingers. Her hand would have fallen off his leg if he hadn't been holding on so tightly.

"Don't count on that."

"I won't."

"Don't hope for it, either."

"You can't dictate my hopes, Beth." His words were softly spoken, but assured. "And neither, it seems, can I. Whether you leave town tonight or live here forever, I'm always going to hope that there'll be a day for us."

Oh, God, why? I begged you not to do this.

"You aren't planning to take no for an answer, are you?" she asked, trying again to blink away unshed tears.

"Not today, I'm not."

Then, she'd just have to try again another day.

And until then, she was going to revel in every bit of the joy being forced upon her.

THE DAY CARE WAS FULL OF ACTIVITY when Beth stopped in later to pick up Ryan.

"He went in the potty today!" Bonnie greeted her at the door.

The news almost made Beth cry again. "You're sure it wasn't just an accident?" she asked her friend. Bonnie knew how concerned Beth had been about Ryan's slow development.

"Positive," Bonnie said. "He grabbed himself, grabbed my finger and pulled me in the direction of the potty chair."

Beth's face almost hurt with the width of her grin. "I was starting to imagine all kinds of things," she said. "He's the biggest boy here still in diapers."

Shrugging, Bonnie walked with Beth through the

groups of children playing contentedly—or not, as was the case with an older boy who was being comforted by one of the day care volunteers—toward the circle of two-year-olds. Ryan lingered on the outer edge as a child-care worker led them through a rousing rendition of "Old MacDonald Had a Farm." "Kids all develop at their own pace," she said. "Where is he on the growth chart for his age?"

"Average." Beth hated the lie, but she felt so lightheaded with relief that she couldn't come up with anything else. She had no idea where Ry was on the chart. He hadn't been measured since she'd been here. And even if he had been, she still wouldn't know. The doctor needed a child's birth date to refer to those charts.

And Ryan's mother didn't know when that was. She didn't know how old her own son was....

"Hi, Bonnie."

Startled, Beth turned with her friend as a well-dressed woman approached them. She was tall and slender. Dark-haired. She seemed to emanate an unusual combination of energy and peace, a quality Beth sensed—and responded to—instantly.

"Becca!" Bonnie greeted the older woman like an old and dear friend.

Becca Parsons. If she wasn't still reeling from the unexpected outcome of her afternoon with Greg and with Ry's news on top of that, Beth would've been intimidated.

"Have you met Beth Allen, Becca?" Bonnie asked, and then, before Becca could reply, she excused herself and went to greet another parent who'd just come in.

"Ryan's mom?" Becca stepped forward, a welcoming smile on her face as she shook Beth's hand. "I've heard so much about you. I'm glad to finally have a chance to meet you face-to-face," she said.

"I don't know what you've heard," Beth said, liking the woman immediately, "but it couldn't be anywhere near as good as what I've heard about you."

"I've heard that you're a single mom who's recently been widowed and is raising a wonderful little boy while also single-handedly starting up a successful cleaning business. I'm very impressed." Becca surprised her by reporting all this.

With warmth spreading under her skin, up her body, Beth attempted to reply with some measure of confidence. "Thank you."

Becca made her sound like a strong, capable woman. Which sure as hell wasn't the way Beth saw herself.

"Bethany's decided she's going to marry Ryan."

"Until a few weeks ago, she was the only girl he'd play with."

Becca grinned. She was a beautiful woman whose composure Beth envied.

"Let's make a promise now," Becca said, leaning close as she lowered her voice. "If they like each other this much when they hit their teens, we'll watch them like hawks."

Becca's words implied Beth would still be in Shelter Valley then. "Got it," Beth said happily, deriving pleasure from that hope—or pretense.

"It's far too early to ask, of course, but Will and I host an annual holiday party up at our place every year. I'd love it if you could come. And bring Ryan. Bethany would have our hides if you came without him."

It was clear who ruled the roost in the three-year-old's home. But Beth also knew Bethany to be a very polite and well-behaved little girl.

"I don't know..." she started to say. A crazed cleaning lady partying with the town's elite? She didn't think so.

Maybe in her other life she could've held her own there, but...

"You can't possibly have another engagement planned this far ahead."

"No."

"Then, please say you'll come. We're planning to invite Sheriff Richards, too. He was several years behind Will and me in school, but we've always known his family and we're so glad he's back in town."

"He told me you helped with his campaign," Beth said, repeating something Greg had told her that Sunday night at her house when they'd sat and talked for so long.

"He was the best man for the job."

Beth grinned at the other woman's confident tone. "Because he's from Shelter Valley?"

Becca grinned back. "That, too. Now back to the party—you have to come! Bonnie tells me you're an incredible pianist, and we have a piano that spends its life being ignored."

Kids were playing and singing around them, the noise level was high, but Becca didn't seem bothered by it. For that matter, neither was Beth.

"I'd like to but—"

"Hey, lady!"

The woman Bonnie had gone to greet was standing behind Becca, holding two sleeping babies, one in each arm. Bonnie had disappeared into another room.

"Phyllis!" Becca said, immediately reaching for one of the two infants. "Let me have her."

"Only for a second," Phyllis said, smiling. "Matt gets impatient if he has to wait too long to see his babies after a long day at school."

"Give me a break," Becca sputtered. "Long day! Will says that man's out of there by three o'clock every day."

"I know—isn't it sweet?" Phyllis said. "Did you realize he used to work so late he actually slept there sometimes?" Phyllis glanced at Beth, who would have moved on except for her fascination with those two babies. And for the intensely cheerful redhead who was obviously their mother.

"I'm sorry, we haven't met," Phyllis said. "I'm Phyllis Sheffield."

"Oh, I'm sorry," Becca said. She quickly finished the introduction between the two women.

Phyllis offered her one free hand. "Beth Allen. You've got the new cleaning business," she said. "I've been anxious to meet you."

"Good to meet you, too," Beth said, overwhelmed by the other woman's friendliness, but entranced just the same. "How old are they?" She nodded toward the babies.

"Four months."

"Both girls?"

"Nope. One of each. This little fella's Calvin. And that—" she pointed to the sleeping baby in Becca's arms "—is Clarissa."

Though surprised by the depth of her envy as she thought of having not one but two babies to love, Beth smiled. "They must keep you busy."

"Which is why I've been wanting to meet you,"

Phyllis said. "My husband and I both teach at Montford, and between our students and these guys, I'm failing miserably at housecleaning."

"And Phyllis can't stand to fail at anything," Becca teased. "Her biggest problem has always been thinking she can do it all."

Phyllis playfully elbowed Becca in the side. "Shut up," she said, her voice warm with familiarity and affection. Beth wanted a friend like that.

"And she's more than just a teacher," Becca continued, giving her a sly look. "Phyllis is not only the best psychology professor at the university, she's also Shelter Valley's resident psychologist."

The red haze slowly ascended. "You have a practice here in town?" She hadn't known there was anyone local.

"No." Phyllis laughed.

"Yes," Becca said at the same time. "It's just not official. Ask any of her friends. She's helped every one of us through pretty serious crises."

"I have not!" Phyllis said, jiggling her arm a little when Calvin frowned at her excited response to Becca. The baby settled back down. "I've done nothing more than be a friend."

"She's counseled every one of us, at one time or another," Becca said again. "Which is why there are so many happy women in this town."

Shelter Valley *did* seem to have an awful lot of happy people.

"That's the town's doing, not mine," Phyllis said.

The redhead did not look like a woman who'd recently given birth to twins. She was slim and almost as elegant as Becca in her business suit.

"It's *her* doing," Becca said to Beth. "Take our

friend Tory. Phyllis rescued her from an abusive past that probably would've killed her.''

"Tory Evans," Beth whispered.

"Sanders now," Becca said.

Both women were watching her closely. "You know Tory?" Phyllis asked, protectiveness evident in her tone of voice, in her posture and even the look in her eyes.

"No," Beth quickly assured her. "I read an article about her in a magazine a while back. The article talked about the welcome Tory received here. It's why I chose Shelter Valley as a place to start over...."

"Not just Tory," Becca said, her gaze full of compassion. "Living in Shelter Valley seems to give all of us a renewed sense of confidence at one time or another."

"Including me," Phyllis said. "This place changed my life."

Beth glanced at the other woman, surprised. "You haven't always lived here?" Judging by Phyllis's closeness to everyone, her acceptance as a solid member of the community, her involvement, Beth had assumed the woman had grown up in Shelter Valley. That she and her friends had known each other all their lives.

"Unfortunately, no," Phyllis said. "I just moved here a little over three years ago."

"I was very pregnant with Bethany at the time," Becca said. "My marriage was on the rocks, and Phyllis flew in and immediately set Will and me straight."

Phyllis had only been here three years? And was a

completely accepted member of the Shelter Valley family?

So there was hope.

Maybe.

"Then, how'd you get to know everyone so fast?" Beth couldn't help asking. Not that she could do the same. The fewer people she was close to, the better. For now.

"She and Cassie Tate do pet therapy together," Becca said. "That's part of it. They helped Cassie's stepdaughter talk again after more than a year of trauma-induced silence...."

Trauma-induced silence. Beth felt cold. And sick.

And very, very threatened. Was Ry's near-silence also trauma-induced? And was help for Beth standing right there in front of her? Did she have the courage to find out?

"She helped me save my marriage," Becca said, her voice softening as she smiled at her friend.

"She's making me sound like much more than I am, and I'll never be able to live up to it. Just take everything Becca says about me with an ear to the flattery involved. She wants my babies," Phyllis teased. "What I want to know is, do you have room for one more client?"

"Of course I do," Beth answered automatically. She'd put in longer hours. Make it work.

And if she took on one more client after this, she'd have to hire help.

Under the table, of course.

Meanwhile, she had to collect Ryan, go home and dye their hair—get herself to the safety of her own space, her regular routine—before the red haze became more than a warning. Her mind was overwhelmed, taking in too much to process at one time.

There were just far too many questions. And no answers.

CHAPTER ELEVEN

AT HIS KITCHEN TABLE on that second Monday in October, Greg studied the four-foot-square collection of clippings and reports, plus the couple of photos he'd had at home—copies of the official photos taken of his father's accident. He and Burt had a meeting in the morning, and Greg knew Burt was going to recommend closing the case—all the carjacking cases—insofar as an unsolved case could be closed. Burt was ready to dismiss the incidents as random, continuing to be on the lookout for any information that might lead to suspects but not actively pursuing clues.

Greg refused to accept that verdict a second time. Not only had he assigned deputies to question people, but he and Burt had gone around interviewing everyone in the vicinity of the carjackings; they'd posted radio news announcements and put out requests on all of the Arizona television stations asking for anyone with information to call.

Burt had personally dealt with every single one of the hundred or more calls they'd received.

They'd turned up nothing. Burt had also, in deference to Greg's ambition to see this case solved, questioned most of the key witnesses himself rather than assigning less experienced officers to handle the legwork for him.

Again, he turned up nothing.

But there *had* to be something. Something right there in front of him, if Greg could only see it. No matter how many nights he spent poring over the reports, the figures, the graphs, the measurements and the photos, he couldn't piece it all together. Or even figure out which piece was missing.

Rubbing the back of his neck, Greg straightened and grabbed a cola from the fridge, hoping the caffeine would be the jump-start he needed. His whole life seemed to consist of looking for missing puzzle pieces. Professionally and personally.

Beth was hiding more pieces from him than she was giving him. Leaning against the counter, Greg drank the soda from the can, staring out the big window above his sink to the resortlike backyard he and Beth had spent those few short hours in.

She'd almost made love to him that night. He'd almost died when she hadn't.

He had to stop thinking about that night.

He couldn't believe Burt hadn't come up with anything substantial at all. He was the best. Which meant there was nothing to find.

Then, why did Greg feel so certain there was?

Can in hand, he moved back to the table, and stood there studying all the bits and pieces. If he viewed them from a different angle, would they reveal something new?

They didn't. Even sideways he saw the same words, the same pencil sketches, same figures, same images…

From Greg's vantage point, that dented front end looked like a rabbit. The largest rabbit Greg had ever seen in his life.

He froze. Stared. Then, every movement deliberate,

he slowly rounded the table, his gaze never leaving that rabbit-shaped dent. Only when he was facing the photograph did his eyes stray to the other pictures.

They were all of the same car. His dad's Thunderbird. Taken from different angles, different perspectives of the crime scene, the photos didn't all show the front of the car. But in every one that did—of the few left since the lab disaster—that dent looked like a rabbit.

One he recognized. "I'll be damned." There were rabbits and then there were rabbits. This one was missing its head; the front end hadn't reached that high. It was missing its bottom and feet, too. They would've been below the level of the bumper. But that middle, with the "paw" raised at a jaunty angle, was unmistakable. If he hadn't just been horseback riding with Beth, noticing shapes in the rock formations of the mountains that he usually overlooked, he might not have recognized the rabbit now.

But Greg remembered that particular formation. It was an infamous landmark to him, as it marked the spot of one of the worst nights of his life. He'd once been invited to a party at Rabbit Rock—he'd been sixteen, feeling privileged to be let in on the whereabouts of the secret gathering place. About thirty miles from Shelter Valley, in the heart of the most undeveloped, unpopulated portion of Kachina County, there was a clearing that abutted the south side of the mountains. The clearing was surrounded by an unusually thick grouping of palo verde trees, enclosing it, hiding it from the rest of the world. Making it the perfect place for teenagers to engage in illicit activities.

He'd been a fool then. A reckless teenage kid

who'd thought he was invincible, and worse, strong enough to take on anything. He'd only seen the rock that one time, but he'd seen it in many different forms. When the hallucinations had been at their worst, he and that rabbit were the only two things in the world.

Tossing his can in the trash, Greg paced his kitchen. Went to the phone. Picked it up. Put it back down. What was he thinking here? Every one of the cars that had been stolen ten years ago, as well as every one that had been taken this summer, had been rammed into the side of a mountain out in a clearing no one but a group of rowdy boys had known about. It sounded even more implausible when he spelled it out.

He'd taken some long shots in his life, but he'd never reached quite this far. Greg rubbed his face. Rinsed it with cold water.

He reached for the phone again. He had to call Burt. This couldn't wait until morning.

Unless he really was losing perspective. How insane was he going to sound when he laid this on his deputy? How much credibility was he going to lose?

And how sure was he that he wasn't dreaming up the whole thing? Making something happen because he was crazy with determination to avenge his father's attack?

Phone in hand, he walked back to the table. Looked at the photos. The rabbit was still there.

He couldn't let this go. Greg knew what he had to do. He dialed.

"Hello?"

"Beth?" he asked, trying to stay calm. He wasn't too eager to have her thinking he was a mental case.

"Greg? What's wrong?"

"Nothing," he said quickly, hating the instant alarm he heard in her voice. She was so easily made nervous, and that bothered him. "I need to run something by an impartial party. Someone I can trust to be honest with me," he added, to reassure her, but also to make sure that he didn't talk himself out of asking for her help.

"Of course," she said, her voice completely different. Soft. Beckoning. "What's up?"

He glanced out at the pool. It would be light for at least another hour, maybe an hour and a half. "Have you eaten yet?"

"No, Ryan and I just got home. Today was my day to clean the Willises'. You want me to throw something in the microwave for him and then call you back?"

"How about if I come get you, we pick up something for dinner and take a drive?"

"Why do I get the feeling this is more than just an impromptu invitation to a picnic?"

Greg stared at the photos. "There's something I want you to see," he said slowly. And then he amended that. "Something I *need* you to see."

"What?"

"That's just it, I don't want to say." He knew he sounded way too mysterious. "I'm doing a sanity check," he finally admitted. "I've come up with this crazy hypothesis, and before I go any further with it, I'd like to show you the evidence and see if you think I'm off base."

"Of course," she said, her instant capitulation filling Greg with a sense of a righted world.

One way or another, he was going to have some answers.

"But if I'm going to have to look at something gross, I'd better not have dinner."

He chuckled. "I wouldn't ask you to look at anything gross," he said. "Usually when the evidence is graphic, wrongdoing is relatively easy to prove. Labs are wonderful things."

"Does this have to do with your father's case?"

Sobering, Greg carefully picked up the photos and slid them back into their envelope. "Yes."

"Give me ten minutes."

GREG CALLED the Valley Diner and placed a take-out order. Chicken nuggets and fries for Ryan. Grilled chicken sandwiches for him and Beth. He didn't take time to change out of his uniform. He wanted to get to the rabbit before dark. At the last minute, he grabbed the spotlight from the trunk of his squad car, just in case.

The drive wasn't nearly as tense as it might've been if he'd been making it alone, dwelling on his obsession. With Ryan in his car seat between them, a sweet little guy in blue jeans and a tiny plain white sweatshirt, he and Beth had their dinner and spoke about superficial things. She mentioned someone she'd met in town that day—a woman he'd gone to school with. He talked about a tentative plan to turn his third bedroom into a weight room. She told him a couple of "toilet lady" jokes she'd made up while working that week.

Ryan, a soggy French fry in each hand, looked up at Greg when he laughed out loud at the last one.

"At least he likes the fries," he said, running a

hand across the top of the little boy's head. The toddler hadn't touched his chicken.

"Sha sha," Ryan said.

"What, sweetie?" Voice eager, Beth leaned toward him, her shiny auburn hair falling forward over her shoulders. "What did you say?"

Ryan held up both hands, showing her his fries. "Sha sha," he said again.

"French fries?" Beth asked. She was wearing jeans, too, and an off-white sweater that hugged those perfect breasts and tapered at her waist.

Ryan nodded. "Sha sha." He then attempted to put both fries in his mouth at once.

"One at a time, Ry," Beth said, pulling her son's left hand away from his mouth. It struck Greg that they were painting a family picture right there. He'd had no idea so much pleasure could be taken from such a simple thing.

It was still light when he pulled off the road, onto a dirt path, and then, putting the truck into four-wheel drive when the path came to an abrupt end, continued on. The adrenaline he'd managed to contain during the past hour came rushing to the forefront again when he noticed the tire tracks just off to his left. They weren't fresh. But they weren't twenty years old, either.

Judging by the lack of regrowth, they were less than a year old.

His excitement grew when he wound his way into the clearing and his gaze alighted immediately on the rabbit. It was almost exactly as he'd remembered. A little smaller, maybe. More weathered. There'd been more growth on the mountain back when he was a teenager.

He stopped the truck, although he didn't get out. Ryan's legs were bouncing a little in his seat, but with a French fry in one hand and a plastic truck in the other, he was amazingly content.

Beth's son did not act like any other two-year-old he'd ever met.

"This is what we came to see?" Beth asked, glancing around the clearing.

Greg pointed. "That's what we came to see."

She looked toward the rocky side of the mountain. Ryan looked, too, dropping his French fry as he leaned forward.

"Sha sha," he said. Greg automatically reached for another one and handed it to the boy. Ryan took it without hesitation.

Greg didn't think anything of the act until he glanced up from the toddler to see Beth staring at him. "What?"

She shook her head. Greg was fairly certain he'd seen moisture in her eyes. "It's just nice, seeing him interact with you...."

So she was sensing it, too. This family feeling. Greg was glad that—at least on this—he wasn't alone.

"What is it about this rock that has you concerned?" she asked, turning to look out the window again.

"Look at it for a minute," Greg said, not all that eager to test his hypothesis. Now that he was there, he was more certain than ever that he was on to something. But if Beth didn't see any connection between that rock and the photos, he might have to concede that he was so desperate to get someplace, he was inventing a reason to continue the search.

Greg gave Ryan another French fry. "Do you see any shapes in that rock?" he asked.

"Looks kind of like something waving, doesn't it?" she said, her brows drawn together in concentration. "Like there's an arm going from the round part up there, off to the side."

"An arm—or a paw?"

"Yeah!" she said, grinning at him. "It's definitely a paw."

Greg nodded.

She glanced from him to the rock and back. "So, are we playing a game, or is this leading somewhere?"

"Look again." Greg nodded toward the mountain. "Can you see the rabbit attached to that paw?"

"Sha sha," Ryan said, his plastic truck falling to the floor as he reached for the bag that contained his dinner.

Greg picked up the truck and the bag, letting Ryan poke his hand in for a fry. The child used one hand and then the other, coming out with double the bounty.

"Smart guy," Greg said approvingly.

He sobered, though, as he looked once again at the mountain in front of them. The sun was going down. It would be dark soon.

"Is that its head?" Beth asked. "That round thing? And his ears go up from there to the right? It's a jackrabbit."

Bingo.

Carjackings. Jackrabbit. It was a long stretch.

Too long.

And yet...maybe this was part of his answer. The missing piece.

"We used to call this Rabbit Rock when I was kid," he said gravely.

"Way out here? How'd kids ever find this spot?"

"I'm not sure," Greg said. It wasn't anything he'd ever thought about. "I just know that certain kids talked about the parties they'd have out here. Only the coolest kids were invited."

"Then, you were invited for sure."

"Not right away," he said. "Not until my junior year in high school."

"Were the parties as good as you'd heard?"

Greg couldn't meet her eyes. Ryan was starting to droop, his head resting against the car seat as he chewed on a French fry.

"I only came to one," Greg said, staring at the rock. "It was one of the most horrible nights of my life."

Even in the growing dusk, he could see that her blue eyes had filled with compassion.

"What happened?" she asked.

"I was an idiot," he said. "Like a lot of sixteen-year-old boys, I was certain that the need to be careful didn't apply to me. I was young. Strong. Succeeded at most everything I set my mind to. Popular. Nothing was going to happen to me."

"I take it something did."

Ryan's eyes were slowly closing.

Greg nodded. "Drinking a few beers wasn't new to me," Greg related softly. "Didn't faze me at all. So, of course, I was certain that little mushroom thing wouldn't, either.

"The worst part was, I didn't even want the damn thing," he continued. "What I'd wanted was to preserve my reputation. I put a lot of stock in being one of the cool guys.''

"Don't most people?''

He was tempted to ask if she had. But didn't.

"Probably. In a small place like Shelter Valley, word gets around quickly. If a guy chickened out or acted like a wimp, he might as well empty his locker in the training room and move in with the nerds.''

"So what happened?''

He loved that voice. The one that wrapped him in warmth.

"I had a bad mescaline trip. Thought I was dying. The other guys were in another world, playing some version of football I couldn't figure out. I couldn't run. I couldn't breathe. They told me afterward that I stood in front of that rock for more than an hour. What I remember was knowing that some freak thing had happened to the world and only that rabbit and I were left. If I took my eyes off it, it might be gone, too, and then there'd only be me.''

"My God, that must have been horrible. You were just a kid!''

"Yeah, well, that wasn't the worst part. That came when one of the guys dropped me off at my house and I had to face Bonnie and my dad. She took one look at my face and was terrified that I was going to die. My father knew better. He checked me out and then sent me to my room.

"I'll never forget the disappointment on his face as I walked away. I lost my father's unconditional trust that night.''

"I'll bet you never did drugs again.''

"Never.''

"And you regained his trust.''

"Eventually," Greg sighed. "But trust is a funny thing. Once you lose it, you never regain it in its original form."

THE SOLEMNITY IN GREG'S WORDS, and in the mood between them, touched Beth deeply. She had no memory of personal trust. And yet her heart understood exactly what Greg was saying.

"I thought we were on an outing to solve a case," she said softly, hoping to bring him out of a reverie that couldn't be pleasant.

"We are."

"Here?"

He nodded, and slowly pulled an envelope out of his pocket. Handing it to her, he flipped on the overhead light in the truck. But not before draping Ryan's blanket over the top and sides of his car seat, shielding the sleeping child from the harsh light.

Such a simple gesture. One that brought tears to Beth's eyes for the second time in less than an hour.

"Look at these and tell me what you think," he said.

Baffled by the lack of explanation, Beth took the envelope. There were pictures inside. She slid them out, curious. There were several pictures of the same car, taken from different angles. It appeared that the only real damage had been to the front end.

Until she exposed the image of the car's interior. It was little more than a black frame, burned-out.

Beth swallowed, aching inside. "Your father's car."

"Yes." He glanced at the photos. "Do you see anything at all that reminds you of something else?"

Frowning, Beth looked again, trying to help him.

To find what he needed her to find. But he was being so vague, and—

"The paw waving," she said suddenly. She could feel the blood drain from her face as she raised her eyes from the photo to the rock outside, still recognizable as it gleamed in the headlights Greg had flipped on. "You think someone ran this car into that mountain."

The look Greg gave her was piercing. Demanding total honesty.

"Do you?"

"I think it's definitely possible. That paw is so distinctive."

"That's what I thought."

She couldn't bear to see any more. Slipping the photos back into their envelope, she passed the envelope to Greg. "Was your father found near here?"

"Not really."

"So his injuries were from a car accident?"

Greg shook his head. "He'd been beaten with some kind of blunt object, possibly fists."

"Why would someone beat him up and then ram his car into a rock?"

"Good question. And it wasn't just his car." Greg was tapping the envelope against his steering wheel. "All of the cars that were involved in carjackings that summer, and then again this summer, bore similar dents in their front ends."

Shivering, Beth gazed around at the dark desert night. They were all alone out there. Miles from civilization. "It's the connection you've been looking for," she said slowly.

"More than that, it's a place to look for the reason.

There can't be too many people who know about this place.''

"Where do you even start looking?''

"First thing I'm going to do is talk to Burt. He was the one who combed this area in August. And then there's an old hermit who lives about ten miles from here. The guys I partied with that night used to talk about him.''

"That was twenty years ago. You think he'll still be around?''

"Maybe. He wasn't all that old back then. Story was, his wife had been raped and murdered in their home someplace in Tucson while he was at work. Had a life insurance policy that made him wealthy. He bought some land out here and wouldn't let anyone near the place. He was pretty warped from the whole thing. Unless he's dead, chances are he's still here.''

Beth shivered again. Greg told the story as if it were an everyday occurrence. To him, the sheriff of an entire county, that probably wasn't far from the truth. She didn't want to live in a world where violence was commonplace. Where you had to fear the evil that lurked in unexpected places, at unexpected times.

She wasn't even aware that panic was starting to descend until she automatically initiated relaxation techniques. Why did she have such a strong premonition that evil could not be escaped?

CHAPTER TWELVE

RYAN WAS SLEEPING SOUNDLY, his head resting against the padded side of his car seat. "I'd like to check one more thing before we head back, if you don't mind," Greg said to Beth.

"Of course I don't mind."

Grabbing his spotlight, he climbed out of the truck, careful to shut the door softly behind him. His gun was a welcome weight against his thigh.

Approaching the mountain's rock face, Greg shone the light all over the ground, looking for tire tracks. While he couldn't make out one distinct and single set of tracks that led to the rabbit-shaped rock, it was obvious that the clearing had been used recently. And often. There were many sets of tire tracks, ranging in size from mountain bikes to four-wheel-drive trucks like Greg's, all crisscrossing each other.

"Looks like there's been some kind of racing going on through here."

He hadn't known Beth was with him. She'd left the truck door slightly open, obviously so they could hear if Ryan woke up.

"Or maybe just kids spinning their wheels, doing fishtails, practicing mountain bike tricks, that sort of thing. I feel like such a fool, with all this going on right under my nose."

"How could you have known?"

"I knew this place was here. I just thought everyone else had forgotten about it. About eight years ago, I started haunting this place regularly, busting up the kind of party I'd attended. Some kind of idea of making restitution to my dad for what I'd done."

"When was the last time you were here?"

"About four years ago. At that point, there hadn't been anyone out here in a couple of years, and I figured my job was done."

With her toe Beth smoothed a clump of dirt in the middle of one of the tracks. "I guess if you were looking for tracks that would prove your theory, this spoils that, huh?"

"Not necessarily," Greg said. He shone the light up to the edge of the mountain. "Look."

"No tracks," Beth said, sounding almost as though she felt sorry for him.

"Yeah," Greg said, walking more quickly. "No tracks, and an unnatural pattern in the dirt. Someone did this deliberately."

"To wipe out tracks?"

"That would be my guess." With the mountain now in the spotlight, Greg studied every inch of the rabbit formation. "But that's not what I was looking for," he said.

A moment later, heart pounding, he added. "*This* was."

Seething with mixed emotions, Greg stood there and stared at the paint mark in the middle of the rabbit's paw. Anger was in the forefront, but some elation and a curious kind of relief were there, as well. The paint wasn't from his father's car, of course; that would've long since worn away.

"It's the exact color of the car stolen from a young

U of A dancer back in August," he said. "I'm surprised Burt missed it."

"Unless he didn't know about the clearing."

That had to be it. Though if anybody could find this little-known gathering place, it would be his star deputy.

Feeling an urgent need for connection, Greg slid his arm around Beth. Her long hair covered the sleeve of his uniform. Motioning back to the truck with his head, he asked, "Does he usually sleep this soundly?"

She nodded, her hair brushing his shoulder. "Unless he has a nightmare. He should be out for the night."

"He won't wake up when you get him home? Change him?"

"Maybe, but he'll go right back to sleep."

"He's a great kid."

"Yeah." Greg was curious about the sound of worry, not pride, in her voice.

He could no longer deny his suspicion that Beth was dealing with much more than the death of her husband. She was immediately nervous anytime he surprised her, which was definitely a giveaway. Although *what* it revealed he didn't know. When he'd called her that night, she'd been instantly defensive. Or that time he'd surprised her at the Mathers when she'd been cleaning. And the time he'd shown up unannounced on her doorstep. She was afraid, that much was obvious—but why? Of what—or whom?

The darkness, the solitude, the idea that they were all alone out here, miles from anywhere, the fact that she hadn't moved away from him, gave Greg an unusual sense of security where she was concerned. "Can I ask you something?" he said.

She stiffened. "Yes."

"And you'll give me an honest answer?"

"If I can."

He almost changed his mind. But if what he suspected was true, she might need help—protection even. And he couldn't provide it until he knew where the enemy lived. Inside her? That was a possibility; it could certainly be part of the answer. Or was the enemy someplace else? Perhaps wherever she'd come from...

"Was your husband murdered?"

"What?" Beth turned to face him. "Why do you ask that?" Her arms were wrapped around herself, and she was as defensive as he'd ever seen her. He'd hit a raw nerve.

"I'm wondering, actually, if you might somehow have witnessed the murder," he said, determining to at least get it all out. "It would explain so much." He wanted to reach for her, pull her against him. And yet he understood that it would be the worst thing he could do. "Your complete inability to talk about your life before you came to Shelter Valley, your nervousness, which surfaces at unexpected times. Maybe even the reaction you had that night at the casino. Was he killed at one of your concerts? And is that why playing the piano seems almost painful for you?"

"Can we go home now?"

Without waiting for a reply, Beth hurried back to the truck. She strapped herself in and waited.

Resigned, disappointed, Greg followed her. But he

didn't immediately start the truck. "Beth, I want to help."

"I know." She sat stiffly, facing front.

"I can't do that if I don't know what I'm helping with."

"I need to go home."

Had there been any feeling at all in her voice, he might have pressured her a little more, tried harder. As it was, there didn't seem to be much point. It didn't matter whether he kept Beth there with him or not. She'd already left.

Because he'd hit too close to the truth? And if so, would she come to him, talk to him about it when she got over the shock of his having guessed?

Or maybe he was conjuring this up, too, to help him accept the fact that the woman he was falling in love with wasn't nearly as willing to open her heart— and her life—to him.

IN THE APARTMENT'S ONLY BEDROOM late that night, Beth sat on the floor in the dark by her son's crib and shook. The glow from the cheap shell-shaped night-light plugged into the wall was her focus. She kept her vision trained there.

Had she witnessed her husband's murder? Was that the horrible truth awaiting her if she ever fought her way out of her mental prison?

Was her lie about being a widow not a lie at all?

Cold, light-headed, she tried to find her way in the darkness of her mind, searched for anything familiar, any bit of recognition. A picture. A single memory.

Even a name.

Her son moved and her eyes were drawn toward the crib. Had Ryan witnessed the murder, too? Was that the trauma that had brought about his silence? From the very beginning of this nightmare, her baby boy had said his name. And hers. But never once had she heard him say "da da." One of the first words most babies seemed to say.

Pulling her knees up to her chest, she hugged them tightly, her hands clutching her upper arms. The shivers were uncontrollable. She couldn't get up to retrieve the quilt from her bed. Didn't want to be trapped beneath it, anyway.

What if she'd killed her husband? What if that was why she'd witnessed the murder?

Maybe it was why she'd run away with her son, only a gym bag, two-thousand dollars cash and a couple of diapers in her possession.

"Oh God, Ry," she whispered brokenly. "What have I done? What am I doing to you?"

There were no answers, not from the sleeping little boy, not from inside her. Only debilitating fear.

Beth sat there long into the night, trying to find a way to go on.

"I KNOW NOTHING about any such clearing," Burt told Greg early the next morning. The two men, dressed in full uniform, were in Burt's office in the county sheriff's building, nearly twenty miles from Shelter Valley. Greg's own office was two floors down.

"What about the hermit who lives out near the foot of the mountains?" Greg asked. "Did you talk to him?"

Burt shook his head. "Far as I could tell, he's long gone. That shack of his looked deserted. I checked back a couple times and there was no sign of life."

Damn. The old guy had been his best lead. Or at least the easiest one.

Greg went over every detail of the case with Burt again, knocking ideas around, seeking his deputy's invaluable reasoning ability. In the end, they'd come up with nothing more than an agreement to continue searching.

"How soon can you and I take a trip out to Rabbit Rock?" Greg asked as he stood to leave.

Burt looked at his watch. "This afternoon?" he asked. "Around three?"

Greg was disappointed that Culver couldn't make it before then. But he smiled, shook Burt's hand, made plans to meet him back at the office later that afternoon.

Taking the elevator down to the first floor where his own suite of offices was, Greg tried to shake an uneasy feeling. Burt hadn't been brushing him off. The deputy was as eager as Greg to get to work on this latest development. Which was most likely why he'd picked up the phone and started dialing before Greg had shut the office door behind him.

Greg didn't turn right as he'd intended when he got off the elevator. He strode straight through the front doors of the county building and headed to his car, his other "office."

Keeping busy had always been a cure for the restlessness that sometimes nagged at him. That was the only reason he was going to drive out to visit that hermit's cabin for himself.

It was something to pass the time until he and Burt took their little field trip that afternoon. He was very eager to hear what kind of evidence his deputy would turn up before then.

If anyone could find the missing pieces that would make some sense out of a bunch of senseless crimes, Burt Culver could.

He was the best damn cop Greg had ever known.

THE HERMIT, JOE FRANCIS—although Greg had never heard anyone use his name—was still around. Greg smelled old cooking grease when he got out of his car on the old man's property. Calling it a front yard would be too generous. The weathered gray logs and boarded-up windows made the shack appear deserted. But that smell. Someone had been cooking there recently.

"Joe?" Greg called, with no idea if the old guy even considered the name his own anymore. Looking cautiously around, he stood still, hoping for a chance to explain before he got shot at.

Not that the hermit had ever been considered dangerous. As far as Greg had ever heard, Francis wasn't violent or out to hurt anyone. He just wanted to be left alone.

"Joe Francis?" he called again. "You here?"

As impatient as he'd been with Burt that morning, he was patient now. He hoped Joe would show himself eventually; Greg wasn't going to be able to leave without checking out that cabin. And he was loath to trespass on the man's private sanctuary without an invitation.

"Joe, you there?" he called again, taking a step away from the car. "I'm just here to introduce myself," he said. "I'm the new sheriff in this county. My name's Greg Richards."

He almost missed the set of eyes peering at him

from a tall clump of desert brush off to the right of the shack. "Is that you, Joe?" he asked the clump.

It moved. And the eyes were gone.

"I mean you no harm," Greg said in the direction of the clump. Joe—or someone—had to be back there. The clump, surrounded by low-lying desert brush, was the only coverage for several yards. "I'm on official business, as you've probably figured out," he added. "But it has nothing to do with you. There's a slight chance you might be able to help me, though."

The earth was completely still. Hotter than most October days, that Tuesday wasn't providing even a bit of a breeze.

Moving around to the front of his car, Greg leaned against the hood, one hand on either side of him, ready to grab his weapon if he had to. That and his bullet-proof vest were all he had to protect himself, but he was prepared to take whatever risk was necessary. This mattered too much not to do everything he could. "There's no real reason you should want to," Greg continued. "But the way I see it, you and I have something in common. I'm guessing we both feel a need to have justice done. To know that at least one crime has been avenged, the perpetrator behind bars where he belongs, not out walking the streets. Free. Laughing. Having a good time. Capable of hurting more innocent people."

No movement.

"I'm not speaking as a cop here," Greg said. If nothing else came of this maybe it would be cathartic to just say these things to someone who'd been there. "My father, an economics professor at Montford, was beaten and left for dead not too far from here about ten years ago. He lived the rest of his life paralyzed until he died last year.'' He stopped. Crossed his legs. Peered at that clump of brown scrub, willing it to move. ''Last night I found some pretty substantial evidence at the base of this mountain. There's a good chance you're the only one who could help me out with it.''

If that didn't work, Greg was going to have to give up. At least for now. Between Beth and this old hermit, he was beginning to feel like he'd lost all his talent for interrogation.

Or maybe he'd just forgotten how to talk to people outside of work and Bonnie's house.

''Okay, well, I'll leave you alone, then,'' Greg said, backing up to the driver's door of his car.

He pulled out a business card and tossed it in front of him. ''If you know anything about the clearing on the south side of the mountain and you ever want to contact me about it, there's my card.''

Frustrated beyond trusting himself to be compassionate Greg knew it was time to go.

''I told the other sheriff.''

The voice was gravelly. Old and cracked. And not very loud.

But it was loud enough for Greg to hear.

Slowly, carefully, he got out of his car. ''Sheriff Foltz?''

No answer.

''What did you tell him?''

''Ten years ago. When the kids were banging their cars into the side of the mountain.''

Greg had no idea if he was talking to a bent and gray, skinny old man, maybe with a long beard, or a sturdy muscled woodsman in the prime of his later years. He gave the brush an intent stare.

"You told Sheriff Foltz there were kids ramming cars into the mountain."

"Ten years ago. I couldn't stand to have them violating nature that way. They stopped right after."

There'd been no report....

Greg was sweating. Yet his mind felt clear and sharp. "You keep an eye on the place since then?" he asked.

"This mountain's good to me, I'm good to it. I hike over there every now and then."

"Still?"

"Yes. I spend a lot of nights on top of that mountain."

Which could explain why Culver hadn't found the old man. Then, too, Francis was pretty adept at not being seen.

"Have you noticed any activity in the clearing in the past few years?" Greg continued to address the clump of desert brush.

"The kids came back with their loud parties this summer. And they're running their cars into the side of the mountain again. I hiked all the way up the mountain to find some peace, and instead, heard that partying going on below. Went on all night long."

Considering the huge expanse of open ground around the shack, Greg found it a little odd that the old man regularly put himself through a rigorous mountain hike. He supposed most people thought they had to leave the life they had in order to find peace.

That was something he'd like to discuss with Beth sometime. He'd bet she had a theory on it.

"If you hear them again and have a way to get in touch with me, I'd sure appreciate a phone call," Greg said. "And in the meantime, if you ever need anything, let me know."

"Groceries," the old man said.

Greg frowned at the tree. "You need groceries?" He didn't know how mountain men provided for themselves, but he'd always assumed they hunted or grew whatever sustenance they needed.

"The walk into town's not bad, but I'm getting a little old for the walk back with all the groceries."

Hochie, the closest town, was a good fifteen miles away.

"Once every two weeks enough?"

"It's more than I go myself."

"Then, I'll be here two weeks from today."

He was eager to see what the old man looked like.

BETH SPENT ALL TUESDAY AFTERNOON at the library, looking up death notices. And searching for articles on murder in a several-hundred-mile radius of Snowflake.

She got about as much from the computer files, microfiche and Internet sites she visited as she did from her own memory. It felt like the whole world was in collusion against her.

To celebrate that they hadn't been murdered, she took Ryan out for ice cream. And ran into Katie and Greg at the ice-cream parlor. He was still in his uniform, while Beth was in her "toilet lady" clothes. Sweats, with her hair up in a ponytail.

"Ryan!" Katie squealed. Ry walked over to his friend and stood there, watching her eat her ice-cream cone.

Greg walked over to Beth, too, but he wasn't as silent. "I tried to call you."

"I was at the library."

He seemed a little curious, but mostly preoccupied. "How about we take the kids to the park and let them drip ice cream over everything there?" he suggested.

She laughed and nodded, ordering quickly, and then the four of them strolled to the park adjacent to Shelter Valley's town square.

It didn't take Greg long to fill Beth in on the events of his day. The progress of the case. She'd been wondering about him, hoping she'd hear from him.

"So what happened when you met with Burt at three?"

Sitting on a bench beside her, but far enough away that they weren't touching, Greg shrugged. He was watching Katie and Ryan, who were attempting to sit on a miniature merry-go-round while they ate. The thing kept moving and the result was a combination of comedy and frustration. Depending, he supposed, on whether you were observer or participant.

"We drove out. He'd never seen the place before, and he saw that as a failure. Took it personally. He felt he'd let me down. Foltz told him nothing about the Francis complaint ten years ago."

Never having met Burt, Beth had no grounds on which to judge, but something didn't quite add up. The best cop in the entire county and he'd failed in so many areas. The clearing. The hermit. Evidence from the past.

"Are you sure Burt's telling the truth?"

Greg's look of surprise was answer enough. "I don't doubt it for a second. I trust the man with my life every single day I go to work. And he trusts me with his. Burt's a good cop. And that's all he is. He's married to the job. Ten years older than me with no wife, no kids. Just those horses.''

"So what now? Do you talk to Foltz?''

"Burt's going to.''

"This case is important to you. Maybe you should do that.''

"Technically, it's Burt's case. And he's kicking himself enough as it is. I don't want my top deputy losing confidence in himself.''

He knew better than she. He knew Burt. And at the moment she was viewing the whole world with suspicion.

"That old hermit said something today that struck me, and I wondered what you'd think about it,'' Greg said a couple of seconds later. The kids had finished their ice cream and, with sticky hands and faces, were crawling around in their jeans and sweatshirts on the merry-go-round.

"What did he say?'' She wished he were sitting closer.

"You know how people always say grass is greener on the other side?''

"Yeah.'' She grinned at him. "But they obviously haven't seen the grass in Shelter Valley.''

"Cultured,'' Greg said. He gave her a grin and quickly sobered. "Francis lives out there in the middle of God's country, with nothing but nature for company, and puts himself through miles of rigorous climbing to find peace.''

"And you're thinking that peace is as elusive as the greener grass?''

"I'm wondering.''

Peace was something Beth thought about a lot. "I guess for some it is that way. I prefer to think that if we try hard enough, we can quit thinking we have to run away from our lives and instead, find contentment in the little things that bring us pleasure or serenity."

Sounded kind of lofty when she put it into words. But the idea had kept her sane and functioning for more than seven months.

"Is that what you're doing?" he asked, giving her a sideways glance. "Trying not to run away anymore?"

"I'm trying to find peace in the little things," Beth said. The running wasn't something she could help.

She couldn't expect him to understand that.

CHAPTER THIRTEEN

"GRADY'S WORKING OUT VERY WELL." James Silverman was sitting with Peter Sterling in the state-of-the-art kitchen of the doctor's three-hundred-thousand dollar condo.

"We're very blessed to have found him," Sterling said, sipping his early-morning herbal tea with care. James had made it too hot, but Peter didn't complain.

"He's on fire for the cause." Silverman smiled. "Almost reminds me of myself when I first met you."

Sterling eyed him carefully over the top of his cup. "You aren't still on fire?"

"More so than ever." There was no hesitation in James's reply. Or his heart. "It's just good to know there are others to help with the work. Gives me hope for the difference we'll be able to make someday."

The doctor nodded, smiled, but the smile wasn't as enthusiastic as it might have been. As it once had been. Lately, the doctor had been looking more tired than usual. His face more lined.

Something had to be done about the Beth situation. Now. Too much time had passed. It was taking its toll. They couldn't do this work without Dr. Sterling. He was a prophet—their prophet. His energy must be preserved at all cost.

"Still no news?" Peter asked, his brows creased, his eyes sad.

James bit back his own pain. His own feelings of betrayal, of loss, were nothing compared to the damage that had been done to Sterling Silver. "None," he said, not at all surprised that Peter had been thinking along the same lines.

And every day, the danger grew.

"I'm afraid I'm starting to obsess," Peter said, his head low as he shook it slowly. "I'm losing my positive outlook. I don't know how much longer I can go on."

Neither of them knew if someone might come to the door someday and try to shut them down. Someone from the police or the government. Someone who didn't understand.

"We're on the cusp of doing great work. We have so many dedicated people ready and willing to spread the good news. People like Grady, relying on us for a better life. Willing to make that happen. Not just for themselves, but for the rest of the world."

James's heart swelled with a sense of certainty that their work was right and good. True. That certainty drove him every second of every day.

"I don't understand why we didn't sense the negative forces," Peter said.

James sipped his tea, not even having to hold back a grimace anymore. He detested the taste, but after years of the morning ritual, he'd grown so used to it that he was no longer fazed.

"We're still men." James finally spoke aloud the conclusion he'd had to accept. "Which means we can be blinded by lustful desires."

"Sex twice a week probably fed that."

"I'm sure it did. As important a purpose as it serves, it appears to have led me into dangerous territory."

Peter glanced up. "So what's the answer?" he asked. "No more women for the two of us?"

James had been giving the idea much consideration. "I can't speak for you, but that's probably my answer."

Peter nodded, his eyes weary. "For me, too." He sighed. "I'm trying to hold on, but I don't know how much longer I've got."

Alarm raced through James. "Don't say that, Peter," he said. "We'll take care of this."

"I don't know what to do."

"Of course not—you're a doctor. Tracking criminals isn't your job. Your job is here. Full-time. But I'm still a prosecuting attorney. I have the means."

"And you've been using them."

"I've been using aboveboard means." James set down his cup, leaned toward his mentor. "And now I'll use ones that are more...creative and equally accessible."

"Illegal activities often bring about negative energies," Peter warned, his eyes serious.

"I've weighed the consequences and know in my heart that this is the right thing to do. Which in itself brings positive energies."

Silently Peter watched him. "So this will be done soon?" he asked, sounding like a needy child.

That need, the fact that Peter placed it in him, sealed James's decision. "It will be done."

"Will there be violence involved?"

"If the need arises, I will not hesitate to give that decree."

"You're a good man, James Silverman," Peter said, his face relaxing. "And you're doing the right thing."

"We both are," James said, smiling. Reaching over, he grasped Peter's shoulder. "We both are, Peter."

They were as angels, Peter and he, doing a work far greater than most mortals ever attempted.

Everything else paled in comparison.

Including the cost.

WHILE BURT FOLLOWED UP with Foltz on Wednesday morning, Greg dealt with a staff issue, approved some budgets and signed off a completed community service order being served by Thelma Hopkins for attempting to lure a man from the Valley Diner to her apartment for a one-hundred-dollar hour of entertainment. By mid-morning, with all immediate business out of the way, he called Burt's office, only to find that the deputy was still out.

Greg was a little surprised at the relief washing over him as he hung up the phone. Had he really had doubts that his deputy would give the matter as much attention as Greg knew it deserved?

"Unit 1 to dispatch," Greg said, forty-five minutes later as he drove through downtown Shelter Valley.

"Dispatch, go ahead."

"I'm going to be off radio." He raised his voice enough for it to travel clearly. "If I'm needed, use my cell."

"Roger, Unit 1."

Greg turned off Main Street toward the mountain, thankful once again for everything Shelter Valley had to offer—small-town life, yet cultural and educational opportunities, too. Enough to keep enough of its young people from moving on. Made his job a hell of a lot easier sometimes—like now.

True, not everyone Greg had gone to high school with was still in town. Few of the teenaged party gang had hung around. Shelter Valley's small-town restrictions—as they'd seen them—had been responsible for the parties to begin with.

But Len Wagner was there. He'd played football at Montford and then for the Phoenix Cardinals—maintaining a decent five-year career in spite of the losing team. And then, when a big offer came that would take him to the East Coast, he'd surprised the world by retiring to marry a Shelter Valley High School teacher, three years older than himself, settling down and starting a family. Len had kids at the elementary school and at Little Spirits, as well. He also had interests in several lucrative business ventures and was one of Shelter Valley's most generous contributors. In his spare time he traveled all over the world fulfilling various philanthropic duties for the many boards he sat on.

Len Wagner was a changed man from the rebellious, daredevil teenager Greg had known.

On this Wednesday morning, he was at home in Shelter Valley with a sick first-grader.

"Kaylee's had a sore throat for over a week," Len told Greg, inviting him in for a cup of coffee. The Wagners' home was just down the mountain, a quarter of a mile from Will and Becca Parsons' place. Greg had never been to either home, but had heard from his sister that he'd be receiving an invitation to a holiday party at the Parsons. If he did, he was hoping to talk Beth into going with him.

Wagner's kitchen was as big as all three bedrooms in Greg's house combined. And the ex-football player seemed quite at home in the kitchen as he ground coffee beans and turned on the espresso machine—in spite of the huge hands that dwarfed the little measuring utensils he was using.

"You cook, too, Len?" Greg asked with a grin. Who would've thought, twenty years before, that the most hard-ass, irresponsible partier of them all would turn out to be a Mr. Mom.

It had been rumored during their junior and senior years that Len spent more time out at Rabbit Rock than he did at home. Greg was hoping the rumors were true.

"I can cook if I have to," Len said. "But Peggy loves to do it and I don't. Match made in heaven." He smiled with complete contentment.

Because of that smile, Greg had to ask, "You really mean that, don't you."

"Yep." His once-rebellious acquaintance didn't even pretend to be manly in that tough-guy way he used to affect. These days he wasn't ashamed to let the world know about his softer side.

For a second there, listening to Len openly confess his love, Greg envied the guy.

"So, what'd you need to see me about?" Len asked moments later as the two men sat at a huge butcher-block table in Len's kitchen. "The county need some money, Sheriff? You know you didn't need to make a trip all the way out here for that. A phone call would've done it."

Greg sat forward, his gun a familiar weight against his thigh. He had to go carefully here. He couldn't be sure of what Len knew—or even if what he *did* know could implicate him or someone else who wouldn't take kindly to the involvement. He figured, too, that Len wasn't going to mess up everything he had going here.

"I need some help, Len," he said.

The blond man shrugged his broad shoulders. "Sure," he said. "I'll do what I can." And then, setting down the mug he'd been about to sip from, he murmured, "Official help?"

Hands around his own mug on the table, Greg nodded. "Tell me what you know about Rabbit Rock."

Len frowned. "You want to talk about Rabbit Rock?"

Greg nodded again.

"That's not exactly the kind of help I expected you to need."

Rolling up the sleeves of his uniform, Greg sat back, one forearm resting on the table. "It's important, Len."

"I figured as much," the ex-linebacker said. "Or else you wouldn't be coming to me."

"So what can you tell me?"

"I wasted two years there, made the biggest mistakes of my life, and am damn lucky I didn't die there, too."

Tensing, Greg forced himself to maintain his casual position. "From the partying?" Or was there more? Things he didn't want to know about Len? He needed information. But seeing Len such a changed man, in his beautiful home, caring for his sick kid, Greg sure as hell didn't want to be the one who sent it all crashing down around him.

"I suppose you could blame all the times I took my life in my hands on the partying."

Eyes narrowed, Greg asked, "How did you risk your life? What did you do?"

"Jumping off cliffs because I thought I could fly. Fishtailing my rig so close to the edge of the cliff it should have flown. Filling my body with so many chemicals I didn't know who or what I was. Having sex with so many people I couldn't even begin to tell you who they were." Len paused, his somber expression the antithesis of his earlier smiles. "You can stop me anytime."

Greg tapped the side of his thumb against the table. "Was there anything else going on up there, besides the partying?"

Len glanced away. "Maybe. Why?"

"I have some pretty conclusive evidence that says someone's been driving cars into Rabbit Rock."

Len paled. "Again?"

Buzzing with adrenaline, Greg sat forward as he held the other man's gaze. "What do you mean *again?*"

Shrugging, Len looked directly into his eyes. "Years ago Culver came asking if I knew of any Phoenix kids who were hanging around out in Kachina County," he said. "I guess maybe you didn't hear about the whole mess, since it was just about the time your dad got hurt."

"You told Culver." Greg's entire body froze.

"Yeah." Len nodded. "I wasn't partying up at the Rock anymore, but I knew some of the punks who were, kid brothers of old friends."

Greg was going to forget about Culver for the moment. "And they were driving cars into Rabbit Rock?"

"Hell, no. They were damn pissed about the whole

thing. Some street gang from Phoenix had taken over the place and pretty much told them that if they showed their faces there again, they were as good as dead.''

A street gang.

''What gang?''

''The Bloodhounds. I told Culver about them. And I was told they disbanded not too long after that.''

Which might explain why Greg had never heard of them.

Mind spinning, he asked, ''So, if your friends stayed away, how do you know about the car thing?''

''Come on, Greg, think back. Do you think any of the stupid punks who went up to Rabbit Rock would walk away just because these bastards told them to?''

Of course he didn't. He knew what they would've done. ''They went up the mountain and spied on them.''

''Bingo.''

''And watched them drive cars into the Rock?''

''Only once. I heard that after they saw what was going on, they decided the gang members were crazy enough to follow through on their death threats, and they found themselves a new place to party.''

A street gang. Greg didn't like the sound of it. Any of it.

''You said Deputy Culver knew about the Bloodhounds?'' It just didn't fit.

''I told him myself.''

''You're sure it was Burt Culver?''

''Positive, man,'' Len's voice was dry. ''He'd just picked me up for DUI a couple of months before.''

Greg stood to excuse himself almost immediately. He had to get out, to think.

To make sense of this chaos, this confusion.

"I hear you're still living in that house of yours all alone, buddy," Len said, walking him to the door.

Preoccupied, Greg nodded.

"I've still got some connections," the big man said, grinning, as he patted Greg on the shoulder. "More beautiful women than you'd know what to do with. Just one phone call is all it'd take...."

"Thanks," Greg said. Any other time he'd have left it at that. Today, though, because the world had apparently spun off its axis and nothing was predictable anymore, he added, "But I've already found the woman who's going to move in." He clung to that thought. Something to hold on to. To believe in.

"Do I know her?" Len's grin had widened.

"Nope," Greg said, already regretting the words. "And she doesn't know she's marrying me yet, so keep this one to yourself...."

IT WAS A TOSS-UP—who should he see first? Greg drove around town, inventing reasons for Culver to keep Len's information from him—and passing by the houses of various people he knew were clients of Beth's, looking for her car parked outside.

He found it outside the Sheffields' three-bedroom bungalow.

"Greg?" The toilet brush in her hand didn't make the expression on her face seem any less frightened, any less hunted.

"Nothing's wrong," he said, used to the drill by now, even if he wasn't really any closer to understanding the reason for it.

"You don't *look* like nothing's wrong."

The alarm in her eyes gave way to compassion. And he knew why he'd come.

"How long till you're finished here?"

"Another half hour. I still have to finish the master bath and vacuum the bedrooms."

"I'll vacuum."

"Absolutely not," she said, but stepped back as he came in the door.

She looked adorable in her black sweats and white sweatshirt, her auburn hair up in the usual ponytail.

"You aren't going to vacuum this house!"

"Sure I am. You'll be finished sooner." And he really needed that.

"You're in uniform!"

"It's seen a whole lot worse than lint on carpet."

Beth shook her head. "Greg—"

"Beth," he interrupted, slowing himself down with effort. "I really need to talk to you and I don't have a lot of time. Please, may I help you finish here so we can have a few minutes?"

After one long searching look, she nodded and silently led him to the back of the house.

That was when Greg knew for sure he'd met the woman he wanted to have living in his house.

"I'VE KNOWN CULVER most of my life," Greg told Beth half an hour later as they sat together in his squad car parked just outside town. "I know there's got to be an explanation. I just can't figure out what it is. And I can't go to see him with my head full of doubts."

Her eyes were serious. "Maybe the doubts need to be there."

He couldn't accept that. "After all my years in law

enforcement, I know there are very few things you can believe in, very few things you can count on. But loyalty to and from those closest to you is one of those things."

This was a tough one for him, something he struggled with. Trusting. Having faith in people. Shelby's defection—the way she'd just left without any warning after a lifetime of building trust, of loving—had robbed him of so many years, had rendered him incapable of developing a close relationship with anyone else. He wasn't going to let it taint him for the rest of his life.

"Just look at the facts, Greg. Burt missed Rabbit Rock. He missed the hermit. He's the only one talking with Sheriff Foltz, and there's nothing to say that he's giving you all the information he's getting. And now this…"

"Burt Culver knew my father. Hell, he was one of our most frequent visitors during those last years. He used to come over and talk with my dad for hours. Never gave the old man a hint that the conversation wasn't perfectly normal. Never lost patience with the repetition." Greg's mind was made up. "This is not a man who would've hidden evidence from me. Especially evidence involving my father."

"Unless they were guilt visits."

Fighting back a surge of anger, Greg tried to listen with an open mind. After all, he'd asked Beth to help him sort this out. He was too close to the situation; he knew that. And then he shook his head.

"He and my dad were golf buddies from way back. Culver's visits didn't just start when my dad got hurt."

"Okay," Beth said, hands crossed demurely in her

lap. "Maybe something was driving him to act completely out of character when he withheld that information. You have no idea what circumstances prompted any of this. Maybe there's something here that involves a member of Burt's family. A person acting out of character normally does so to protect what matters most to him."

"Burt doesn't have any family."

"Then, what really matters to him?"

"His job." And there was no way Burt would jeopardize that. Not ever.

He couldn't even guess why Burt would've kept Len's information from him, but talking with Beth had allowed him to straighten out his own thoughts. One thing had become very clear. Knowing Burt's reason wasn't even important; Greg already felt sure it would be an acceptable one. Because he knew Burt Culver. Had faith in his deputy. Trusted him. And what, after all, was faith if a man didn't keep it in the face of difficulties? If he only believed when belief was easy?

It was nothing.

And without faith, life was nothing.

Greg had faith in Burt Culver.

And that was that.

CHAPTER FOURTEEN

"HE LOOKED ME STRAIGHT IN THE EYE and lied to me," Greg said, his expression hard as he stood, still in his uniform, by her front door later that same night. The look on his face, the acute effect Culver's dishonesty was having on him, struck Beth with fear. There was none of the compassion she'd come to associate with him. She realized something about Greg Richards: he did not tolerate liars.

Heart heavy with dread, Beth tried to maintain her equilibrium. Tried not to panic over something that had nothing to do with her.

"Please come in and sit down," she said. She'd already said it once, when he'd first arrived. He was intimidating in his uniform, so tall—and justifiably indignant.

He led the way over to the sofa. He even sat down. But then he stood up again, his hands shoved deep in his pockets as he paced.

Beth felt at a definite disadvantage, still wearing sweats she'd worn earlier in the afternoon. Ryan had been unusually difficult that night, and he'd kept her running from the time they got home until he'd dropped off to sleep just half an hour ago.

She'd thought longingly of a shower. But she'd known she should do her bookkeeping before she was too exhausted to keep the numbers straight. Paperwork was spread all over the small desk at one end of the living room.

Should she stand there, toe to toe with Greg? Or sit down and pretend she wasn't affected by his imposing stature? She sat. In the rocking chair that gave her a sense of security.

"What did Burt say?" she asked, because she wanted to help Greg. She didn't want to hear about Burt. She'd been ready to see the man exposed only hours before, and now was filled with this odd need to defend him.

As though his fate and hers were somehow tied together.

Greg was staring at her, but his gaze was vacant. She had a feeling he was replaying, word for word, his afternoon meeting with Burt Culver.

She wished this wasn't happening. Wished she didn't have so much at stake.

That she didn't care so much for Greg.

Or hate herself so much for deceiving him.

Beth lost her mental battle—she feared that the anger he was now directing toward Burt Culver would one day be directed at her. She and Burt were both liars.

And Greg's reaction to one could apply equally to the other.

She'd been furious when she'd thought of Burt double-crossing Greg. Because she'd been thinking only of Greg. Her vision had changed since that afternoon. To include Burt. And herself.

Shaking his head suddenly, Greg shrugged. "What did you just ask me?"

"What Burt said." Even if she wasn't sure she wanted to know...

"Not much. It didn't really get that far."

She frowned. "What do you mean?"

"I asked him if he remembered Len Wagner." Greg's expression was steely. Had there been any sign of emotion—even disillusionment—she'd have taken hope.

Greg started to pace, over to the window, around her paper-covered desk.

That paperwork made her nervous. There was no way Greg could know what she'd been doing—that every month she figured how much she'd owe in taxes and put that money away at the bottom of her towel drawer.

No way for him to tell, just by looking at the stuff on her desk, that she paid all her bills in cash—that she had no bank accounts.

But Greg was the sheriff. And a damn good cop. He could see things no one else even knew were there.

Like rabbit shapes in the front ends of smashed cars.

"I wasn't asking any leading questions," Greg said. Clearly the day's events were hard for him to accept.

"There was no thought in my mind of testing him or trapping him. I asked the question casually, as a way to open the conversation."

Her neck stiff from looking up at him, Beth guessed what had happened. "Burt said he'd never met Len."

Greg nodded.

"So maybe he forgot. It was ten years ago. Do you remember the name and face of every single person you've questioned over the past ten years?"

"Of course not."

"Well, there you go, then," she said, feeling a little more in control.

"Len Wagner holds an NFL record for yards run in a single season," Greg said, his voice devoid of emotion. "Culver's second love, next to police work, is football. He'd remember if he was ever in the same room with Len, let alone questioned him."

"But Len wasn't famous then, was he?"

"He hadn't set the record yet, but he was playing pro ball."

Okay, Culver had secrets. But sometimes good people did, for any number of reasons. Beth hated how quick she'd been to condemn Burt Culver only hours before. What kind of person did that make her? She'd been so heartless—so unforgiving—until she'd pictured herself in the same place.

She felt a little sick.

"What explanation did he give when you told him you knew he'd questioned Culver?"

"He didn't."

"He just said nothing?" Beth couldn't imagine being able to stand up to Greg that way. Not unless something was life-or-death important.

Greg dropped to the edge of the couch, running a hand wearily through his dark curls. "I didn't tell him I'd talked to Len," he said, the first note of uncertainty creeping into his voice. "Since I have no idea why he's lying, I can't trust him with my progress on this case. I have a better chance of finding the missing pieces if he isn't going around hiding them from me."

"Wouldn't he already have hidden whatever evidence he could?"

"Not until he has to," Greg said. When he glanced

over at her, Beth felt the prickling of tears. The steely look was gone. She almost wished it back. The disillusionment in Greg's eyes, the draining away of all the strength and confidence that made him Greg, was heartbreaking.

She could hate Culver for doing this to him.

But then she'd have to hate herself, as well.

"The more Culver tampers with things, the greater the likelihood that I'll catch him at it. Those photos that were mysteriously damaged, for instance. It was a risky move, but one I now suspect he was behind. I was getting too close."

"What do you think is going on?"

"I can't even guess," he said, his head leaning against the back of the couch.

She'd never seen him so exhausted.

"But you can rest assured I'll find out."

Beth did not doubt it for a second.

Which made him a dangerous companion for someone with secrets... Someone like her.

"Come here," he said softly.

Heart pounding, Beth stared at him. He held out his arms to her. "Please?"

It was the undisguised need in his voice that she couldn't resist. Beth had no idea if she gave her heart lightly. Frequently. Or if she'd never fully given it before. She knew only the here and now, and that she'd rather hurt herself than Greg.

She felt an overwhelming helplessness at the knowledge that hurting him was something she might not be able to avoid. Some things were completely out of her control.

And Ryan came first. That was the one constant in her life.

"Please?" he asked again.

There were some things within her control, too.

Trembling, Beth stood and went to him. If sex had been all he was asking for, she could have refused— for his sake as well as her own. But tonight Greg needed comforting.

Without a word he closed his arms around her, pulling her so tight against him she could hardly breathe.

"I'm sorry," she whispered, her lips against his throat. Sorry for whatever Burt Culver was up to. And sorrier still for the things she couldn't tell him.

She felt terrible guilt about that. But worse, she felt terrible fear of what she didn't know. Of whatever Greg might find out if she told him the truth, of what he might have to do with that knowledge. To her. And to Ryan.

His arms tightened briefly. Then his touch changed, lightened. He was cradling her, holding her, not hugging her. She could feel his heart beating beneath the palm she had on his chest. Felt the beat grow heavier. Faster.

She knew what that meant.

It was no surprise when his lips came down over hers, possessing hers. His kiss was not tentative. Or searching. It was the kiss of a man who desired the woman he held. Desired her deeply.

Beth desired him, too. Just as deeply.

Opening her mouth, Beth not only gave Greg everything he asked, she participated in the exploration. She'd been starving herself, denying every single personal need she'd had for so long, she just couldn't do it anymore. Not when allowing herself to need Greg was helping him, too.

She ran her hands over his shoulders, the cool cotton of his uniform shirt like a soft sheet beneath her fingers. She knew that whatever life asked of her from here on out, she'd always be thankful she'd known these moments. A perfect merging of body and mind. No, not mind so much as *feeling*.

Her unrestrained fingers wove themselves through his hair, satisfaction shooting through her as the strands curled around her fingers, almost as though they were holding her there, a part of him.

"Do you have any idea how good that feels?" he groaned, burying his face in her neck.

Beth didn't say anything. She couldn't. She just felt. And allowed those feelings to carry her...

He needed her touch. Needed reassurance in a world gone crazy with broken promises and broken rules. She knew he wanted to lose himself in the flames that had been smoldering between them for months.

God help her, Beth needed that, too. She was living on the edge. Her time could be up any day. She was fighting for the strength to endure, to shoulder her burdens and make the right decisions.

She needed him as badly as he needed her.

His hands skimmed her sides, touching her breasts, moving over her ribs, her waist, down to her hips, pulling her against the rock-hard length beneath the zipper of his slacks.

Still fully clothed, Beth unfastened the top button of his uniform shirt. Driven by an almost panicked urgency, she didn't listen to the voice of reason, or of caution. She didn't listen to any voices at all. She just kept unbuttoning as quickly as her trembling fingers could manage, revealing his muscular chest, and when she'd unfastened enough buttons, she pulled the shirt open, discovering his tight little nipples, dipping her head to run her tongue over them.

Greg groaned, tightening his hold on her hips, increasing her desperation. And then he relaxed his hands.

"If you don't stop that, I'm not going to be able to stop at all."

His voice was so husky she hardly recognized it. Beth wanted to pretend she hadn't heard him. To just kiss her way down his body and not be accountable at all. But no matter how intense her passion, she wasn't made that way. Couldn't be so irresponsible.

She also couldn't bear the thought of his leaving there tonight without making love to her first. As life in Shelter Valley continued and nothing happened— she wasn't finding herself or being found—she felt more and more uncertain, as though each day was a gift and she couldn't count on the next. She was consumed by the fear that if she didn't take this chance, she'd never have the opportunity again.

She lifted her head from his chest, then slid down between his legs until her knees touched the floor. She met his gaze directly. The desire she read there, the fact that he wasn't even attempting to bank it, had her belly spiraling with heat even as she attempted to calm herself, to think straight.

"I want to make love to you."

His words made it hard for her to think at all. "Nothing's changed." She wasn't even sure what the words meant. Only that she had to say them. "I can't make any promises beyond this moment."

He surveyed her silently for longer than she thought she could stand. Yet, because of her hope that the night might not be ending, she withstood the scrutiny.

"Can't make promises because you *can't?* Or because you don't want to?"

"Because I can't." It was painful to look at him. The thought of looking away was unbearable.

"But you want to."

"I want to be able to."

He nodded, looking like the sheriff hero of some western film, as he lay there sprawled on her cheap used couch with his shirt undone and that holster still hanging by his side.

"It's more than just sex," he said.

"Far more." Beth couldn't believe how great it felt to have something about which she could be totally honest.

"I'm a fool to let you do this to me," he said, his voice seductive. He pulled her up. Kissed her gently. "To accept your secrets…"

Beth kissed him back. Shivered when he ran his tongue along her lips. "There are so many things I don't understand," she said, acutely feeling the pain—and the ecstasy—of loving him. "But I can promise you that as soon as I do, you'll be the first to know." It was a promise she meant to keep. No matter what.

"Why—" he kissed her "—can't you—" he kissed her again "—let me help you understand them?" He asked the question, but prevented her from answering with a kiss that took away any chance she had of regaining control.

Beth Allen, or whoever she was, was about to have sex for the first time since she'd come into being.

GREG KNEW DAMN WELL he shouldn't do this. Even as he kissed Beth, kissed her and made himself sense-less, he couldn't escape the foreboding sense of wrong. Wrong timing. Wrong circumstances.

But not wrong woman.

That was what drove him. Beth *was* the right woman for him. He had control over so little where she was concerned. Certainly not her and—as he'd just begun to realize—not himself, either. His heart had given itself away in spite of his repeated warn-ings.

If he could at least have this, the most intimate communication there was between two people, if he could feel they'd shared something that was for the two of them alone, he would have one certainty to hold on to.

He stripped her slowly, reaching beneath her shirt to undo her bra, pulling it off through the sleeve of her sweatshirt. As their eyes met and held, his hands cupped her breasts through the shirt.

"You have the most perfectly shaped breasts," he whispered, and welcomed the ache in his groin when her eyes darkened.

Lifting her shirt, he exposed her womanliness. His entire body was heavy with desire as he gazed at the white skin contrasted with the dark nipples that tight-ened while he watched.

"You don't have a bedroom where we can shut the door." That had just occurred to him when he'd re-alized that what he wanted to do next was pull that shirt right off her. "Ryan's way too young to get this kind of education."

"It's okay." She cleared her throat but her next

words were just as husky. "He can't climb out of his crib yet. If he wakes up, he'll call out to me."

Greg did not even recognize the man who stripped off Beth's clothes and his own, then donned a condom without any finesse at all. He was taken off guard by the energy that coursed through him so strongly. Despite that, he could slow down, caress her gently, bring her to the same point as he. Lying back on the couch, he lifted her up.

Then he lowered her immediately, sheathing his aching penis inside her. He had to stop for a second, not just because she was so tight and he didn't want to hurt her, not even because she was so tight and he didn't want to come immediately, but because she felt so incredibly *good*. He needed to savor that moment. To remember it always. To know how glorious it felt to be part of her, and she of him.

Beth groaned, fell forward until she was lying on his chest, planting her breasts against him, and began to rock. She loved him confidently, sliding along him with exquisite slowness, then knowing just when to move harder, faster, and when to use slow, seductive strokes.

I love you. The words repeated themselves over and over in his mind. She raised her upper body, and Greg suckled her nipple, briefly afraid that he'd said them aloud.

She was seductress and nurturer all at once, and he couldn't get enough. Couldn't possess enough of her or give enough of himself. He felt the orgasm coming and tried desperately to hang on. He didn't want this experience to end. Didn't want to return to the real world—a place where he didn't share her life.

And then he felt her tightening around him, her

body pulsating with the power of release, and he spilled himself inside her, the spasms coming over and over again. In his mind there were shouts of incredible bliss, a brilliance beyond anything he could imagine, an awareness that he was someplace he'd never been before.

The end was different, too. Instead of deflation settling in, leaving him tired and ready for sleep, a serene joy spread through him. It gave him a sense of great peace. *I love you,* his mind said. Over and over. *I love you, Beth.*

And in that moment of grand awareness, he was almost able to pretend that she loved him back.

BETH CRAWLED INTO BED sometime in the small hours of the morning. Her body was sore in places she'd hardly noticed before, and that made her feel fully alive for the first time since Beth Allen had come into existence. Her skin, her nerves, were tingling with an awareness of what she'd just done. She felt healthier. Stronger. Calmer. And strangely, like she'd just done something she'd been commanded to do.

Suddenly shaking, cold sweat breaking out while the skin of her face burned so hot it was scaring her, Beth sat straight up.

Commanded to do?

What an odd thought to have. An incredibly frightening thought, somehow. Where had it come from?

Why did it feel so real? As though having sex because she'd been *told* to was a natural part of her life?

Who would have commanded her to have sex? And why?

God forbid, had she been a prostitute? Had it been

her pimp who'd beaten her up? Was he the person she'd been running from? Trying to save her son from being part of such a sordid life?

Squeezing her eyes shut, she tried to return to the state of mind she'd been in seconds before, when the commandment thought had slipped out. She tried to recapture anything at all that might have been there. To get even a single clue to the truth.

And found nothing.

Great big damn nothing.

"I hate you," she whispered to the woman she'd once been, as tears dripped from her eyelids. "I hate you so much."

But whoever was hiding inside her didn't respond. That person remained numb and uncaring.

She eventually lay back down, automatically using relaxation techniques, and eventually drifted off to sleep.

If she had any dreams, she didn't remember them in the morning.

CHAPTER FIFTEEN

PUTTING PUZZLES TOGETHER might be a pastime for some. For Greg it was, in every sense, a vocation. Standing over the card table in his office, he studied the thousand pieces of a jigsaw rendition of cops' badges Katie had given him for his birthday a couple of months before. Bonnie had special-ordered it from a puzzle club she'd joined just for the purpose of keeping Greg challenged. Shaped like a badge, with no clearly defined edge pieces, it'd been a hell of a thing to get started.

The going was faster now that he was three-quarters of the way done.

Greg found the piece he'd spent at least an hour searching for—if he added up all the moments like this one, when he wandered over from his desk. A small piece, it had a rounded top and two interlocking notches. Its bottom left corner had the distinct darker silver that indicated it belonged to a badge on the right side of the puzzle.

Sliding the piece into place brought him great satisfaction.

With a few phone calls first thing that morning, he'd found it surprisingly easy to learn most of what he'd wanted to know about the Bloodhounds, the gang that, according to Len Wagner, had taken over Rabbit Rock ten years before. They'd been based out of Hohokom High School, and while no charges had ever officially been brought against them, they'd had the reputation of being one of the roughest gangs in Phoenix. They'd been accused of drug dealing, robbery, even rape, although no decisive proof had ever materialized. Obviously their leader had been a professional. Knew what he was doing. And how to get away with it.

Then, ten years before, the gang had indeed disbanded, just as Len had reported. There'd been no record of any connection to car crimes in the gang's history. No police intervention, period, which made the whole disbanding appear odd.

As far as Greg was concerned, too odd.

He was looking for a piece with a pear-shaped prong. A light-silver tip. He picked one up.

Piece in hand, he strode across the tile floor to his desk. He had an old buddy from the Phoenix police department on the phone in ten seconds.

"Cliff, check something for me," he said without introduction or other social preamble.

"Sure, what've you got?"

"I need a list of possible members of a gang called the Bloodhounds. They reportedly disbanded about ten years ago."

"Ten-four."

Back at the puzzle, Greg put in his second piece of the morning. A good sign; his luck was changing.

Third piece in hand, he stopped to stare out the window. He knew he'd make headway on his father's case. The sky was more blue, the sun more vibrant.

Greg's heart was lighter than it had ever been.

He'd made love with Beth. She'd let him see her

naked. Touch her. Love her. She'd given herself to him in the most ultimate sense.

Life was good.

His phone rang. "I think I have what you're looking for." It had taken Cliff an hour.

"What?" He hadn't known for sure that he was looking for anything.

"Don't know how any of this connects, but one of my sources from Hohokom High tells me Colby Foltz was a member of the Bloodhounds at the time they disbanded."

Dropping the puzzle piece, Greg frowned. "Foltz?" he asked. "Any relation to Hugh?"

"Kid brother."

"Foltz never mentioned him."

"Didn't know him well," Cliff said. "Story goes that after her divorce, Mrs. Foltz moved to Phoenix with her youngest son. Hugh didn't see him much."

I'll be damned. Greg kept his breathing steady. "Thanks, man, I owe you one."

"Yeah, right," Cliff said. "In a million years maybe…"

Ignoring the puzzle piece on his desk, Greg hung up the phone and sat down.

A powerful street gang disbands for no apparent reason. A sheriff's younger brother is a member. There's a carjacking involving the father of one of that sheriff's deputies.

The sheriff's younger brother. A powerful street gang disbands.

Burt Culver, a man with no family, a man married to his job, a man whose superior was his closest friend.

A hermit who'd talked to the sheriff. An ex-football player who'd talked to Culver.

Dazed, Greg continued to sit at his desk. There were still some missing pieces. Like why a gang as professional and able as the Bloodhounds had resorted to carjacking. There were easier ways to make money. A lot more money...

And what kind of connection could there be between the current string of carjackings and a gang that had been disbanded for ten years?

How deep into this was Culver?

All were questions that needed answers. But at this point they were merely inconveniences, not problems.

Greg had the important answers. Before this day was out, he was going to be well on his way to avenging the senseless waste of his father's life.

He had to call Beth. And Bonnie. To let out a victory cheer.

Except that following too closely on its heels was a howl of anger. The pain of betrayal made a far greater impact than the satisfaction of victory.

He had to get Burt Culver off the streets.

And pay a visit to his mentor and predecessor, Hugh Foltz—a man he'd spent most of life admiring. A man who'd covered up the crime that had killed Greg's father.

And Culver—all those times he'd come to see Dad. Sat in his house, ate at his table...

Insides shaking with dangerous emotion, Greg made himself stay at his desk, weighing the facts, formulating a logical plan of action. The weight of the holster on his hip was a reminder of who he was. What he could and could not—would and would not—do.

Perhaps another puzzle piece or two was his best choice for a first move. Picking up the piece he'd dropped, Greg still didn't get up. His heart wasn't in the completion of a jigsaw puzzle. His mind raged too fast to allow for the quiet contemplation that accompanied puzzle building.

Instead of adding another piece to the badge puzzle, Greg stared sightlessly at the small stack of mail lying on his desk. A missing person postcard was on top; he recognized the familiar layout.

He got them all the time. They were part of a national program and had nothing to do with him or his job. They were sent biweekly to all Arizona mailing addresses in the hope that someone, somewhere, might recognize the person in the picture. Nine times out of ten they depicted children, and most often the disappearances involved known abductions, frequently due to custody disputes.

Out of habit, and because he was still too filled with energy to make his next move, Greg picked up the card and looked at it. Chances were slim that he'd ever be instrumental in finding any of these poor children, or in the arrest of someone vile enough to steal a child from home, but he looked diligently. Every week. Every time the card came.

Just in case.

Leaning back in his chair, he studied the statistics first. *Brian Silverman.* There was a birth date and the date he'd disappeared. The boy was not quite two years old. Had been gone for more than eight months. He had curly blond hair. Blue eyes. Was missing from Houston, Texas.

He'd last been seen with Beth Silverman. His mother, presumably.

Beth. God, Greg needed to talk to his Beth.

This woman was thirty-four years old. Had blond hair and blue eyes. Was last seen in Houston, Texas.

As he always did, Greg looked at the pictures last. His mind suddenly numb, he looked again. The hair color was different.

He should never have had breakfast. The pancake syrup was not sitting well in his stomach.

Greg put the card down. His hands weren't shaking, he decided. He'd probably just thought they were because he was a little disoriented from the news about his father. And Culver. And Foltz.

Really, he was fine.

Just to prove it, Greg picked up the postcard again. Gave it a glance.

It fell to the floor as he made a run for the bathroom.

His breakfast was horrible the second time around.

"MERRILY WE ROLL ALONG, roll along, roll along," Beth sang under her breath as she pushed the vacuum cleaner back and forth across the floor of the Mathers' master bedroom. In deference to the unusually warm day, she was wearing a T-shirt with her cutoff navy sweatpants. The navy-and-white designer emblem across the front of the shirt made the ensemble a toss-up between a cleaning uniform and a fashion statement. What Beth liked most was the five dollars the duo had cost her at a close-out sale.

Close-out sales. And clean toilets. Ryan to pick up in half an hour. Greg naked. Beth's thoughts, running along only pleasant lines as she finished her last job of the day, entertained her. She hummed more of the song she'd been singing, since she couldn't recall any more words.

She thought she heard the doorbell.

Turning off the vacuum cleaner, she listened.

Yes. The doorbell rang again.

Hurrying to answer it, hoping—rather pointlessly, she knew—that it was Greg, she pulled open the heavy wooden front door with more energy than usual. She'd done everything with more energy than usual that day.

"Greg!" she said, thrilled that her wayward wish had been answered. She could get used to this very quickly.

"How long until you're finished?" he asked.

"A few minutes," Beth reported, feeling pleased. And then she really looked at him. Past the smiling lips and cordial eyes, to the man she knew.

Something was wrong.

Of course. *Burt.* Greg had found out something.

"I'll just be another five minutes and then I'll need time to load up my gear."

"I'll be in my truck."

He was still dressed in his uniform, but driving his personal vehicle. In the middle of the afternoon. That was odd. Greg always drove his squad car when he was on duty. The truck didn't have a radio.

Even odder, he didn't meet her eyes when she glanced back up at him.

Rushing, her need to get to Greg, to help him, comfort him, far greater than her usual need to pack everything in the order she'd determined was most efficient, Beth threw things together. She gathered everything and made her way to the car, toilet brush and broom sticking out from under one arm, a bucket overflowing with supplies suspended from that hand, her vacuum clutched in the other.

She slammed her trunk on the tools of her trade and locked the car, knowing it would be just fine parked out on the street, then hurried over to Greg's truck.

Staring straight ahead, shoulders stiff, jaw implacable, he didn't notice her coming. The passenger door was locked. He hit the button on his side, letting her in. He didn't come around to open her door. Didn't look at her as she climbed in.

"What's up?" she asked, hoping it wasn't as bad as it appeared. Her earlier good mood hadn't been strong to begin with, and the usual dread that was always so close at hand was already beginning to seep in.

Just once she wanted to be whole and able for Greg. Wanted to be there for him one-hundred percent, not busy dealing with her own problems. He'd done so much for her. Given her back so much of herself, if only in the form of the confidence she was gaining since he'd started to care so much about her.

Still without a word, without a look, he reached for a postcard on the seat beside him. Handed it to her.

Confused, Beth looked at it.

And couldn't move.

Couldn't breathe. Arrows were stabbing inside her skull. She had no idea where she was. What she was doing. She sat, head bent, simply reacting. Letting the unreality wash over her. Her heart beat far too fast, and she did nothing. Her skin was cold, clammy, yet her face burned. She didn't move, allowing the red haze to consume her vision.

"That's some secret you've been keeping."

The words were bitingly harsh. She wasn't sure what they meant. Didn't recognize the voice saying them. Wasn't even sure they were directed at her.

"I don't know what part of this you found so hard to explain." The same bitter tone.

The words made little sense. Other than that, they were like little pellets, pummeling her at a time she wasn't equipped to handle them.

"Take me home," she said. Nothing mattered but that she get someplace safe.

On some level she was coherent enough to know that Ryan was safer where he was for the moment. And yet, she desperately needed to hold her son in her arms, needed him close.

This was an emergency. They might not have much time.

The engine started, the rumble a strange kind of comfort beneath her. At least she was going somewhere.

She didn't see the houses they passed, didn't notice the streets or the turns, didn't see a single person or sign. She saw nothing but that crumpled card in her fingers.

Fear escalated almost to the point of madness when the rumbling beneath her stopped. She waited for whatever was going to happen next.

Nothing did.

Beth looked up to see that she was parked outside her own duplex. For some reason she felt extremely relieved to be there. As though she'd been prepared to find herself somewhere else entirely.

"Thanks for the ride," she said very politely, inanely, and opened the truck door. Her exit might have been made cleanly if her knees hadn't given out on her as she attempted to jump down from the big truck. She caught herself with both hands on the seat, hitting her knuckles on the doorjamb.

The pain brought tears to her eyes. She welcomed the pain as something she recognized. Something she could concentrate on.

It gave her the strength to get herself to her door, find her key, put it in the lock. She saw no one, heard nothing. Just the key. In the lock. Open the door. Get inside.

The door didn't close behind her. It hit something big and solid.

The man who'd followed her in.

She might have screamed then. Might have broken into hysterical tears if she hadn't glanced up and seen the pain shining from eyes she'd grown to love. Eyes that had made such promises of love and safety the night before.

"I need some answers," Greg said. His voice was still that of a stranger.

A frightening, intimidating stranger. He was wearing a uniform. A gun. If he chose to detain her, take her away, she wouldn't be able to stop him.

Her eyes fell. Recognized the shape and width of those hands. This was the man who'd been naked in her arms.

She nodded. Turning unsteadily, Beth made her way into the living room. She wanted to sit in her rocker, but was afraid of the unsteady movement. She dropped to the old couch instead, bracing herself in a corner.

Afraid of Greg's reaction, she didn't look at that card again, although she wanted to. She desperately wanted to know what it said.

What it could tell her.

She was unsure what he was going to do to her. Would he just arrest her and never speak to her again? Turn her over to some other authorities and never speak to her again? Take her son away and never speak to—

"I'm listening."

He was also standing. Too close. Telling her quite plainly who was in charge.

Beth opened her mouth, intending to say something. She realized he deserved answers. She wanted to give them to him.

She had nothing to say. She had to look at that card.

"Beth, now's not a good time to play me for a fool." The warning in his voice was more powerful than the words.

She was scared to death of him, yet she didn't fear he'd hurt her. Not physically. The danger he threatened was far worse than that.

"I've never played you for anything," she said. She tried to hold his gaze, but couldn't. She couldn't stand to see the stranger staring back at her.

"And you've never given me one damn answer, either," he said, jamming his hands in his pockets as he started to pace in front of her. "I'm giving you an opportunity to do so now. If you still refuse, you leave me with no choice but to take you in."

Did that mean there was a chance, even the slimmest of chances, that he might not?

She glanced at the card. Her name was still Beth. Odd, considering the circumstances, but she found a small bit of joy in that fact.

Beth Silverman. Fighting down panic, Beth found she still had no idea who that was.

"I woke up in a motel room a week before I came to Shelter Valley," she said.

She was thirty-four years old. That felt odd. A couple of years younger than she'd thought.

And her gaze landed on her son's precious face. *Brian Silverman.* Not Ryan at all. Tears pooled in her eyes, blinding her to the rest of his information for the second it took her to blink them away. And then, just before her eyes filled again, she saw his birth date.

"He's not even two yet," she whispered. Her baby boy had been barely a year old when she'd brought him here. Big for his age and much younger than she'd assumed. No wonder he couldn't talk! And potty-training him before he was two; it was ludicrous. Not fair at all to a little body that couldn't possibly be experiencing all the sensations he needed to, in order to be successful at that important venture.

"I'm running out of patience."

Stronger now, as though finally having possession of her son's birth date made all the difference, Beth looked up at Greg. Even through her tears she could see his jaw twitching with the effort it was taking him to be civil.

She held out the card to him. "This is what I know," she said. "It's all I know."

She was from Houston. She didn't feel any affiliation with the place at all.

"What do you mean it's all you know?" His tone was not getting any friendlier.

"Almost eight months ago, I woke up in a motel room in Snowflake, Arizona, with a splitting headache, a bad gash on my forehead and another one on the back of my skull. I had a bag that said 'Beth' on it, with some diaper essentials and a change of clothes for Ryan...." She couldn't think of him as anyone else. "An exercise outfit for myself and two-thousand dollars in cash."

"Go on." He was still standing but had, at least, stopped pacing.

She shrugged, then met his gaze. "I had a baby with me who called me Mama. When I asked him what his name was, he just kept saying Ryan."

"From Brian?"

"I guess." She had a feeling he was always going to be Ryan to her.

"Then later, when I bathed him, I noticed a funny little V-shaped freckle mark on his knee. I have one, too."

Greg sat down, not next to her, but not on the other end of the couch, either. "So why were you there?"

The world was getting smaller again. Her vision was tinged with red.

"How did you get hurt?"

"I don't know." The words were a whisper.

Not only was she frightened to death at her lack of ability to help herself, her powerlessness, but she was also ashamed to admit the truth to him. What kind of a basket case ran away from herself?

"What do you mean you don't know?"

"I don't know," she said again, staring down at her hands. The gig was up. Unless...

Could she talk him into not turning her in? Could she get even one more night? Long enough to collect Ryan and run away?

Did she actually think she could hide from a lawman like Greg Richards?

"I don't remember anything." Finally, because she knew she had to, Beth looked over at him, saw the card in his hand. "Until you brought that, I didn't even know my own name, my son's age, where we were from. Nothing."

His eyes narrowed. "You're telling me you have amnesia."

Beth nodded, humiliated, scared, placing her life in hands she wasn't sure were ever going to be gentle with her again.

"I can't buy that."

"*What?*"

"You expect me to believe you don't remember anything about yourself?"

She nodded.

"Come on, Beth. It's not that I doubt amnesia happens, but I've been around you for months, and there hasn't been one sign of mental confusion. And it's not just me. It's Bonnie and her family, the people you clean for, everyone you've known in the more than eight months you've lived here. You'd have to be a pretty good actress to fool an entire town."

"It's the truth." And then, when the doubt in his eyes only grew more severe, Beth became desperate. It hadn't dawned on her that he wouldn't believe her. She'd expected him to be angry, yes. Do what he had to do, yes. But... "You *have* to believe me, Greg."

"You've done nothing but keep secrets from me since the beginning. And now, when I find out why, you come up with a story that's utterly fantastic. How can you possibly expect me to believe you?" he asked, his voice devoid of any of the warmth she'd come to depend on.

Because last night you made the most incredible love to me. Because I think I actually trust you. I need you. Because I love... "Because I'm telling the truth."

CHAPTER SIXTEEN

YEAH.

Sure she was telling the truth.

Another day, he might have believed her. Greg slumped back against the couch cushion, thankful in a highly ironic sense that he'd just found unquestionable proof that his deputy and his superior had betrayed him. That experience was going to save his butt now. He'd been such a lovesick kid with Beth, so willing to have faith and believe in something that he couldn't see or prove, that she'd probably be able to string him along even now, if not for his deputy's timely lesson.

And unlike Culver and Foltz, Beth had struck at the very foundation of his life. For one thing, harboring a criminal could've cost him his job. For another, she'd undermined his newfound ability to trust.

That auburn hair wasn't natural. He couldn't get over it.

A cover. Just like the amnesia was a cover. Smart, really, the way she'd kept her secrets. Made the whole thing almost plausible. And that much more damning. She'd obviously been planning this all along. She had her cover all ready in case she got caught before she got out.

He was sure he should be feeling something—anger at the very least—but for now, he was going to go with the numbness that was all he seemed able to dredge up.

Surely she'd figured that she would be found out eventually. It was one of the first rules of conduct for people on the run. Always be ready, with no notice, to run again. To keep running.

He was lounging on her couch as though he had all day. Nothing to do. No crises to sort out. "It would've meant a lot if you'd been honest with me from the start."

"I was as honest as I knew how to be."

The intimacy in those warm blue eyes seared him. Just the night before, it had been as if God's angel had reached right down and touched him. His gaze roamed to the rocker behind her left shoulder. What was true and what was false?

"You aren't trying to tell me you didn't know you were betraying me?" he muttered.

He glanced over—and saw the bitter truth in her eyes before she closed them.

"I didn't think so."

"Greg."

There was such pleading in her voice that he could've been forgiven for feeling a twinge of caring. Of hope. Thankfully it wasn't a forgiveness he'd need to seek. Braced, he waited for her to continue.

"I know this is hard for you."

"It's not hard at all." He wasn't lying. He couldn't feel a thing. And he damn sure wasn't going to have her feeling sorry for him on top of everything else. He might have been taken for a fool, but he could handle it.

And recover.

With all parts still working fine.

"Please listen," she whispered.

"I heard every word you said," he told her in his best cop's voice. "And a lot you haven't."

"I know—" She bowed her head.

He could barely see her in his peripheral vision.

"—but I need you not just to hear but to really *listen* to what I have to tell you."

That was rich. Now that she was in trouble, she suddenly had things to tell him. Because the only difference between that moment and twelve hours before, when she'd lain naked beneath him right there on that couch, was the crumpled white card with the incriminating pictures.

He wanted to tell her that, but didn't see any point in dragging himself through the series of quickly fabricated lies that would follow.

"I'm scared to death, Greg," she said.

For a split second her raw emotion started to work on him. But only for a second. His armor had grown thicker than that. It would sustain him through this.

"For eight months now, that fear has been the only constant in my life."

No. He wasn't going to be sucked in. She was an expert at it.

If he wasn't so sickened by his own part in the whole thing, he'd probably admire her for those abilities.

"I have no idea who I am—why I was in that motel room—how I got hurt—who might be after me. Or worse, Ryan."

Greg studied his gun. He'd polished it early that

morning, while he was waiting for people to get to work.

Of course, then, much of his extra energy had been a result of the incredible night he'd spent. The excitement he'd still been feeling. Yeah. Well...

"It was pretty obvious that I'd been in danger, enough so that I took my son in such a hurry that I didn't even grab my identification. I got cash from someplace and ran. But because I have no idea what that danger is, I can't fight it. I can't even be prepared for what I might have to run from, or what might be coming at me."

"Maybe you weren't running at all," Greg said, pretty sure his intent was to poke holes in her story. "Perhaps you'd just had your purse snatched, got roughed up in the process, but got away."

"I've considered that," Beth said slowly. "But then, why did I check into that motel under the name of Beth Allen if my name is really—" she paused, glancing down at the card lying between them "—Silverman," she finished. "And why would I have been carrying two-thousand dollars in cash?"

Okay, so the purse-snatcher idea wasn't his best. He couldn't even imagine how horrifying it would've been for a young mother to wake up to the reality Beth said she'd found in that Snowflake motel. Or how strong that woman would have to be to cope all alone....

No. Greg shook his head. He wasn't going to let anyone make a fool of him again. He'd just come off a ten-year term. He wasn't doing it again.

Ever.

"Have you seen a doctor?"

"Of course not." She shook her head. "I'm in hiding."

That was convenient. "Like I said, Beth, amnesia happens, but not without symptoms and signs. I saw my father through years of therapy and I encountered more head-injury patients than I can count, so I have personal experience with these things. I just don't see how I can possibly believe you."

"By listening to your heart?"

He could tell she didn't really expect that to fly.

"You made one critical mistake," he told her now, in control of his faculties again. Fully numb once more.

"What?" she asked, turning, one leg on the couch as she faced him.

Her puzzled frown would have sold him on her innocence just a day earlier.

"I've gone over and over this so many times," she whispered, "it's all one big foggy mess to me. What did I miss?"

He wasn't going to play her game. Wasn't going to be a participant—a pawn—in whatever ugly scheme she might be creating.

Out of the blue, a mental picture of Beth up at Rabbit Rock flashed through his mind. The way she'd given everything she had to him that night, to comfort him, to help him fight his own demons. The way she'd understood...

No. He couldn't let himself go soft.

"Today," he said, a little less complacent. "You made the mistake today. Now. When I confronted you with the truth and you knew you'd been caught. If you'd just come clean, told me what this is really all about, I'd have done everything I could to help you.''

Greg was barely aware that his voice had trailed off. That *was* all it would've taken. A plausible story. Hell, he'd been going along with her all these months, having faith in spite of her silence, understanding that she'd needed time. But he had to draw the line somewhere. There was a point when a man's belief wasn't a matter of faith but of *wanting* to have faith. It could make a fool of him.

With Culver and Foltz, he'd drawn the line in the wrong place. He couldn't do that again.

Not if he was ever going to trust his own judgment again.

''Even now you can't trust me with the truth,'' he said, regretting the words when he heard the emotion he hadn't meant to express.

He needed a drink. If this anesthetic ever wore off, he was going to hurt like hell. He should've taken time that morning to polish the leather of his holster, as well. Its scuffed surface wasn't doing much for the gun.

''That's just it, Greg,'' she said. He heard the tears in her voice but didn't look up to see if she was crying. ''I *am* trusting you. For the first time in eight months, I'm able to trust my life, Ryan's life, to someone else.''

God, that hurt. If only she'd said those words the night before... ''Funny how that trust magically coincides with the very moment I discovered the truth on my own.''

''It's not the truth.''

She could've played it better if she'd injected a

note of defensiveness into her voice rather than sounding like she was giving up so easily.

Greg picked up the postcard. Made himself study it. To remember the facts. "You're saying that this woman is not you? That the boy who's been missing for eight months isn't Ryan? That's not true?"

"No."

He was disappointed in her answer. As though, after all this, he'd still been holding on to some nebulous hope.

"Of course it's us," she said, leaning over to glance at the photos.

The expression on her face surprised him. She looked more hurt than anything else.

Yet *he* was the one who'd been lied to. Betrayed. Wasn't he?

"What's *not* true is that I knew who we were before today," she said quietly, sliding back to the corner of the couch, her arms wrapped around her chest. "I see now that I should have told you," she said. Again, her voice was resigned, not Beth-like. "And yet, what would've happened if I had? You'd have had to go looking for me and you'd have found out that I'd kidnapped my son and it would all be over."

She'd been fighting him since the first day they'd met, but suddenly there was no fight left.

And she should still be fighting him if she hoped to convince him not to turn her over to the FBI without so much as a goodbye to the baby boy she loved.

And she did love her son. There was no doubting that.

A mother didn't exist who loved her son more than

Beth loved Ryan. Nor was there a mother who looked out for her baby's welfare more than Beth.

"Maybe I made a mistake, but I was doing the best I knew how," she said. "The best I was capable of doing. I have no idea why I'm running. And until I do, how can I possibly know how to proceed in any direction at all? How can I predict what kind of hell you might create?"

He wasn't used to going around creating hell for people, but okay.

"Think about it," she said. "I tell you—a cop, no less—and you start to investigate. You find out I've done something against the law and you're bound by your office to turn me in. Because I don't remember what happened, I can't even defend myself. I lose Ryan. I go to jail. And there's not a damn thing I can do about any of it."

He thought about that.

"Or what if I am in danger? What if whoever beat me up is itching to finish the job? To hurt Ryan? Your digging into things might alert someone. And before we even know *who* we're alerting, he's here. And it's too late."

That wouldn't have happened. He'd have protected her.

"I also went through a lot of times when I didn't want to know. Whatever I'm running from—not physically, but mentally, emotionally, inside me— must be pretty horrific if my mind's gone to such lengths to protect me against it. I spend a lot of time scared to death to find out what it is. What if, when I do, I still can't face it? What if I don't deal with it any better the second time around? What if I lose my mind and they lock me up in some nuthouse? How am I going to take care of Ryan?''

He remembered that night at the casino. The way she'd reacted to whatever had set her off.

If Greg's chest got any tighter, he was going to have go outside for some fresh air. Might not be a bad idea in any event.

She sure has a career in storytelling if cleaning toilets ever ceases to satisfy her.

That last thought was beneath him.

But how in the hell could he possibly know what was the truth? And how much of his reaction was simply a matter of Greg Richards, Mr. Nice Guy, being taken in again?

When would he learn? If the heartbreak with Shelby had been like kindergarten in this life lesson, Culver and Foltz were surely on the college level. So what was he doing now? Going for a doctorate in how to have his trust abused?

''Besides, how did I know I could trust you?'' Beth asked, startling him with a question too closely related to his own thoughts. ''I couldn't even trust myself.''

In the past twenty-four hours he'd certainly learned how *that* felt. ''You might've thought of that before you slept with me.''

''I did.'' The simple words, emitted without hesitation, held a depth of emotion. ''A lot. In the end, making love with you was between you and me. It was personal. I could trust in that. But this is far bigger. This is my son's life.''

A pretty damn good reason to spin this incredible tale.

She'd almost had him.

"So what was your plan?" he asked, more out of curiosity than anything else. And maybe to find out if she could produce one.

Beth shrugged. "Nothing too fancy," she said. "Nothing really even too logical. For a lot of the time, I've focused on just surviving."

Basic. But a good answer.

"I've been searching everywhere I could think of, trying to find out whatever I could on my own."

He was impressed when she listed all the work she'd done in the library, on the Internet. The hundreds of hours she'd spent searching.

He could verify that she'd spent a lot of time at the library.

Of course, she knew he knew that, so she could be using this to convince him, when, in reality, she'd been doing something incriminating that entire time. Like working on whatever criminal activity she was involved with. Making contact with coconspirators. Perpetrating some kind of scam. Or creating permanent new identities for her and her son. Researching other places to run. Other jobs.

"I've also done a lot of studying on amnesia," she said softly. "My best guess is that this is hysterical retrograde amnesia. That means I could regain my memory at any time. And then I'd have my answers. I'd have the ammunition necessary to fight whatever battle awaits. I'd have a clue as to where and how to proceed."

Like he'd told himself many times in the past hour, it was a fantastic, incredible story. One he might even believe, if only...

"Why didn't you tell me this last night, Beth? You had the perfect opportunity."

"I had no idea what to say, no control over what you'd do with the information."

Her words were deadening his heart again. She'd been manipulating him, just as he'd feared.

"You're a cop, Greg. In some ways, the obligation that goes with the territory limits your choices."

"It also makes my ability to help you that much greater."

"Maybe."

He waited for her to say more. Needed her to say more, to offer him assurance, some kind of entrance into her most private thoughts. When she didn't, the armor surrounding him grew another degree heavier.

"Would you have told me today, now, anytime soon, if I hadn't found out?" Damn, it was almost as though he were begging her to give him enough rope... Inventing reasons he could still believe. Still justify this insane idea that faith wasn't faith unless it endured to the end.

"Probably not."

She'd cut the rope. He didn't fall nearly as far this time—it hardly hurt at all.

"So, the bottom line is, you didn't trust me enough to tell me."

Her eyes brimmed with sorrow as she held his gaze. "I guess—" She choked on the words.

"Then, how can you expect me to trust you?"

"I can't."

BETH WAS COLD. Her skin had goose bumps. Her fingers and toes and nose were freezing, as though she'd been outside in Maine during the dead of winter. But this chill was coming from inside.

She'd lost.

Maybe everything: A mysterious and frightening game for which she still had no definition or rules. Her one chance to know what real love could be. *Her son.*

Oh God. Ry. *What have I done to you, my precious baby?* Shivering, Beth sat up, forcing her mind to concentrate, considering only the next few moments. She couldn't think about Ryan and stay coherent. Not when losing him, losing the right even to see him, was so real—possibly imminent.

Over her dead body.

A strength of will she did not recognize passed through her, held her in its grasp. "I will give up my life before I let them have him," she said. And then frowned. As she sat there, she had no doubt whatsoever of the conviction in her words. She just had no idea where they'd come from.

"We're talking about Ryan?"

When she looked at Greg, it was almost as though he'd left and come back. She was seeing him differently.

The adversary? Or the negotiator? Was saying anything saying too much? She wasn't sure; she knew only that she had to tell him. "Yes."

"Who's them?" He sounded like a cop.

But a good one. A cop who cared about seeing the right thing done. Or was that just her own bias? Was she projecting upon Greg the things she needed to find in him?

She had to make a decision. Work with him. Or

find a way to make things work in spite of him. Her time was up.

Beth took a long breath. Let it out slowly. Forced her mind to focus on only one thing. "I don't know," she said, taking the plunge. She wished she hadn't, when the shuttered expression darkened his face.

"I'm telling you the honest-to-God truth, Greg. Just now, I had a very deep and certain feeling that there's someone out there who's a danger to me and my son. Someone I'm protecting Ryan from. I don't know who. I'm assuming the 'where' is Houston, but I don't know that, either. I don't know why. I just know with complete conviction that I will die before I see him go back to *them*."

"There's more than one of them, then?"

"Yes," she said, surprised to be able to answer without hesitation. "I have no rational basis for knowing this, but I've never been more certain of anything."

"This isn't just a custody battle gone bad? It's not just Ryan's father you're running from?"

He still didn't believe her. He thought she knew more than she'd told him. But he'd called her son Ryan. That meant something.

"Maybe it is a custody battle," she said. "Perhaps one involving a powerful family or something."

The idea wasn't completely foreign to her. And yet, it didn't seem quite right, either.

His glance brooding, he sat there, an imposing figure in full uniform. He was the same man who'd made her feel so incredibly safe and secure—and loved—the night before. And yet...

Did he believe her, even a little? She couldn't tell. But she could only take his silence for so long.

She needed to get Ryan. To get out.

And how could she do that with the sheriff of Shelter Valley sitting in her living room?

She switched to the rocking chair. Dizzy now, as well as freezing, she was afraid she was going to be sick.

The red haze continued to come and go, a companion so frequent she almost didn't notice. Except for the horrible sense of helplessness that accompanied it.

If not for her son, she'd give in and let it just take her—and be done with it.

"What happens next?" she finally asked, when it appeared he might sit there forever. He'd shut himself off from her, leaving her no idea what he was thinking. What he was waiting for.

Or what he had planned for her.

She was so damn tired of being afraid. And yet, every corner of her mind was filled with terror. There was nothing else.

"I'm trying to decide that."

Her legs were shaking visibly. She couldn't stop them. "Are you going to call the FBI?" She had no idea how all that worked. Would she be spending the night in jail? What would they do with Ryan?

Light-headed, Beth began to rock, to concentrate on her breathing. To try to think. She had so damn little experience to draw on, to guide her.

Had she ever been in jail? Would she survive even one night there? Would she survive having Greg turn her in?

What would they do with Ryan?

Greg sat forward, elbows on spread knees, his hands lightly clasped between them. "Because there are some possible extenuating circumstances and because, as the sheriff of this town, it is my sworn duty to protect its citizens and because you are currently one of those citizens, I would like to do some more investigating before making any irrevocable decisions."

It was a mouthful. Spoken in a monotone. They could have been discussing a baseball game.

Beth continued to rock. To shake. "Okay."

She didn't know if she'd just been given a reprieve. Or a jail sentence. She just knew that, for the moment, she was out of choices.

CHAPTER SEVENTEEN

"I CAN'T LEAVE YOU HERE ALONE." Greg might have sounded embarrassed or apologetic. He didn't.

"Why not?" The question was out, and then the obvious answer hit her. "You don't trust me not to run."

"Can you assure me you won't?"

"No."

He nodded. "Wouldn't matter, anyway. You've already run once, which proves you're capable of doing it again. I would be remiss in my duties if I gave you the opportunity."

"So you're arresting me?" Where was the strength that had rescued her moments earlier?

Head slightly bent, he looked at her. "No. But I will if I have to."

This from the man who'd held her so tenderly less than twenty-four hours before.

Rock. Back, forth, back, forth. That was all she could do. Just rock.

"I don't suppose it would do any good to ask for a little more time?" He couldn't, in all conscience, give it to her; she understood that. She wasn't even sure what she'd do with it if she had it. What could she do that she hadn't already done? All of which had led her nowhere.

He didn't bother with an answer other than a long,

serious stare. Heart pounding, she held her own, eyes focused on his. He was telling her something. She just wasn't sure what.

"I have a proposal to put to you," he said finally, breaking another lengthy silence. "Before I present it, I'd like you to bear in mind that this is not your only option."

Beth's throat was dry. She wasn't sure she was going to make it through the explanation without losing the contents of her stomach. The nausea had been steadily rising. If only she could wrap herself in the blanket that was folded neatly at the bottom of Ry's crib. Right where she'd left it when she'd made their beds that morning. Then she'd be okay. Maybe...

"This suggestion is based partially on the fact that I have no knowledge of what kind of enemy we might be fighting. As the possibility exists that you or your son could be in danger, I feel it would be best, initially at least, to conduct a quiet, unofficial investigation of Beth Silverman."

"Can you do that? Unofficially, I mean?"

He nodded. "I have connections. Favors to call in. I should be able to get information without alerting anyone that we're looking. That way, I can also get the background facts without giving any reason for needing them."

She liked that a lot. If only...

"But when you get the answers, you'll have to act on them." A sharp pain shot through her middle as she considered what that might entail.

"One way or another, yes." He nodded again.

He was doing a lot of that. Nodding. And very little looking at her. She was close to believing that she'd imagined the warm and wonderful feeling he'd so recently brought into her home—her heart.

She could believe she'd imagined one night. But she couldn't have concocted the past couple of months, could she?

Beth didn't think so. But then, her mind had a history of playing tricks on her.

HE WAS AN IDIOT. A complete and total fool.

But if he was going to fall, at least he'd go down true to himself. He would endure to the end. No matter how many times he listed the reasons he should have his finger on the dial that very moment, calling the FBI, he couldn't turn his back on Beth.

The thought of what could happen to her son—months in foster care, to start with—were also wreaking havoc on his repeated admonitions to wise up.

"Pack a bag for yourself and the boy." If he was going to get through this, he had to be businesslike.

The rocking stopped. She didn't get up. "Where are we going?"

"To my place." He'd already figured out it was the only way. "You and Ryan are moving in with me."

He'd never actually seen someone's jaw drop before.

"What will people think?" she asked while he stood there, waiting.

"That we're shacking up, of course." It was the only way.

Beth stood straight, met him eye to eye. "We can't do that," she said with more gumption than he thought he'd ever seen her show. "It's not like this is Houston, Greg. You know as well as I do that if we did something like that, everyone in Shelter Valley would know by nightfall.''

"I'm counting on that.''

"What?''

He took a strange satisfaction in seeing *her* with all the questions for once. And didn't feel a twinge of guilt, either.

Of course, he was trying hard not to feel much of anything.

"Look,'' he said, as coolly as he could, considering that he was doing exactly what he'd dreamed about—bringing the woman who belonged in his house home to live with him. "I cannot take you to jail, and I have to keep you someplace where I can be certain you won't run out on me. All the windows in my home have an alarm system that alerts me immediately if there's any tampering, and the doors have dead bolts that lock from the outside with a key.''

She wasn't going anywhere.

And no one else would be getting in, either.

He wondered how often she had to color her hair—and Ryan's—to conceal the blond.

"Why can't you take me to jail?''

Why in hell couldn't she concentrate on the key-from-the-outside part? Dammit, he'd just told the woman he'd slept with, that she was now in essence his prisoner. Couldn't she at least yell at him about that?

Something had to make this job easier to execute.

"Because.'' He gave her question the succinct answer it deserved. The fact that it was also the only answer he had didn't matter.

"I still don't get why you'd do this to yourself, have the entire town talking about you. About us.''

She was good. Playing the "concerned about him" card.

Or…she was the Beth he'd grown to love.

Either way, his answer was the same.

"Everyone knows we've been seeing each other," he told her, treading in dangerous waters. Dangerous to his determination not to feel. He was strangely reluctant, as well, to point out something that she apparently had not yet considered. "Because we have no idea of the enemy we might be up against, you're going to need all the protection I can muster," he said. "When everyone else in town sees their mail today, there are bound to be some questions. Sadly, most people don't pay attention to those cards, but the ones who do are going to be suspicious."

She paled, sank back to the rocker as the truth dawned on her. Clearly she'd given no thought to the seriousness of her current situation.

"They might not know you well, Beth, but they've known me all my life. They trust me. If I show them that you deserve our protection, not our condemnation, they will protect you without question. At least for a while. They would no more let anything happen to their sheriff, or anyone he loved, than they would to one of their own children."

"That's expecting an awful lot from people who don't even know me. To harbor me and Ryan with such…such conclusive evidence against me."

He wondered if she'd intended part of that comment for him.

"Anywhere else, and I'd agree with you," he said. "But not here. If I put out the word that there are extenuating circumstances and that people should hold tight, they will. They're bound to speculate

among themselves, but they won't talk to strangers."
He was thankful he was the only law officer living in
Shelter Valley, the only one who knew Beth. And
once he had her safely ensconced in his home, he
wouldn't have to worry about the townspeople or
what they thought.

He and Beth had other, more critical matters facing
them.

Like the criminal charges he should probably be
filing against her.

Ryan's future.

And the fact that if he was wrong about Beth, the
people of Shelter Valley would not trust him a second
time.

He wasn't even going to consider the state of his
heart. That was no longer relevant.

BETH COULDN'T BELIEVE the speed with which Greg
upended—and then resettled—her entire life. A call
to the Willises had Ryan safely out of the way for an
extra couple of hours. A second call to her landlord,
and she was out of her lease. A run for boxes, a trip
or two with his truck, calls to her clients canceling
jobs. Five minutes to shower and change into the
jeans and sweater she'd left unpacked. Finally, for the
last time, she walked out of the dingy little apartment
she'd grown to love.

During the whole time they packed and cleaned,
she was never alone. Even when she showered, he'd
insisted she not lock the bathroom door, and had been
right outside when she came out.

Greg didn't trust her.

She wasn't even sure he particularly liked her anymore. His conversation was civil, bordering on kind—but distant. He was working.

Last night, she'd been his lover. Now she was a job.

And when he had to go into the office—a meeting with Burt Culver he'd told her nothing about—he dropped her at the day care with his sister. He could have locked her and Ryan in his home, and Beth didn't doubt that was coming, but he'd wanted to announce their liaison to the town as soon as possible.

Bonnie's day care would take care of that.

He'd told his sister not to let Beth close to Ryan; he insisted that Beth was exhausted and needed a rest. In effect, he'd put her under house arrest at Bonnie's. Bonnie loved him and trusted him so she'd gone along with it.

Beth didn't think she'd have run, anyway. Where could she go? And why? Greg might be her best chance at finding the answers she had to have. She'd decided to let him try. Life without him was unpalatable. As unpalatable as subjecting Ryan to a life on the run.

"You really love my brother," Bonnie said, her cheery smile cheerier than usual as she sat behind the closed door of her office on the main floor of the day care. Through the window, they could see the children playing. Ryan and Katie were off in a corner, Katie giving Ryan a tea party. The few other children left that late in the day were coloring at a table with one of the college students who came in after school when the day care teachers went home.

"I do," Beth said, barely managing to look Bonnie in the eye. Greg had told her how she had to play this.

But she didn't want to be playing. Not with his sister. Bonnie was the only "family" she had.

"I know he loves you," the other woman said, her gaze intelligent but happy, as well.

It amazed Beth how Bonnie, with her plump cheerfulness, her short body and lively dark curls, could still emanate such authority.

"I knew months ago that you two were meant for each other. I just wasn't sure either of you would figure it out."

Beth smiled, but her lips were trembling. If Bonnie only realized how impossible it was for Beth to figure *anything* out.

"Hold on to that thought," she said, pulling the crumpled card from the canvas bag monogrammed with her first name. "You might not be so happy in another second or two."

Bonnie leaned forward across her desk, grabbing Beth's hand. "Of course I will be," she said. "You're an answer to many years of prayer. I knew it when I first saw you with Ryan. You're strong yet sensitive, not afraid to nurture. You're intelligent. Independent when you need to be. Capable. When something bad happens, you land on your feet. You're exactly the type of woman Greg needs. Has needed for a long, long time. You would never have been scared off by Greg's responsibilities with my dad. If you'd been with him then, you'd have settled in and helped. Because you care. you know what's right and it's important to you to *do* what's right."

She wasn't going to cry; she couldn't afford to. But Beth had never been so close to just laying down her head and letting everything go, releasing all the emotion inside her. Tears in her eyes, she looked at Bonnie. ''Thank you,'' she whispered.

Bonnie couldn't possibly realize how much harder she'd just made the next few minutes.

Silently, she handed Bonnie the postcard. It wasn't part of Greg's plan. He'd determined that they should downplay the whole thing in an effort not to bring it to the attention of those who weren't going to notice it, anyway. According to him, that was most of Shelter Valley.

Bonnie's face paled visibly. Dropping Beth's hand, she sat up straight, every bit the intimidating administrator in spite of the brightly colored balloons painted across her shirt.

''Has Greg seen this?''

Beth met and held her gaze. Bonnie deserved that much. ''Yes.''

''He has?'' Bonnie scrutinized her.

''Yes.''

Taken aback, Beth watched as the other woman visibly relaxed. Her posture, as she sank down again. The expression on her face, from formal back to friend. And her eyes, changing from careful to compassionate. All in the space of a second.

''Then, we don't have anything to worry about.''

''Bonnie...''

Bonnie forestalled her with a raised hand. ''It's okay,'' she said. ''It's not that I'm not dying of curiosity, and of course as your friend I want to know what's going on, but you don't owe me anything, Beth. I trust you. There's a damn good explanation for this. Whatever it is, you were left with no other choice.''

''You didn't think that a minute ago, before I told

you that Greg knew," she said bleakly. "Your reaction was pretty obvious." Not that Beth blamed her. She had doubts about herself, too. As far as the law was concerned, she was a criminal. The distribution of that card meant kidnapping charges had been pressed. And who knew what else she might have done?

"Of course I thought that!" Bonnie's brows drew together. "My reaction was panic, pure and simple. If he didn't know, he had to be told immediately, so he could get to work."

"So he could find out if I was worth trusting?"

Because she was looking down, Beth didn't see Bonnie's hand slide back across the desk. Was startled when she felt the other woman's comforting touch.

"So he could protect you," Bonnie said softly.

"What about protecting *him?*" Beth asked. "Until we get this straightened out, he is, in fact, harboring a criminal."

Bonnie shook her head emphatically. "I don't know what's going on and I suspect, since Greg didn't tell me, it's best that I not know—much as I might want to," she added with a grin that disappeared quickly. "But I have complete faith in my brother. He'll do the right thing."

The right thing. The words were a comfort to her, speaking to something elemental inside Beth. She had a very real sense that was all she'd ever wanted: to do the right thing.

"I'M NOT LYING," Burt Culver told his superior for the fourth time. His gut was one hard rock as he stood before Greg Richards's desk, watching his entire life turn to dust. "I've told you everything I know."

The sheriff tilted back in his chair, but Burt wasn't fooled by the seemingly nonchalant pose. Greg Richards was doing battle. And he was going to win.

He always did.

Because he chose his battles carefully and fought only for what he believed in. It was probably the quality Burt admired most about Greg.

He'd just never figured he'd be on the other side during one of those fights.

But somehow Burt had to win, too. The job was everything to him. Always had been. His only motive had been to protect his right to be a cop.

Greg perused him silently. Waiting for him to crack, to say more. Burt had witnessed the tactic more times than he could count.

He was immune to it.

But not to the desperation driving him. If Greg Richards thought he was going to take his job away from him...

"I swear, Sheriff," he said, using Greg's title although he didn't often do so. "I was only on an information-gathering mission when Len Wagner told me about the Bloodhounds taking up residence in some clearing about thirty miles from Shelter Valley. I had no idea what the significance of the information was or why we should care. I reported back to Foltz and that was that."

"And the hermit?" Greg said, his tone implacable.

"I tried three times to find him, just like I told you. The place was boarded up. Looked deserted."

He was relieved when Richards nodded. But not really surprised. The sheriff had told him he'd been out to the place himself. And he'd be fair in his assessment of the truth.

"And the photographs?" Greg asked.

Eyes focused on the freshly painted ceiling, Burt gritted his teeth. He thought about lying to his superior. He *had* to lie. Just like that day he'd damaged the photos, he had no choice.

Sweating, Culver stood there. Time stretched before him. Empty. Pointless.

He wasn't at fault here. He'd done nothing but follow orders. He wasn't going to lose everything, when he'd done exactly what he'd sworn to do. He couldn't.

And then his gaze met Richards's.

It was over. He'd done his job. He'd had no idea there was a connection between the two series of crimes. Foltz had sworn to him... And then, when Greg had shown him the photos, he'd known. Damn! He'd only done what he was told, done his best. And it was all over, anyway.

Foltz, you son of a bitch, I have a new boss now. Until he crucifies me.

"I distracted the technician, put all the photos together, loosened the cap on some kind of fluid..."

"Why?"

Humiliation was hell. A lesson he could have done without.

"Because if I don't have my job, I've got nothing."

Greg's feet landed on the tile floor with a *snap*. He stood, fists on his desk, as he leaned forward. "And where did you ever get the idea that tampering with evidence would preserve your job?" The words were no less deadly for their softness.

His coffin was lying before him. There was no longer any reason to follow orders. Or to care what happened if he didn't.

"Unless I destroyed those pictures, I was going to be implicated in the series of carjackings that killed your father."

If it was possible to hate himself any further, Burt would have when Greg dropped back into his chair, the aura of unshakable authority falling away for an instant.

"You?" Greg asked, hardly able to look at Burt. "*You* were behind the carjackings?"

"Hell, no!" He hadn't meant to be so loud, glanced around to see if anyone was coming into the room to see what was going on.

No one did.

He stepped forward, careful to keep his hands folded in front of him and nowhere near the revolver Greg had asked him to place on his desk at the beginning of the interview.

The beginning of the end.

"I knew nothing about them," Burt said, consciously lowering his voice. "Back then, I didn't even know that the questions I'd been asking had anything to do with the carjackings. I'd picked Len up on a DUI a few months before. It wasn't the first time—he was a heavy-duty partier. Foltz sent me to question him, trying to find a link to a...problem he was having out in the desert."

Greg was listening intently, one fist at his lips.

"Then, out of the blue, I get this call from Foltz. He tells me that I worked on the case ten years ago. That I turned up incriminating evidence—evidence I didn't act on—and that he had enough witnesses who'd incriminate me. We could both go down, he said. He had some reports I'd signed. Investigations I'd done for him—always under the guise of something else. He had me neatly framed. I was the officer in charge and it looked like I'd closed a case in spite of hard evidence. He was taking care of things on his end and just needed me to watch things here.''

"And to hell with protecting the safety of this year's innocent victims?''

Burt shook his head, surprised to find how badly it ached. "He told me about the Bloodhounds. But they'd disbanded. There was no way the two sets of crimes were related.''

"He told you the Bloodhounds killed my father.''

Shame was worse than humiliation. Burt would prefer death. "He told me they were responsible for the carjackings.''

"Before or after you told me that my interest in the case was bordering on unprofessional because of my personal involvement?''

"Before.''

"So what was it, some kind of game to them? A pastime? See whose car you can bump on the highway, get them to pull over, and then—like deciding on a flavor of ice cream—choose what you're going to do to the victim?''

Head bowed, Burt prayed the interview would end soon. Damn Richards for not seeing that he'd only done what he had to do. He was the best damn cop Richards had. He might have damaged some old pictures, but he'd been told no one would get hurt. That there couldn't possibly be a connection between the crimes ten years ago and these new ones. If he'd had any idea, he never would have listened to Foltz. He'd never have knowingly endangered the people he was sworn to protect.

"I don't know," he said.

"Did you know that Foltz's younger brother was a Bloodhound?"

"Colby?" Burt asked. "No way. Foltz was just telling me about him. Kid graduated with honors, went to Harvard. He's some hotshot law professor at one of them Ivy League schools."

"I'll just bet he is—" Greg said.

Burt had never heard such bitterness in his superior's voice.

"After sending my father straight to hell."

Culver felt the first nail seal that coffin shut.

BETH COULDN'T SLEEP. The night was too dark. The room was too dark. Her life was too dark. Nothing but black holes and shadows. Everywhere she looked.

The night-light was across the hall in Ryan's room. She'd wanted to keep the baby with her, but Greg hadn't budged. The boy needed his own space, he'd said. It wasn't natural or fair to have him so used to sleeping with his mother.

And it would be harder for Beth to steal away into the night if she had to cross the hall and pass Greg's open door first.

All their doors were open. Something else he'd insisted upon. Not that he ever crossed the threshold of her room. Or invited her to cross his.

Turning over, she tried to find in the hallway a brief glimmer from Ry's night-light. It was on a far wall, near the corner. Lighting his crib area but not the hall.

Beth sat up, bunched the pillows on the double bed in Greg's guest room, lay back down and waited impatiently for her relaxation techniques to kick in. This was her third night at Greg's house, her third night since she'd learned her own name, and those techniques had been cruelly absent the entire time.

She'd been able to play the piano to her heart's content, though. Had spent hours letting her soul speak to her without her mind's intervention.

Greg had never mentioned that he had a piano, too. One that wasn't as new as Bonnie's.

Sitting up again in the dark, she wondered what she could do without disturbing her reluctant keeper. She'd spent the past hour, the past three days, trying to remember. Poring over Internet information about Houston on Greg's computer, hoping to find something familiar.

Her mind was as vacant as the blackness surrounding her.

When it started to close in on her rather than merely surround her, Beth flew out of bed. Quietly she tiptoed down the hall to the kitchen at the back of the house. A place where she could safely turn on a light without waking Greg from his much-needed sleep. She'd known he was a busy man, but now that she was living with him—staying in his house, she quickly amended—she saw what an impossible schedule he kept.

Sliding the kitchen drawer slowly out so she could get the pad of paper she knew was inside, she wondered if the citizens of Kachina County had any idea how lucky they were to have Greg serving them—

"What are you doing?"

She dropped the pencil she'd been lifting from a tray in the front of the drawer.

"Getting ready to take notes," she said, hating how

shaky her voice was. Shaky because it was Greg, not because he was a lawman.

Afraid to turn around, to see what he was or wasn't wearing, she stared at the contents of a junk drawer she'd just cleaned out the day before. She was in sweats and a T-shirt. Looked like she wasn't going to be needing them as uniforms anymore. Her business had quietly closed when she'd moved in with the sheriff.

"Notes for what?"

He came far enough into the room that she could see him out of the corner of her eye. He was wearing sweats, too. Black ones. And a white ribbed tank T-shirt. The kind muscle men wore in ads.

It looked better on him.

Beth turned. "Sometimes I write things down, free associating, hoping that when I read it over, something will make sense."

He frowned, his big frame dwarfing the small but elegantly modern kitchen. "That's something you can't do during the day?"

"I couldn't sleep."

She'd thought it was hard going from being strangers to lovers. That was nothing compared to the journey back. She looked at his hands, reaching for the refrigerator door, pulling out a bottle of water, taking off the lid, bringing it to his lips—and remembered how intimately she'd known those hands, those lips.

She watched him and wanted to cry. She'd already lost her past. Losing him meant giving up all the fragile new hope she'd had for the future.

Bottle in hand, he faced her. "You often have trouble sleeping?"

"Not often." She held the notepad and pencil in

front of her, providing a shield between them—between her and the pain of being this close to him with everything falling apart.

"Is there something wrong with your room? The bed's too hard? Too soft?"

"No." And then, because she'd decided three days ago that she was going to trust him, tell him everything in case there was some important detail that she might miss, and to prove to him that she was never going to keep anything from him again, she admitted the embarrassing truth. "Since the…accident…I haven't slept without a light on."

"Oh." The answer seemed to shake him. Pulling out a chair, he sat at the table he hadn't shared with her since she'd been there. He'd eaten all his meals out. She'd had hers alone with Ryan.

She wondered if she'd be around to see Ryan graduate from a baby spoon to the real thing.

Greg didn't say anything. Just sat there. Beth sat down, too.

He seemed different, suddenly. As though she'd caught a glimpse of the man she'd known…

"I know you said it would be a few days before we hear anything, since your police contact is camping with his family for the weekend, but is there anything we can find out on our own?"

"You've done the people search on the Internet."

"It just gave me an address and phone number."

"Even if Gary wasn t on R and R, we probably still wouldn't know much. The clandestine kind of checking we'll be doing takes time. At this point I don't want anyone to be able to trace anything, not even a phone call."

"So nothing can be traced back to you." She understood and fully supported that decision.

"So nothing can be traced to *you*," he said, his eyes soft as he looked at her—really looked at her—for the first time in three days. "Until we figure out what you were running from, I have no way of knowing what kind of danger you might be in."

Beth was so glad to be able to talk to her friend that she almost cried. "What if you find something terrible?" She was trusting him when she didn't trust her own judgment.

He shrugged, seemed to be considering something, and then said, "I don't know."

Her stomach churned. She looked away. "After we made love the other night, I had this strange sensation that I'd...done well because I did what I'd been commanded to do. I seemed to accept quite naturally that that was something I did. Had sex on command."

When she glanced over, he was watching her broodingly, his expression somber. "Maybe you're running from an abusive husband."

Instantly, Beth shook her head. "I can't be married."

"If you don't remember anything, how can you be so sure?"

"I wasn't wearing a wedding ring."

"A point, but not a conclusive one."

"I don't *feel* married."

"Did you feel like a mother when you woke up in that motel room?"

She didn't want to answer him. "No." And when he remained silent, leaving her case full of holes, she said, "I can't be married, Greg. Not after what we—"

Beth broke off. Embarrassed. And far too sad when she thought about what might have been.

He left her words hanging there, too, and she had no idea what he was feeling.

CHAPTER EIGHTEEN

"I'M AFRAID I MIGHT HAVE BEEN A PROSTITUTE."

Greg just couldn't remain immune. For better or worse—fearing it was only going to get worse—he was connected to this woman.

"You were not a prostitute," he said. Criminal she might be; a whore she was not.

"It would fit," she said, her beautiful blue eyes huge with anguish. "Sex on command is a way of life. Maybe my pimp was beating me. Maybe he was threatening to do something to Ryan and I had to escape to save him. Or maybe he refused to let me stop and I had to run to get Ryan away from that life. Makes sense about the money, too. Clients would pay in cash, wouldn't they?"

Greg sat there calmly while his mind raged. She'd obviously given this a lot of thought. Seemed truly distressed by the ludicrous idea. Surely, if she were faking the amnesia...

"Sex is instinctive," he said, trying to convince himself that he could talk to her about her nakedness and not feel the burning of desire. "An animal drive. The way you respond is also instinctive."

And oh, she'd been so sweet. And hot. And... "You did not respond like a woman to whom sex was a job."

Her eyes were fixed on the pad of paper she'd set in front of her.

"Maybe I forgot that, too. That sex was a job."

In spite of himself, he thought of all the months they'd spent together, getting to know each other—not the things they'd done, necessarily, but the spirit he'd come to know. He remembered the time he'd kissed her right there, out by his pool, and the way she'd stopped him. Because she couldn't make love lightly. And he thought of their one incredible night together.

"Beth, take my word for it, you didn't have anything to forget." And then he tried to concentrate on business because, contrary to his admonitions, his blood was running hot. "This 'on command' feeling you had—were there other feelings that accompanied it? Fear, maybe? Or disgust?"

She thought for a moment, still concentrating on that blank pad of paper and the little pieces she was ripping off the top page. "No." She peeked up at him and went back to the business of making confetti. "It was odd. Just a sense of having done what I was supposed to. But in a positive sense. Like what I'd done was right and good."

Greg was so focused on trying to analyze every clue, he didn't immediately notice that something was wrong. Beth had stopped talking, but she'd finished her previous sentence, so that wasn't particularly striking. She didn't fall out of her chair. Didn't make any sound at all.

She just stopped. Her hands froze, a dime-size piece of paper pressed between her thumb and index finger. Her entire body was stiff, unmoving. Her eyes alerted him first. They were focused on him, but it was as though she were blind, staring sightlessly through him.

"Beth?"

Greg leaned forward, tension gathering as he tried to assess her condition.

She didn't even seem to hear him.

He tried to remember everything he'd said. Everything she'd said. And drew a blank. An uncomfortable occurrence in itself for a man who depended on close observation to do his job.

"Beth," he said again, more firmly.

Oh God. Horror descended as the thought struck him. She'd taken something. Pills. Liquor. Both. Gulped them down when she'd come to the kitchen, and they were only now having their effect. He grabbed her hand, started to haul her out to the pool if that was what it took to rouse her from that catatonic state.

"No!" The shriek that filled his house was a sound he'd never heard before. "No!" The cry was terrifying, high and shrill and animalistic.

Pulling her hand away, Beth jumped up. The crashing of her chair went unnoticed. "No!" she shrieked a third time.

"Okay!" Greg spoke loudly enough for her to hear, but also as soothingly as he could. "It's okay, Beth," he said over and over, moving as she moved so that he stayed in front of her, trying to catch her gaze with his own. "It's okay, honey. It's okay."

It was a wonder Ryan wasn't awake and calling out to them. Greg hoped the little guy managed to sleep through whatever the next moments were going to bring.

Beth was turning in circles on the tile floor, not particularly fast but not slowly, either, as though she were looking for something.

"No, no, no, no, no..."

It seemed to be the only thing she could say. But she'd quieted down considerably. Was speaking more than shrieking.

"Okay, we won't," Greg said. He needed a doctor. Wondered who he could call in Shelter Valley in the middle of the night. It wasn't like they had a twenty-four hour emergency clinic downtown.

Phyllis Sheffield. Greg landed on the name.

Phyllis would know what to do. He reached for the phone. Beth stopped turning and stared at him, the look in those blue eyes hard, determined.

And then, in one blink, as she really saw him, they softened.

"No."

What he suspected had begun as a shriek came out more as a wail.

"No," she said again, tears in her voice, as her shoulders fell, defeated.

"Sweetie?" Dropping the phone, Greg grabbed her, gently but quickly, under the arms, afraid she might collapse onto the floor. Like a rag doll, she sagged against him, her limbs uncoordinated. She was far too skinny, and yet became dead weight in his hands.

Thinking of the portable phone in the living room—from which he could call Phyllis—Greg lifted Beth, one arm under her knees, one behind her back, and carried her out of the kitchen. He'd meant to lay her down on the couch, but unable to let her go, sat with her instead.

Cradling her like a baby, her head against his shoulder, he pushed the hair from her face. "Beth?"

She was crying. Silently. Tears dripped slowly down her face. Her eyes, when she opened them, were dull but no longer vacant. She looked ill. Exhausted. Shadows seemed to form under her eyes even as he watched.

"Beth?" he said again, battling an unfamiliar panic.

"Oh, Greg, it's bad."

That was when tears choked the back of his throat.

SHE WAS SHAKING SO HARD her teeth were chattering. Phyllis Sheffield had told her that was normal under the circumstances. Beth wasn't in physical shock. Her vital signs were okay. Phyllis had had Greg check them when he'd first called her, and she'd checked them herself when she arrived and again right before she left.

There were rough times ahead. But nothing she couldn't handle, the compassionate psychologist had assured her. Her memory wouldn't be returning if she wasn't ready to face whatever her mind had been hiding.

Beth still didn't know much, only vague recollections of feelings, but disconnected thoughts and flash visions were attacking her from every angle.

"Phyllis told you to relax and let them come, sweetie," Greg said softly, holding her. She hadn't left his couch since he'd first brought her in from the kitchen almost two hours before. It would be dawn in another few hours.

"I know," she said, her jaws vibrating. The way it had some winter, when she'd been locked out of her house. She was in New York. She'd forgotten her key....

Beth tried to grasp the memory. To see more. She was young. Junior high, probably.

And...

It was gone.

She was tired. So damn tired.

Phyllis had also said that if they could get through this without medication, it would make things easier. She'd said that, then told Greg to call a doctor in the morning to get a prescription, just in case.

"Whenever you're ready to tell me, I'm here to listen," Greg said.

Phyllis had suggested he say that. Beth had heard them talking quietly by the door.

So far she hadn't told either of them anything. Except that she was having flashes. Of severe pain. And of pictures she recognized but that didn't go together.

She didn't know how to make sense of anything. Not really. But...

She was going to trust Greg. She couldn't trust herself, so she'd decided to trust him. She'd made a promise to herself three days ago. Couldn't let herself down. She had to trust him.

Trust him.

Don't keep secrets.

"I'm afraid."

"I know. But we'll get through this, Beth."

"It's bad." Worse than an abusive husband. She had a feeling it was even worse than being a prostitute.

"We'll handle it."

Phyllis had told him not to pressure her. She wondered if it was hard for him not to ask questions. She'd had her eyes closed when he and Phyllis were talking by the door. They'd probably thought she'd fallen asleep.

As if she could. She'd been trapped in a haze of pain and fear.

Talk. That was what she had to do. But to do that, she had to think.

Her heart pounding as panic sliced through her, Beth wished the red haze would carry her away.

"We had to say *right and good* at least four times during a session." She barely opened her mouth as she spoke.

Not missing a beat, Greg continued to stroke the hair away from her face. She loved him so much.

A picture of a padded table flashed before her eyes. A room, mostly in darkness, music playing, strong scents.

"They were massage sessions. I was a masseuse."

She thought about it. Knew it to be true. Yet rejected the idea at the same time. She didn't *feel* like a masseuse. Was more comfortable with the idea of cleaning toilets.

Greg still said nothing, just continued to stroke her, to give her something to concentrate on so she could stay in touch with reality. Beth wondered what he was thinking and turned to look up at him.

He smiled down at her, his eyes filled with such warmth, such strength, she wanted to die right then and there. During a perfect moment. And escape all the horrible things to come.

"I had to say *right and good* at least once every quarter of an hour. More often when the subject appeared amenable."

"Subject's a funny word to use," Greg said, his tone nonjudgmental. "Aren't people who have massages usually referred to as clients?"

"I suppose so." Beth tried to get back to that room, but another pain shot through her skull. "I don't know why I said that."

"I have to ask you something," Greg said slowly, "but please understand that I'm not trying to pressure you, nor will the answer change how I feel about you."

She looked up at him again, and a sense of fresh air penetrated the suffocating darkness. "How do you feel about me?"

His eyes grew brighter, giving her the distinct impression that he'd had something very definite to say and then changed his mind. "I believe in you."

It was enough.

Probably as much as she was ready to hear.

"What were you going to ask me?"

"Were you being forced to do what you were doing? Was it against your will?"

Her chest constricted. The red haze circled her vision. "Yes." And then, just as clearly, "No." She stopped. Begged herself for answers, for anything that would make sense of the debilitating emotions consuming her. "I believed strongly in what I was doing. It was right and good."

She didn't even hear the words she'd said until she felt Greg stiffen, and thought back over them.

"What does it mean?" she whispered, a tiny child huddled in a corner. "Why do I keep saying that? And why do those words scare me so much?"

"I don't know, sweetie." His voice came from far off. "But I can promise you we're going to find out."

"GREG?"

It was very late. Or very early. He'd carried her to his bed and, still dressed in their sweats, they were lying together on top of the sheet. She'd been too hot for covers.

"Yeah?"

He'd told her to try to sleep. With her head on his chest, she thought she felt secure enough to do so. Ryan would be up in another couple of hours.

"What's going to happen if whatever we find out means we can't be together?"

He didn't say anything, just pulled her closer.

"I know you might not even want a future with me, but what if we don't have that option?"

"We'll have it."

"I'm scared to death I did something horrible. That I'm in trouble."

He didn't say anything.

"Tell me what you're thinking. Please." She was starting to cry. She didn't want to. She just couldn't seem to help it.

His sigh was more telling than any words. "I'm scared, too."

GREG WAS HOME all day Sunday. Word had spread around town that Beth was living with him, and that she'd been "set up" with the postcard thing—he wasn't sure where that had come from, but suspected his sister—and the phone rang on and off all day. When it woke Beth for the second time, he unplugged it.

He spent a good part of the day playing quietly with Ryan. The little guy was an amazing kid, perceptive far beyond his age. Whenever he glanced over at his sleeping mother, his wide-eyed look seemed to tell Greg that he understood and that everything would be all right.

The toddler was probably seeking reassurance, not giving it, but Greg felt better, anyway.

He napped when Ryan napped, ate when the little boy seemed hungry, and at seven-thirty that night, when Ryan lay down in his crib, Greg climbed into his own bed across the hall, took Beth into his arms and willed himself to sleep.

His gut twisted at the thought of the next day, the answers he was going to get, one way or another. Burt. Foltz. His father.

And Beth.

He had to know.

And then he had to have the strength to endure whatever came next.

Beth sighed, her body pressing a little more closely against him, as though, even in her sleep, she needed the assurance that he was there.

He was. And he would be in the days to come. Somehow.

With that decision made, an evanescent peace

passed through him, calming him enough to let him sleep.

GREG HAD HUGH FOLTZ AND BURT CULVER in his office by nine o'clock Monday morning. His buddy, Gary Miller, an old partner from the Phoenix police department who'd gone undercover when Greg went over to the sheriff's department, was moving mountains in Houston. And while Greg waited impatiently to find out what kind of challenges awaited him there, he tackled his own mountainous problem in Kachina County.

"I'm sorry." Hugh Foltz sat in the chair in front of Greg's desk. There wasn't even a hint of the bravado Greg had never, until that moment, seen him without. Just the slumped shoulders of a man who knew he'd come up wanting.

"Sorry's not good enough." Greg was seething, ready to tear somebody's throat out. Ready to howl with pain and trying to pretend he wasn't.

"He was just a kid, Greg. A sweet kid who got suckered by some punks, at a school he never should've been attending, with promises of protection and friendship. And by the time he figured out that he wanted no part of what was going on, he knew too much. They had their hooks in him and wouldn't let go. Threatened to kill his mother. My mother." Foltz wasn't crying on Greg's shoulder. Wasn't whining or courting sympathy. He was stating the facts. Unemotionally. Honestly. Just like Greg would have done.

Culver sat in the chair next to his ex-boss, facing his current one, his expression that of a man who'd lived too long, seen too much. He was pulling at his ear.

"When our mother left our dad," Foltz continued, "she took the kid—he was only a baby then—and moved to Phoenix with the first of many boyfriends. I finished college, had a life, paid far too little attention to this kid who needed a father figure. That should've been me." He shrugged. "I started investigating those carjackings, found out what was happening with the Bloodhounds and went in to bust them all. That's when I learned Colby was involved. It was up to me whether or not I sent him to jail. What kind of cop would I be if I couldn't protect my own kid brother?"

"An honest one?" Greg suggested harshly, threatened by the compassion he felt for the older man—a man he'd once admired above all others. Including his own father.

"My position was going to allow me to do something I needed to do. It was going to let me make something right. I was going to save my brother's life. Holding the incident over his head, I was able to force him to run all his decisions by me from then on and to make the right ones."

Culver looked at Greg.

"What about that little matter of justice?" Greg asked. "What about the citizens you'd sworn to protect?"

"I did protect them," Foltz said. "Not in the way you would have." His right hand gestured in Greg's direction. "Not in the way the law would have me do, but they were nonetheless protected."

Culver shook his head.

"There was nothing I could do about the victims," Foltz went on, "but I could make damn certain the carjackings stopped for good. Which was more than any judge would've been able to do. The courts would never have gotten a conviction."

Len had intimated the Bloodhounds were that good.

"I went in with death threats that weren't empty, and I got the kid out. By the end of that month, the driving force behind the Bloodhounds was out of the country."

"Then, tell me why I've spent the summer cleaning up after a series of crimes that resemble those carjackings of ten years ago—right down to the indentations on their front ends."

"Rabbit Rock," Foltz said.

Greg nodded.

"The carjackings weren't a joyride," Foltz said, his eyes deadly serious. "They were an initiation process."

Greg sat forward, giving his full attention to the retired sheriff.

"Each pair of *applicants*—" the older man practically spat when he said the word "—had to steal a car. They could do whatever they wished with the victims, but it was understood that if they went easy, they weren't right for the Bloodhounds. In that case, they should count themselves or their loved ones as good as dead. Once the victim was disposed of in some fashion, they were to drive the car to Rabbit Rock, where the rest of the gang would be waiting. In order to prove they had no fear and that they'd do whatever they were told, the potential Bloodhounds had to drive that car full speed into Rabbit Rock. If they survived, then they were in.''

"How many kids died in the process?'' Greg asked quietly.

"Only one that I know of.'' Foltz's mouth was turned down at the corners. "Most of them were so strung out by the time they got to that point, they rolled like rubber with the blow.''

"We've got another gang on our hands.'' Culver sat forward, speaking for the first time. "It's the only explanation. And I'm guessing either the drug traffickers Hugh scared out of the country crossed back over the border, or some punk who was once a Bloodhound decided to go into business for himself.''

"God, I'm sorry,'' Foltz said, looking at Greg. "I'd rather be dead myself than know I'm the cause of the hell that's been happening on the highway this summer. I swear to God I was sure they were unconnected.''

Greg stood. "Yeah, well, we don't have time for sorry. Right now, this county needs you. You're the only one who has the full story from ten years ago. Names, dates, all of it.''

Foltz stood, too, hiking up a pair of jeans over the belly that had started to expand since his retirement. "How do you know I still have any of that?''

"Because I know you,'' Greg said. "Your brain has a record filed away for every single case you ever supervised.''

Hugh nodded. Stepped up to Greg's desk. "About the Bloodhound deal, I'll put it all in writing—''

"Not now, Hugh,'' Greg said, forestalling any more of the contrition he wasn't in the mood to stomach. "What's past might be better just left there. For now, let's concentrate on the bastards messing up my present."

ONCE HE HAD THE INFORMATION he needed, it took Culver a little under six hours to track down the thirty-year-old loser who'd been terrorizing high school drug addicts into joining forces with him. Greg's discovery of the Rabbit Rock connection made an impossible task almost easy. The carjackings were indeed—and once again—an initiation process. They served one purpose: to prove loyalty to the point of death to Steel Crane, an ex-Bloodhound who'd been in and out of prison since his late teens. These crimes also ensured future loyalty, as they gave Crane something to hold over his members' heads. Him or jail. That would be the only choice left to them. And Crane knew guys in jail. Guys who'd make anyone who'd been "disloyal" wish he were dead.

Just after six o'clock that night, with Steel Crane in custody, Foltz and Culver left Greg's office. Greg had requested that they give him some time to consider any future action against either or both of them.

He was tired. Ready to go home. To have dinner with Ryan. And to cuddle up to Ryan's mother for as many hours as he could get away with. Sometime soon, he'd want to do more than cuddle. Sometime soon, he'd want to make love with her again.

He shouldn't, but he'd worry about that when he had to.

His cell phone rang as he was leaving the office. Greg picked it up on his way downstairs. Gary had handled his inquiries carefully—until he'd discovered there was a hit man after Beth Silverman. Then caution be damned; he'd called everyone he knew. The rest of what Greg's old partner had to say turned Greg's blood cold. With the bubble on top of his car, he made the twenty-mile trip to Shelter Valley in a record twelve minutes.

BETH HEARD THE GARAGE DOOR OPEN when Greg got home. She'd fed Ryan, who'd gone to bed an hour and a half early, exhausted from the upheaval of the past couple of days. Her son was already a creature of routine, a little boy who liked his life organized and predictable. Taking after his mother.

She knew it all now. Like a motion picture with scrambled frames, her entire life had scrolled before her throughout that long day—until she'd fallen into a state of numbed acceptance, too weak to be afraid anymore.

It was Beth's own mental weakness that had started the whole thing. Or at least, her part in it. She'd been so culpable. So easy to brainwash.

And the things she'd done...

Feeling dead inside, she got up to open the door from the garage into the house. She'd been waiting for Greg. Waiting to tell him it was all over.

Unlocking the dead bolt, Beth was fully prepared to get through the conversation ahead without crying. Without asking anything for herself. Prepared to beg for Ryan, though. To somehow make Greg promise that he would not abandon her son, that Ryan would never be in the custody of his father or anyone else from Sterling Silver.

She was not prepared for the black-sheathed arm

that came around the door, or the leather-clad hand that grasped her wrist and bent it back until she heard it snap.

Maybe that was why she didn't feel a thing. She opened her mouth to scream but no sound came out.

"Got you, bitch." The muffled growl struck the first chord of fear in her. And once feeling started, it didn't stop. The pain in her wrist was now so sharp she was afraid she might pass out. Or throw up.

Before she could do either, she was outside the house. In the dark, gassy smelling garage, another leathered hand came over her mouth. She couldn't breathe. Couldn't think. She was completely gripped by cold, dead fear.

"We do this easy, or we do it my way," the voice said.

He was enjoying this.

Beth knew then that she was going to die. Somehow that made all the difference. Freed her. She didn't even care all that much about dying if she could get the bastard away from Greg's house. Away from her son.

Greg would be home soon. He'd save Ryan.

"James sent you." She was surprised how easily she found the strength to talk, as he dragged her toward the running car. It was parked under a tree across the street. She wondered how the guy had managed to open the garage door, and then noticed glass from the window on the ground.

He was holding her hand, making it appear as though she were friendly with him, a willing companion. All he had to do was give her fingers the lightest tug and searing pain shot through her wrist, up her arm and into her shoulder. Ensuring her co-operation.

As long as he left her son alone, he didn't have anything to worry about. Her life wasn't worth the struggle. Not after what she'd remembered that day.

She stumbled and he pulled down on her hand. Slowly.

"It's already broken," she muttered. Were her words starting to slur?

The guy grunted.

"So how many years did he get you out of?" she thought about asking, but wasn't sure she'd actually said it aloud.

"Shut up." The words were accompanied by another tug on her wrist.

Oh. The pain was so sharp, spearing through her in white-hot agony. Death was even more painful than she'd imagined it would be. He tugged one more time.

Losing all sense of reality, Beth jerked forward and retched. She vomited all over the driveway, herself and the shoes of the man who appeared to be holding her head, but was in the process of breaking her neck.

He had to let her finish vomiting first. He couldn't get a good enough grip when she kept convulsing away from him. In a semi-delirious state, she wondered if that was supposed to be funny.

Mostly, Beth was just glad she was going to die before she was raped.

If James had sent him, the man gradually adding pressure to her neck was a rapist. A prominent Texas prosecuting attorney, James Silverman had one of the best conviction records in the state—except when it came to rape. During those trials, he often seemed to have commitments elsewhere. Beth hadn't known, until years after she'd married him, that James was not as right and good as she'd thought.

James had purposely thrown more than one case. But only cases of rape... Despite his "spiritual" beliefs, he'd begun to reveal his misogyny, his deep-down contempt for women. And over the years he'd gradually begun to develop sympathy for men who were, as he explained it, so tormented by women that they couldn't help being driven to punish them, to put them in their place. He didn't see it as an act of aggression but one of desperation. He got many of them off and then brought them into Sterling Silver. There, they received protection, sex twice a week and, occasionally, undercover jobs to do.

Lost in the story of her past, as she had been on and off for most of the day, she was hardly aware of the pressure, the nausea, the night.

Thoughts flashed through her mind, obliterating her awareness of the ground below her face, the unbearable pain in her wrist, the fact that she was never going to hold her baby boy again.

Her entire body convulsed with another spasm.

Beth's last thought, as the pressure on her neck increased, was that she'd never be able to tell Greg how much she loved him.

GREG DROVE FAR TOO FAST, taking corners precariously, all the while telling himself that he was overreacting. There was no reason to assume, just because those postcards had gone out, that the man who'd

been hired to track and kill Beth would be tipped off
to where she was.

Beth had been smart these past months, kept a low
profile. Very few people outside Shelter Valley had
seen her.

Except... His blood ran cold. That jerk at the casino. He'd had a good long look at Beth while they'd
waited around for the Reservation police. And while
Greg had been giving his report, as well. The guy had
been in the back seat of the cop car, probably staring
out the window at Beth.

Greg had heard he was out on bail—awaiting trial.
With information like this and an underground net-
work that was more trustworthy than the CIA, he
could've made some good money....

As he came through town, Greg laid on his horn,
an accompaniment to the siren already blaring. The
way cleared miraculously, images of people he'd
known all his life passing by him as if in slow motion.

By the time he reached his street he could hear the
rhythm of his heart in his ears. As soon as he knew
that Beth was okay he'd calm right down. Consider
the things Gary had told him.

For now, he couldn't even think about them.

Greg's heart pounded harder. And then practically
stopped altogether when he saw the circle of people
crowding around something on his driveway. His
practiced eye registered the strange dark sedan parked
with its engine running, across the street from his
house.

The blood drained from his face. He felt it. Just as
he felt the tears fill his eyes.

No.

He took everything in quickly. The neighbors he knew and loved, some crouched, some standing, peering over others' backs.

And then something struck him. That car was still there. Which meant the driver hadn't gotten away.

Could it mean that—

"Greg!" Carl Bush, a retired foreman from the Cactus Jelly plant, pulled open Greg's door as the cruiser screeched to a halt and Greg jumped out. "Thank God, you're here!"

"Where's Beth?"

"There," Carl said, out of breath as he ran beside Greg, pointing to the crowd on the drive. "She's conscious again and I think going to be just fine, but she won't let anybody look at her or touch her. She's holding that baby boy of hers and just keeps crying for you."

"Get out of the way!" someone shouted.

"The sheriff's here!"

"Greg's here!"

"Greg, thank God..."

Greg barely heard the loud chorus of voices that greeted him as the crowd around Beth melted back, making room for him.

"Deputy Culver already took the guy away." Greg recognized that voice. It belonged to his sister. "Sue called from next door. Said Beth wouldn't get up off the driveway. I came right over. She won't move Greg. She..."

He didn't hear another word as he stared at the woman he loved and the baby she was rocking against her. She was a mess. Ryan looked petrified.

"Beth? Sweetie? Let's go inside."

She smelled so bad his eyes watered. Careful to make sure he had a firm grip on Ryan, as well, he lifted Beth to his chest.

"Greg?" Her gaze wasn't quite focused when she looked at him. "I couldn't trust anyone but you." Her eyes closed, scaring him. And then they opened again. "Take care of Ryan," she whispered before her head fell limply back against his arm.

"Somebody call an ambulance," he bellowed.

"It's already been here once." Bonnie was still beside him. "Culver called them. She refused treatment. I'll get them back."

"Geg?" the little boy said, staring solemnly up at him.

"It's okay, buddy, your mama's going to be just fine," Greg said.

And prayed that he wasn't lying.

WITH HER BROKEN WRIST in a cast, Beth sat at the kitchen table, carefully sipping the hot chocolate Greg had just made for her. It was hard to believe it had only been hours, instead of days, since he'd come home to find her incoherent on the driveway.

She didn't remember much about the time she'd spent out there—and figured, from what she did recall, that it was probably a good thing. It was enough to know that the people of Shelter Valley had more than lived up to the faith their sheriff had placed in them when he'd moved her into his home and told her she'd be safe there.

Even before she'd started retching in the driveway, they'd gathered together and formulated a plan—that included flattening all four tires on the sedan. Deputy

Culver had been called immediately, when Carl Bush first noticed the strange car parked in front of his house. But the neighborhood men had already had James Silverman's hired thug under control before the deputy arrived.

"How you doing?" Greg asked softly, sitting down on the chair closest to her as he studied every inch of her face.

"Fine. Better," she amended.

"You should take some of those pills and get some sleep."

She was sure he was right. Still, she shook her head. "I'd rather talk."

He frowned. "The doctor said—"

"That other than an aching wrist and bruised neck, I'm just fine."

"You will be—after a good night's rest."

"Greg, please. I can go to bed, but I won't be able to sleep."

"Thank goodness Ryan went right down. It was way past his bedtime."

Beth smiled. Greg was a natural when it came to the daddy thing. She hoped that meant he'd be willing to grant her her promise.

"Once he saw that you were awake and smiling," Greg continued, "he seemed to take the whole situation in stride."

"I think Ry learned quite a while ago that as long as I was okay, he was okay."

"I imagine—"

"Greg," Beth interrupted, covering his hand with the one she could move. "I remembered everything today."

She saw the concern flicker in his eyes before he quickly doused it, and resumed the mild expression he was using to convince her everything would be fine.

"I'm one of the founding members of a cult," she said. "It's called Sterling Silver and it's located just outside Houston in a little community we built. Last I knew, we had almost four-hundred members, most of whom live in our community."

"Correction," Greg said, his tone serious. "You're married to one of the founding members."

She blinked. "You know?"

Greg nodded. "Gary called just as I was leaving the office."

"I was a willing participant, Greg. We used the spa as a front to find prospective members. I scouted them out from massage clients and administered the first few levels of mind manipulation. Relaxation exercises, accompanied by subtle thought-reformation techniques. Any people who responded positively, I turned over to Peter Sterling."

"This happened only after you'd been brainwashed yourself."

"He'd been sued for malpractice." She summarized what she'd remembered that day. "He met James during the court proceedings, and over drinks the two of them commiserated about the terrible state of the world, the negativism, the destruction. James had been suffering from depression. Being a prosecuting attorney, spending your days face-to-face with the scum of the world, watching some of them walk away, is not an easy thing. Peter understood that. Just as James understood why Peter had allowed a woman to die when she'd begged him to do so. The two of them created a bond that could not be broken. They became inseparable.''

"That must have been hard for you.''

"Not really.'' Beth shook her head, thinking back—relieved that when she looked, there was something there. "James's depression disappeared. It was as though Peter had given him a new lease on life, a new purpose. The two of them were always talking about saving the world. They'd come up with one scheme after another, volunteer for any service project that sounded worthwhile. They were actually quite fun and invigorating to be around. James was a happier man. A better man. A better husband.''

"So what happened?''

Beth shivered as darkness descended. On her mind. And her heart. "I don't know,'' she said slowly. "Eventually it wasn't enough. James's depression started to return. There was always something wrong, in their view, with the projects they were doing, something wrong with the people in charge. They always figured they could do better, think bigger. That was when Peter suggested taking things to a new level. He wanted to really change the world. James had been taking some positive thinking seminars. The two of them were convinced that with them in charge, they could create a new world without negative energy....'' Beth's voice faded as she stared vacantly ahead.

Greg waited patiently for her to continue.

"I was skeptical at first,'' she said, "but their motivations seemed so good...'' She sighed. "One minute we were all on fire, risking everything on a huge shot at making a real difference in the world. And the next…'' She didn't want to have to face the rest. ''They were going to put Ryan through two days of starvation in a dark room all by himself.'' She skipped through the memories. Reached the breaking point.

''While they gave him dialysis to clean any impurities from his system?''

He talked about the atrocities so calmly. Beth nodded, shocked. ''I can't believe you don't find this appalling.''

Greg's chin dropped to his chest for a moment before he peered up at her. ''I find it so goddamn hideous, I want to murder those two men with my bare hands.''

The barely leashed anger might have been frightening; instead, Beth found it reassuring.

''Boys didn't go through cleansing until they were two, but every time Ryan cried, Peter would tell James he—my baby—was filled with aggression. And Ry always seemed so much more aware, following us with his eyes, looking at us as though he understood things. Peter didn't like that, either.''

''Sounds to me like maybe your husband's friend was jealous of your son.''

No. It hadn't been like that.

Or had it?

Beth just didn't know. Couldn't be sure which thoughts were her own and which had been planted….

''For a long time I had no idea what was going on, but by then I knew things were bad. James was a powerful man with an army of loyal followers.'' She gave a convulsive shudder. "I'd had problems with them doing it to other boys, even when their parents approved, but I couldn't let them take Ryan, couldn't let them hurt my son."

She was seeing through red again, her mind cottony, her thoughts unclear. Greg's hand, rubbing her shoulder, brought her at least partway back.

"Of course you couldn't."

"Peter must have guessed..."

"What happened, Beth?"

"I was in a session, but had come out to give my subject a chance to disrobe. I overheard Peter telling James that now was the time. And then they were talking about me, about manipulating me, and James assured Peter he was willing to do whatever it took. He'd do to me whatever was necessary so he could 'save' his son from the aggression threatening to control him."

Tears in her eyes, she peered at Greg. "He was only a baby!"

"But nothing happened to him."

Greg was right. It was okay. She could breathe. "I left my client lying naked on the table. Never went back. All I had in the room was my canvas bag. My purse was in my locker in the women's dressing room. I grabbed the bag, emptied the cash register, took Ryan from the nursery and ran."

"Something tells me it wasn't that easy."

Beth shook her head, every muscle in her upper body aching. "I hitchhiked for three days, but they found me. Peter caught up with me in New Mexico. I think maybe he didn't trust James to bring me back. I don't know. He tried what he called *thought refor-*

mation first. And it worked. At least some. After all, he was my prophet. But when I wouldn't give him Ryan, he got ugly. He touched me—'' She stopped, hot with shame. Couldn't look at Greg. "Reminded me of my commandments. Reminded me that every man in Sterling Silver had to have sex twice a week. That I had a duty. But I fought him. That's when he started hitting me—''

"I'll kill the bastard."

Beth came up out of her own personal darkness to find herself still in Greg's kitchen, her knight there, ready to fight her battles. It was an odd sensation. To realize that she really and truly was not alone. It wasn't just her against the world.

"I'd taken some self-defense classes," she said, "and somehow managed to knock Peter out. I ran. This time I didn't hitchhike. I wasn't going to give them another chance to find me. I dyed my hair and Ry's, paid cash for that car from a sweet old country man who had it for sale on the side of the road, and drove all night."

"To Snowflake."

Beth nodded. She'd checked into the motel under an assumed last name, fallen asleep for the first time in almost twenty-four hours and woken up empty.

"The second day I was there, I found this old magazine with a story about Tory Evans. It told about her sister's accident in New Mexico. About the identity switch at the hospital. About Tory's abusive husband. And something struck a chord in me. Her story had a happy ending. Because of Shelter Valley. So I knew this was where I had to come."

Only, her story wasn't going to end as happily as

Tory's. Beth was a criminal. In love with a lawman. He was going to have to turn her in.

He wouldn't be who he was, the man she loved, if he didn't.

There was only one thing that mattered now. "Peter and James are dangerous men, Greg."

"They'll be put out of commission. For good."

"You'll make sure that they don't get control of Ryan when I'm gone?" she asked. She couldn't think beyond saving Ryan.

Frowning, Greg looked confused. "Where are you going?"

"I'm not sure how these things work, but eventually to jail."

"You aren't going to jail."

"I kidnapped my son."

"You saved his life."

"I brainwashed innocent people."

"You were brainwashed yourself."

Beth's pulse sped up. She started to feel light-headed again. Couldn't even hope to keep up with all the places her mind had been that day. "Greg, are you telling me you honestly think I have a chance of being found innocent?"

"I'm telling you I know for certain there will be no charges pressed against you. My last call, while we were still at the hospital, verified that Sterling and Silverman are already in custody. James's thug talked."

She couldn't believe it. Couldn't believe it might actually be over.

"I think I'm going to pass out." Her voice sounded far off to her own ears.

"I'm here to catch you if you do."

The stars receded, and Beth looked him full in the face. He was there. Warm. Welcoming.

And still in uniform.

"Am I going to have to testify?"

"Yes."

She nodded, her mind returning to the early days of Sterling Silver. They'd all started out with such good intentions. "You know, they only wanted to make the world a better place," she murmured.

"I know you believed that. And perhaps Sterling and Silverman did, too. At first. In their own twisted ways."

Overwhelmed and exhausted, Beth sat staring into the hot chocolate she'd barely touched. "It's odd to think I'm beginning my life all over again. I'm not Beth Allen, but I'm not Beth Silverman, either." She had been nothing more than a puppet on a string. Even her career had been the result of their manipulation.

"You weren't a masseuse before you met James?"

Beth shook her head. "I was a pianist, playing with the Houston Symphony. It was when my agent got me an international tour that James convinced me I was wasting my talent on something as frivolous as music. Told me I could do so much more, that I could be the catalyst that helped save the world from destruction and despair. That I should use my strong hands to create good in the world."

Beth started to panic again when she thought about how easily she'd been duped. And wondered how she'd ever be able to trust her own mind again.

"What about your parents? What did they have to say about it?"

"My parents are both dead," Beth said. She'd grieved a second time when she'd remembered the car accident that had claimed their lives when she was seventeen. That memory, too, had come back earlier in the day. "I'd been living at Juilliard. The money was there for me to continue, so that's what I did. I graduated. And then I went on to college as my parents had always wanted me to. They wanted me to have something to fall back on, in case I didn't make it as a musician. I majored in business, graduated with honors, got the job in Houston and eventually met James."

Drained beyond capacity, Beth gazed sightlessly into the darkness outside Greg's kitchen window. She'd lived, almost literally, two lifetimes in that day. She had no idea how she'd survived.

"It's all over now," Greg said, almost as though he could read her mind.

He could probably read some of it on her face. He'd been studying her so intently all night, reacting immediately to every change in expression, making sure she had everything she needed. God, how she wished she was free to love this man.

Beth shook her head. "I don't think it'll ever be over for me," she said. "I don't know how anyone recovers completely from brainwashing. I mean, sure, thought reformation can be reversed—some of it's been reversed without my even realizing—but now I know how easily my mind can be persuaded to accept alternative realities. I'm such a weak person, I'll never be able to trust my own judgment."

"Stop it, Beth," Greg said, his voice firm. "What happened to you can happen to anyone, weak or strong. That's what makes brainwashing—what Peter Sterling described as thought reformation—such a frightening threat. But the important thing, the only thing that matters, is that you got yourself out. Even when you thought your mind had let you down, you trusted yourself, relied on yourself, made the most of what you had left, and managed to fool an entire town into thinking you were a perfectly normal grieving widow. You carved a whole new life for yourself out of nothing at all. That's strength in its truest sense."

She needed so badly to believe him. But...

"My mind did let me down. I was fighting the biggest battle of my life and it checked out. How can I ever trust myself now? How do I know that every time I'm facing a difficult challenge, it won't just check out again? I have no control whatsoever."

"Uh-uh." Greg shook his head. "You've got it all wrong." The passion in his voice was compelling. "Think about it. Sterling and Silverman had taken control of your thoughts. The only way to be free of those two, to let the so-called reformation wear off, was for you to be separated from those thoughts. Your mind had to go numb, not because you couldn't handle the facts, but so you could free yourself from the brainwashing."

He sounded so sure. Absolutely and completely certain.

"Are you just saying that because I'm at a low point and you know I need to hear it?"

"What good would that do in the long run?"

"None."

"Have you ever known me to lie to you? Or any-one else?"

"No."

"I don't say things unless they're true, Beth. You have every reason to trust your mind. Because it found a way to free you from a state that's considered impossible to escape from without medical help or counseling. Yet you beat all the odds. I'd say that's pretty impressive. I'd say no one else is likely to get away with telling you how to think again."

Tears filled Beth's eyes. Rolled down her cheeks. And kept rolling. Until she was a sobbing mass huddled against Greg's chest.

Lifting her, he carried her, crying so hard she couldn't see, to the living room.

Beth cried until she thought she'd never stop. Years of pent-up tension and confusion and hurt spilled onto Greg's uniform. And then, the tears were gone. Spent. No longer necessary.

"Thank you." They were the first words either of them had spoken in almost an hour.

"You're welcome, Beth."

"I can't believe what a good friend you are to me."

"I love you."

Beth's head fell back, her heart pounding quickly. Scrutinizing Greg, she tried to convince herself that the moment was real. That *she* was real. That it was okay to be feeling what she was feeling.

"I love you, too." What a relief to say those words.

He lifted her face gently, giving her a soft kiss.

Beth answered him as completely as she could with her weary, aching body, finding new energy in his kiss. His mouth opened against hers and she responded instinctively, until she remembered. And pulled away.

"I'm married."

His eyes serious, he held her gaze. "I know."

They'd committed adultery.

Beth got up from the couch, surprised by how shaky she was. She didn't go far. Just to the other end of the couch.

"I have a business degree," she said, looking for something positive. She had no life. Maybe her education was someplace to start.

"You can get a divorce, Beth." Greg moved over, urging her close once again.

She shouldn't let herself walk back into his arms. But he felt so good. And she was tired of being alone—of being strong all by herself.

"I imagine we can get a quick one, considering the circumstances."

"We?"

"I figure I have as much of a stake in this as you do."

She stared at him, hardly daring to hope. "Why?"

He raised one eyebrow. "I can't very well get married until you can."

Beth might have started to cry again if she'd had any tears left. Greg had an uncanny way of making the confused seem clear, the impossible quite manageable. She began to chuckle. And then to laugh out loud.

"What's so funny?" Greg asked. He was trying to sound offended, but the grin on his face ruined the effect.

"Nothing's funny," she said, laughing even as she

tried to explain. "I just feel so good after so much bad, I can't keep it in."

"I take it that's a yes?"

Beth didn't need to be asked twice. She wasn't really sure she'd been asked once, but she didn't care. Sobering, she placed her lips on Greg's, kissing him reverently.

"Of course it's a yes," she whispered.

Greg's arms wrapped around her, and Beth wanted nothing more than to spend the rest of the night, the rest of her life, loving him.

"Greg?"

"Mmm?" he murmured against her lips.

"Can we go to bed now?"

She thought he nodded, knew he lifted her into his arms, but was asleep before they left the living room.

She had all the nights of her life for making love. That night, she just needed to be welcomed home. By Shelter Valley. By the house that had been waiting for her. By the man who'd rescued her, and made her life complete.

She and Ryan had finally found something that was truly right and good.

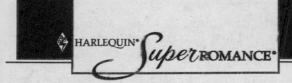

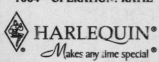

The holidays have descended on

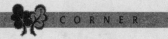
C O O P E R ' S   C O R N E R

providing a touch of seasonal magic!

Coming in November 2002...
MY CHRISTMAS COWBOY
by Kate Hoffmann

Check-in: Bah humbug! That's what single mom
Grace Penrose felt about Christmas this year. All her plans
for the Cooper's Corner Christmas Festival are going wrong—
and now she finds out she has an unexpected houseguest!

Checkout: But sexy cowboy Tucker McCabe is no ordinary
houseguest, and Grace feels her spirits start to lift. Suddenly
she has the craziest urge to stand under the mistletoe...forever!

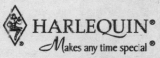

This is the family reunion you've been waiting for!

TRUEBLOOD Christmas

JASMINE CRESSWELL
TARA TAYLOR QUINN
& KATE HOFFMANN

deliver three brand new Trueblood, Texas stories.

After many years, Major Brad Henderson is released from prison, exonerated after almost thirty years for a crime he didn't commit. His mission: to be reunited with his three daughters. How to find them? Contact Dylan Garrett of the Finders Keepers Detective Agency!

Look for it in November 2002.

HARLEQUIN®
Makes any time special ®

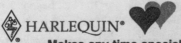